Love Bones and Water

ADAM ZAMEENZAD was brought up in
East Africa before going to Pakistan to
attend university in Lahore. Since then he
has travelled widely in Europe and North
America and has taught in Britain.

In 1987 he published his first novel, *The
Thirteenth House*, which won the David
Higham Prize for Fiction, and in 1988 it
was followed by the highly acclaimed *My
Friend Matt and Hena the Whore*.

Adam Zameenzad lives in Kent.

D0994170

Also by Adam Zameenzad

THE THIRTEENTH HOUSE
MY FRIEND MATT AND HENA THE WHORE

Critical acclaim for *The Thirteenth House*, winner of the 1987 David Higham Prize for Fiction:

'An unusually talented and vigorous first novel'
DORIS LESSING

'Ghost story, nightmare, vision . . . It transposes the reader from a world where even the traumas of political upheaval and police brutality – however appalling – are at least solidly real, to an insubstantial, shimmering world where nothing is what it seems and where the significance of people, events and things trembles tantalizingly just out of focus . . . A forceful, moving and confident debut'
Times Literary Supplement

'Fine narrative wryness of the R. K. Narayan sort. The wryness, though, never once stifles the power' . *Observer*

'If ever comedy was black, this is'
Guardian

Adam Zameenzad

Love Bones and Water

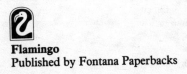

Flamingo
Published by Fontana Paperbacks

First published in 1989 by
Fourth Estate
This Flamingo edition first published
in 1990 by Fontana Paperbacks

Flamingo is an imprint of
Fontana Paperbacks, part of
the Collins Publishing Group,
8 Grafton Street, London W1X 3LA

Printed and bound in Great Britain by
William Collins Sons & Co. Ltd, Glasgow

There can be no life without water, no structure without bones, and nothing without love.

For those who sing unheard, dance unseen, grow old unloved. And for Jasper the cat. Also for you.

Ninochka would have liked this book.

1

The man lay curled up on the beach like a grotesque grey ball with its air booted out.

He was naked, except for a black hood over his head and face. His penis had been crudely carved out, so had his tongue. The wounds had healed. His buttocks were fire-branded, his nipples razor-slashed. The burns and cuts were healed.

The quivering shoreline skirted uncertainly round him: back and forth, back and forth, back and forth . . .

Spewed out by the ocean? About to be swallowed by the waves? Fallen from grace? All set for ascension? Violated by humankind in a most vile manner? Out to subvert the world with self-inflicted hell?

You may wonder, but cannot know. I know but cannot make you know. Not unless you first hear.

So hear.

Hear him well.

For it is your story he tells.

And the story of your child.

And the story of your world.

And he tells it through me.

2

The night was beginning to expel the new day from her womb. The lower parts of the horizon were drenched with blood.

The man lay curled up on the beach like a grotesque grey ball with its air booted out. The quivering shoreline skirted uncertainly round him: back and forth, back and forth, back and forth . . .

He was naked, except for a black hood over his head and face. His penis had been crudely carved out, so had his tongue. The wounds had healed. His buttocks were fire-branded, his nipples razor-slashed. The burns and cuts were healed.

To look at him you would have thought he was dead. I would not have argued.

The pain of cold and cramp, impelled and compounded by some primitive drive to survive, wrenched him out of black blankness and brought him back to life. Letting out a gutteral groan he resumed breathing.

He tried to move his ravaged limbs. They remained stiff and still.

His mouth felt dry and flaky, his face wet and slimy.

He succeeded in forcing his eyelids apart by sheer will-power. He saw black blankness again. Was he still dead? Was it the middle of a thundery starless night? Was he wearing a black hood?

A black hood!

The image caused an explosion within him, galvanising every particle of his being to electric activity. His arms, which only a moment ago were motionless and dead as the charred limbs of a tree struck by lightning, shot up like tongues of frightened snakes. His hands tore the hood off his head and face with robotic efficiency. The face that revealed itself was agonised and old. So agonised and so old that sorrows of centuries were etched on his features in lines of painstaking complexity. The man could not see all that. But he could see.

Yes, he could see. He could see. The sea, the sky, the new-born day.

He was free. He was alive. He could see.

He let out a yell of relief and release. Its hoarse, somewhat unpleasant quality did not adequately express his emotions. In fact, it ended up vaguely disturbing him. To compensate for its lack of *joie de vivre* he decided to sing out loud. What better than waves of the living sea to have as a chorus for his song of life and freedom!

Suddenly he was a child again. 'All things bright and beautiful' came to his mind. Came to his mind, but not to his lips. Could not. The 'song' that did emerge from his lips sounded much like his frightening cry of joy. This time it frightened him.

He tried to say something. Anything. A swear word. A word of prayer. A word of fear.

Nothing.

His body froze once more. His mind seemed to lose consciousness while still conscious. Gradually it homed in on the area of his mouth. It occurred to him that it felt both more empty and more full than it should. It also felt very dry and parched. He could almost see his lips crack. He made as if to stick out his tongue to run over them. Nothing happened. He tried again. Nothing again. There was something wrong there. He tried again. Nothing, yet again.

More puzzled than worried he opened his mouth as wide as he could, brought his right hand up and tried to feel his tongue with his fingers. At first he couldn't, and then he could. Way back. Stumpy and swollen and only a quarter of what it should have been. In confused disbelief he lowered his head in order to facilitate the movement of his fingers to explore within his mouth. The realisation that his tongue had been cut out came at the same moment as his lowered eyes saw his dismembered crotch.

His eyes and his mouth kept opening wider and wider. His hand kept travelling inside his mouth until his fingers entered his throat. He choked. His stomach went into spasms, jerkily squeezing out a sticky acidic liquid from its empty depths. It emerged in a slow trickle out of the man's lower opening, scalding his thighs, and in harsh rasping gasps from his upper opening, burning his fingers with its hot stench.

After an epoch of frozen seconds, up he jumped. Then jumping and squatting by turns – like a frog, only backwards – he began to emit weird wailing sounds. One hand still in his mouth, now covered with the slimy acid that still kept jerking out of his stomach; one hand down between his legs trying to hide, or find, what was no longer there – either to hide or to find.

He continued to jump backwards, now semi-erect, more like a gorilla than a frog; part reeling, part falling, part stumbling; wailing all the while, shitting slime, puking slime and urinating. The urine was going all over his thighs and legs, not having the advantage of a proper spout any more.

I leant backwards in ultimate agony, and jumped and wailed in unison with his jumps and wails; more mute, and as impotent.

No one heard my cries. But a small boy, walking a small dog along the beach, heard the man.

He was nine years old, but looked barely five. His build was tiny, his bones small, his face thin. His golden skin could look pale as the summer moon or coppery as toasted bread. This morning it was shining like the morning star.

He was a late abortion that survived. His mother, who always knew what to do, on the principle that that which is rational is ultimately also good, was for once in doubt. In the end she decided to 'accept' the boy. Her money and political status and the benefits they brought and bought enabled him to develop into a normal child, except for what she chose to call his 'reduced size'. Some problems with breathing occasionally resurfaced, as did water on the lungs, but not much wrong otherwise.

Conquering his initial fear, the boy ran out towards the sea to investigate the source of the unearthly noises that filled the dawn air.

The man saw the boy about the same time as the boy saw the man.

The man's hoarse screams eased into soft hiccuppy yelps, his backward jumps slowed, faltered, and came to a halt. Both man and boy stared at each other motionless. Even the little dog was rigid.

The wind began to increase in velocity. Its singing assumed a higher pitch. The waves quickened their dance. The music of the sea surged alongside. The rising yelps of the dog harmonised with the dying yelps of the man. The wet air stung with its salt freshness.

I knelt down and prayed. *My children who are on Earth. Blessed be your name* . . .

3

Strangely, it was the man who made the first move. Strangely, but not surprisingly. After all, it was he who needed help.

He moved towards the boy, almost managing to hold himself erect. Fortunately, by then, he had succeeded in controlling the distorted noises that he had been emitting. In one sense he was aching to speak, but restraining himself from even trying. In another he was almost relieved that he could not speak. For if he could, he would not have known what to say; apart from asking for help, which he could do wordlessly. Faced with the opportunity to communicate with the boy, he realised with a new and worse kind of horror that he could not recall who he was, what had happened to him, and how he had got wherever he was.

He thought of the best alternative to speech. Squatting on his haunches, still keeping one hand between his thighs, he brought the finger of his other hand down to the pebbly sand as if to write; a plea for some clothes, or food, or shelter? All three?

He couldn't write. Not one word. Not one letter. Couldn't remember how. Maybe never knew.

Instinctively he raised both his arms up in the air in a helpless, supplicating gesture. As he did so, equally instinctively, the boy's eyes lowered to the man's crotch, now in full view. The man saw the movement of the boy's eyes. Before the boy himself could register any expression at the sight, the man realised that he had exposed himself. Whatever it may or may not have meant to the child, to the man it was the climax of his humiliation. Swivelling on his heels like a twin-pointed top, he turned round and began loping back towards the sea, once again a yelping wreck of a creature.

The boy turned and ran as well. Ran all along his own private stretch of beach to a grand beach-house on the re-styled cliff two miles to the west.

The man stumbled over a large yellowy crab that was trying to escape his path, and fell face downwards. He tried to scramble up, but was either physically unable to do so, or lost the will to do so half-way through. He let his head flop sideways on the sand, his knees buckled under his stomach, his arms spread out.

As he lay there without movement, except of the diaphragm, I hesitantly extended my hand to help him up. He extended his, and grasped mine. A miracle!

It was easier for both of us now; easier, but still damned difficult.

. . . *Lead us not into trials, and forgive us our debts, as we forgive . . .*

4

The boy was panting like the dog by the time he reached the hewn-in-the-rocks, sun-and-sea-speckled steps, leading up to the stylised, multi-storeyed, multi-balconied, multi-terraced stone beach house, larger than some hotels.

He paused for breath. The dog was much relieved at this interruption in the morning's romp. There was an easier way up to the house than these steep one hundred and seven steps – the boy had counted them many a time – but it was very much longer, sloping first down and away from the house before turning upon itself and gradually moving upwards in a gentle curve towards the front door. The boy did not want to waste any more time walking, or running. He was bursting with news to tell. Besides, he always enjoyed the challenge of the steps, despite many warnings from his mother, echoed by his father.

A tall, thickly-built man, with a smooth, attractively boyish face came over from the other side of the rocky stairway, walking with easy, powerful strides. He was wearing a loose-fitting dark suit with an open-necked shirt exposing thick black hair right up to the shaving line. The face somehow did not appear to belong to the rest of him.

'I've been looking all over for you,' he said.

'Wrong direction,' replied the boy.

'Very funny. You had me worried.'

The boy hesitated, then made as if to tell the man what he had seen. Before he could say anything, the man spoke again: 'Where *were* you, kid? And how's Trick-s!' He emphasised the k and s separately with a childish glee in his husky voice.

The child's desire to confide evaporated. 'Her name is Trix, not Trick-s. And I am *not* a kid. Kid's grow up to be goats. Like your mother.'

'Watch what you say about my mother.' The man's face and voice changed noticeably. 'And you still haven't told me where you have been. You know I am supposed to keep an eye on you.'

'And *you* know I take Trix out for a walk!'

'You are supposed to take her out for a walk. Not on a journey.' When the boy did not reply and turned to climb the steps, the man spoke again, this time in a more concerned manner: 'You know you are supposed to be careful . . .' He stopped as he remembered that he was not meant to refer to the boy's health '*without GOOD reason*', spread his arms in the air and repeated: 'You know I am supposed to keep an eye on you in the mornings.'

'Well you should do a better job of it then,' the boy piped back.

The man's finely-chiselled nostrils flared, 'What am I supposed to do? Put you on a leash like that stupid dog?'

'Trix is not stupid, you are. Talking to me like that. I'll get Daddy to fire you.'

The man's husky voice smiled again, this time more meaningfully. '*He* can't fire me. He wouldn't da . . .' He checked himself in time, realising he may have already said too much.

Reconciliation was in order. 'I'm sorry kid . . . Peter. It's just that . . . well . . . you know you are not supposed to talk back or talk big. Phil . . . Philip . . . your Dad would be the first to say that.' Which was almost true. He moved forward and put one enormous arm round the boy's shoulders, 'You are not supposed to disappear on your own. First my partner runs off to . . .' He paused, looking flustered, fumbling for words '. . . vanishes. Then you. What am I supposed to . . .'

The man's arm round his shoulders was getting heavier and it annoyed the boy. 'Stop saying "supposed to, supposed to" all the time. "Supposed to" this and "supposed to" that. And let go of me.' He wrenched himself free and began running up the stairs as fast as his little legs could go over the high steps.

The man raised his huge hands up in the air helplessly and tried to think of something to say that would not bring the boy's Mother down on him. 'You are not supposed to . . . meant to, leave the house so early in the morning anyway, walking the dog or not walking the dog. Don't you ever sleep!' he added, shouting louder, 'What do you do at night? Pick the ticks off Trick-s?'

The boy stopped somewhere between the man and the sky and shouted down: 'Wouldn't you like to know!'

'And what's that supposed to mean?' the man shouted back up.

'Supposed to, supposed to . . .' the boy chanted on his way up, wondering what on earth *was* it supposed to mean? 'Wouldn't you like to know?' He had heard adults in the house use the phrase. His parents were both members of the state parliament, Mother in the government, Father in the opposition, so it could have something to do with official secrets. Or perhaps it had something to do with S.E.X. There was a lot of that going on too. At least a lot of talk about it. He was not 'supposed to' know about it, but he did.

He decided to think of nothing but sex all the way up. However after only a few steps he forgot all about it; and about Stewart down below. His mind went back to the strange naked man. Disturbingly the thoughts of sex came back and mingled with the thoughts about the strange naked man. He tried to hurry up even more.

The dog, an ageing, half-blind, totally deaf yellow poodle, had given up barking and was following the boy instead of leading him.

Peter's enchantment with the strange naked man, and the anticipatory joy – even if strongly coloured with concern – of telling his parents about him, over-rode his fatigue. He did not often have much to say to them to which either paid much attention. This was going to be different.

Stopping only for a few heavy breaths at the top of the cliff and in front of the house, he rushed past the two guards in the shopping-mall-sized-porch-cum-verandah, kicked open the dog flap in the ornate rococo door and crawled in before the dog. Inside the massive hall, he pointed the dog to her room and rushed up the winding stairs, along the eastern corridor, past three doors, then left, and through the gilded black door without knocking. 'Mummy, Mummy, I saw a na . . .'

'In God's name, Peter, have you completely taken leave of your senses, *and* your MANNERS!' Eleanor's voice and visage emerged from under a plush duvet splattered with a profusion of gargantuan pink roses. Even in bleary-eyed sleepiness her face could have launched a thousand Harrier jets.

'But Mummy, I saw a . . .'

'I do not want to hear another word until you go back, and . . . and . . .' Raising herself on her elbows she looked straight into Peter's eyes and waited expectantly. 'And . . .' she repeated when Peter remained open-mouthed but silent. Normally he would have responded immediately, but today he was too excited and too exhausted. '*And* . . .' she repeated again, more emphatically but without raising her voice.

'And knock on the door and ask permission to come in, Mummy,' he said at last, softly dropping his shoulders and his eyes. He looked so forlorn and so sorry that Eleanor's heart went out to him in a surge and she could have rushed up to him and wound her arms round him in a loving embrace. But she couldn't. She shouldn't. It would not be good for him. He had to learn to follow the rules. That was the way of the world, and he had to learn to cope with it – he more than most, being smaller and weaker than most. She had to be cruel to be kind.

'Thank you, Peter,' she said gently, and waited.

Peter slowly turned round and started walking out.

'PETER!'

Peter turned round again, 'Sorry, Mother.'

'Sorry what?'

'Sorry to . . . I am sorry I came running in without knocking, and without asking permission.'

'And . . .' she pointed behind him.

'And for not shutting the door behind me.'

'I hope you have not brought Trix upstairs?' she digressed with a new note of anxiety in her voice. The dog was getting old and forgetful of her 'manners' and Eleanor found it difficult to cope with her. She had loved her once, still did; but she did not have enough time to show it any more.

'No, Mummy. I sent her to her room.'

'Thank God for that, darling. And now . . .'

Peter walked out of the open door, shut it gently behind him, it didn't click; he pulled on it, firmly but still gently, until it did; waited for a few seconds, then gently knocked on the door.

'Who is it?' Eleanor asked in honeyed tones reserved for special people, strangers, and occasions when she was not sure who the person was.

'Me,' said Peter, opening the door just a crack in order to better hear and be better heard. This was allowed after the initial response. Eleanor often received messages through the bedroom door, especially when she was working there, which she often did – sometimes in bed with her papers and files on the breakfast table which fixed itself across the bed. He tried to peer through the crack to see her reaction, even though he

23

knew it was useless. Her bed was so placed as to make it impossible. Peter wondered how far his neck could twist itself round the door before he could be accused of entering without permission.

'And who is me?'

'Peter, Mummy.'

'And what do you want, Peter, at this time on a Sunday morning?'

'May I come in, Mummy?'

'Is it something urgent, Peter?'

Peter hesitated. He was not sure if his news was urgent or not. If she had said 'important', he might have risked declaring it important. But urgent? A strange naked man, more than two miles from their house – even if he was on their beach . . . Was it or was it not urgent?

'I am not sure, Mummy,' he said after a bout with his conscience and the urgency within him, which he knew to be of the sort which was rarely, if ever, considered urgent by adults, with the exception of Uncle Paul.

'Well, if you are not sure it is urgent, it cannot be urgent. That's what being urgent is all about. When it is urgent, you *know* it is urgent. Without doubts. Right, Peter?'

'Yes, Mummy.'

'Well then, now that urgent is out, what else can it be? You are not feeling ill are you? You do sound a bit odd?' The concern in her voice was mingled with vexation. There was a very important dinner that night. Peter did have the habit of being ill at the most inconvenient of times.

'No, Mummy.'

Relief.

'Now if it is not urgent, and you are not ill, it can wait. Is that reasonable or is it not?'

'It is, Mummy.'

'It is what, Peter?'

'Reasonable, Mummy.'

'Good boy. Now go downstairs and wait. Remember, Reason is the Mistress, Patience the Handmaiden. Together they can move mountains.'

'Yes, Mummy.'

'And without Intellect, Reason and Patience . . .'

'Disorder, Chaos and Anarchy, Mummy.'

'Good. Now we don't want Disorder, Chaos and Anarchy to reign in this house, do we now?'

'No, Mummy.'

'Very good. Now go down and ask Natalia to make you your breakfast while you have your glass of milk.' Natalia was the au pair. 'Now you know that Sunday is the only day Mummy has a lie-in. Up to eight o'clock. Now that is not asking for much, is it? Considering I work all day and most of the night. Now is it?'

'No, Mummy.'

'But any way, since you have woken me up at – five forty-seven, to be precise, don't you ever sleep? – and since you evidently have something you want to tell me, I will come down in twenty minutes. I will have a cup of coffee with you and give you your Easter egg while you have your breakfast. Then you can tell me all about it. Is that fine? It can wait another twenty minutes, can't it?'

'Yes, Mummy.'

There was a stony silence from within the bedroom. Then, 'Is that all you have to say, "Yes, Mummy"?'

'Sorry, Mummy. Thank you, Mummy.'

'That is better. Now run along. See you in a jiffy.' As she heard his tiny footsteps receding she called out, 'Love you.' She meant it, too.

5

Peter stopped in his retreating tracks, then turned and walked to the top of the balcony. With his head just under the balustrade, he peered out through the iron latticework. Across the dry cliffs and the green cliffs and the bushes and the palm trees and the beach of specially-delivered sand and the real pebbly beach – somewhere out there was the strange naked man. Waiting. Waiting for him. Waiting for him to take him some clothes and some food and to find him a place to live. Perhaps Peter had this in the back of his mind all along; perhaps that was why he was so keen to talk to someone, to get help; but the thought had not occurred to him so directly and starkly before then.

What could he do? He began to think of ways and means, and ended up worrying himself into more of a quandary than he had been to start off with. Twenty minutes was not a long time. But then if his mother said twenty minutes, it could mean anything. Nineteen minutes and forty-five seconds, if it was the Prime Minister; one hour and twenty minutes, if it was a party . . . But then all parties were not the same. She didn't normally keep him waiting too long, but then it was Sunday morning, and he had been rude.

His throat was hoarse from talking round the door to his mother, especially as it had been parched to begin with, after that long run on the beach followed by the climb up the steep rock steps. The idea of going down for some breakfast and a drink of milk began to appear quite appealing.

He was about to turn and make his way down when his eyes focused on the timber chalet to the right of the house, visible through the trees and the vegetation. Strange that he had overlooked it until then. Usually he stood and stared at it for more seconds than he could count. Well above a hundred thousand on many occasions.

The chalet was his Father's extended study-cum-flat. He often slept there as well, especially if he had a lot of reading to do, or needed to catch up on his constituency paper work. This had the added advantage of leaving his mother free to prepare her own papers. Since they belonged to different political parties – she in the ruling, he in the main opposition – this privacy was essential every now and then. They had to be very careful, even though the 'extraordinary bill' introduced by a government MP to force one of them to resign had been defeated and they had won their seats in the following general election with a greatly increased majority. Their popularity was well founded, both with the public and in parliament itself. Not too long ago each had been the youngest MP in either party. When they fell in love it was the most talked about romance of the year. When they married, it kept the popular press going for a few months. Stories of their wedded bliss – or lack of it, depending on which made better copy – still appeared in dailies and weeklies of the sort in which such stories appear.

Each had their own house in the different areas of the city they represented. However, they spent little time in either, and lived mostly in this beach-house which was in another constituency altogether – it belonged to Eleanor, who was the one with the real money. Both were working really hard in their separate quarters these days. Yet another election was due that year.

Peter was forbidden to go to his Father's study 'when he was working'. Since it was impossible for Peter to know when he was or was not working, the rule was that he should not go to the chalet at all. Not unless he was taken. His Mother's voice, when she repeated this instruction from time to time, took on a more than usually sombre tone. Even Peter's father, not always in agreement with his wife, never gave any indication that a surprise visit from his son would be a welcome interruption. Just the opposite. So Peter had never dared.

Today was different. He did not really want to do anything which would bring on a family row – or worse, cause electoral defeat for either of his parents: he had been warned on more than one occasion that if he did this, that, or the other Mummy may lose her seat, or Daddy for that matter; but the compulsion within him to talk about the strange naked man was gaining strength. He should have taken the risk and said 'urgent' to his mother. But it was too late for that. She would not stand for another barge-in. For a specified number of hours – three, five or nine – she would probably refuse to talk to him at all after that. It could even be twelve – which could mean days if he was at school and she was busy working! Fortunately the school was closed for Easter.

Yes, he was going to take the plunge today. Break the big taboo. Circumvent circumspection. Forget milk and breakfast.

There was an outside stairway spiralling down from the balcony into the stone-walled sand garden. Peter was there before he could count forty. He had loosened one stone from the western part of the wall and when he wanted to escape unnoticed he could push it out, crawl through the gap then push back the stone from the other side. He did just that; then on to the short rocky path, past the naturally growing and

28

artificially cultivated trees and shrubs, and towards the timber chalet within the barbed wire area. He knew how to crawl under that without triggering any alarms. Then schlip schlop schlip schlop schlip schlop, his feet sinking into the imported sand; and he was in front of the open-planked steps leading up to the circular balcony which ran round his father's chalet.

After a hesitation count of only three, he was on the stairs and away into the actual study area. It was empty. Of course it would be. Too early. Through it was the bedroom. 'Daddy, Daddy I saw a na . . .' He stopped when he saw that Daddy wasn't here either. Somewhat puzzled but still not slowed down, he ran out of the back door of the bedroom which led once again to the balcony, on the far side of the chalet. There, on Daddy's favourite rocking chair, brought by Mummy only last Easter, two naked men were struggling. Fights frightened Peter, and his fear turned to terror when he saw that one of them was the unmistakable figure of his father, a giant carved out of milk chocolate. The other was a white man, as delicately white and as strikingly blond as his mother.

He need not have not been afraid, for they were not struggling in combat, only struggling to get out of the chair. It is not easy for two big men to jump suddenly out of one rocking chair rocking furiously.

That was not the only worry off Peter's head. Once the man had covered the big meat stick jutting out of his middle – so different from the middle of *his* naked man – with his hands and Peter turned his attention to his face, he recognised him as Tom, Stewart's partner. Thank God he was all right. Stewart had told him Tom had vanished. Without realising it, Peter had been a little worried about him. He was a worrier, Peter. Worried about everything. Even when he was not aware of it. Only when something came out fine and he heaved a sigh of relief or said a prayer of thanks did he realise that he had been worrying about it. Of course if it did not come out fine, then he worried much much more openly, and all the time. He was going to tell Tom that Stewart was worried about him, but

Tom did not wait to listen. He jumped off the balcony and ran off naked.

While he was thinking about Tom and Stewart his father had rushed back into the bedroom, and now came out belting a pair of jeans, and looking as red as he possibly could. Putting a hesitant arm round Peter, he quickly took him back again into the bedroom, away from the scene of 'the crime'.

Peter was sure he would be told off for coming running in like that without permission. He deserved it, too. Philip had his own worries. He tried to speak, but words wouldn't come out. He cleared his throat and tried again, 'What . . . What . . . ahem . . . – do you want? What is . . . ahem the matter . . . son?'

Peter did not know what to say. *I saw a naked man* suddenly did not seem quite right. Or perhaps it was. But then again he did not want to take any more thoughtless risks today.

'I . . . I . . . I'm sorry I came in – without . . .' He would have been in tears only he could not even bring himself to cry. He felt so tired and weak. He just wanted to crawl back into bed. He wished he had not got up. He was not quite sure what had been going on between his father and Tom, but he did know that it was not right for him to have seen it. In the excitement of the morning, and the moment, and the relief of finding Tom safe he had not had time to think. Now that he did start to think, he couldn't. He could only feel: feel sorry and feel ashamed. He hung his head down and looked at his shoes and twiddled his toes inside.

'Are you all right?' said Philip, his voice still shaking, his shame struggling with concern for Peter. The boy did have a habit of falling ill at the most inconvenient of times.

'I'm all right . . . I . . . I think I had better go now. Mummy is coming down to have breakfast with me.' That was a good way out of the situation; and the truth. They didn't often come together.

'Is that what you came to tell me?' Philip sounded surprised and relieved.

'N . . . Yes. Yes,' he said hurriedly, grateful for another easy explanation.

'Oh, all right then. Go wait in the study, or the . . . er . . . balcony, if you like, and I'll come over in a minute. We can go together and have breakfast with Mummy. That will be nice, won't it?'

'Will you, Daddy? Yes, that will be nice. Thank you.' Peter's wan face brightened. 'Thank you, Daddy.' He was about to run out of the room, but Philip held him back.

'You . . . you . . .' He was again having difficulty with words, 'You won't tell Mummy . . . about Tom, Thomas, will you? We . . . We were just . . . exercising. Yes, exercising.' He was more confident now, having fumbled upon what he thought was a good excuse. 'And you know Mummy does not like me exercising. Not too much. You know . . . Not good for the heart, she says. You know?'

Peter said nothing. He knew there were many things that did not meet with Mummy's approval. Exercise was not one of them. In fact she quite definitely approved of it. Especially for the heart. On the other hand, she was known to change her mind.

'You won't now? Will you?' Philip said again, trying to keep the desperation out of his voice, while at the same time wondering why he should care. After all, she knew. In fact, she had known before he had. At least, she had articulated it before he had found the guts to admit it even to himself: that he was undeniably and unchangeably homosexual, and not just having affairs with men 'for a change'. Some men did, but he was just straight homosexual. There was nothing 'bi' about him. He could get no pleasure from women sexually. He could, perhaps, give them some pleasure. He had often given Eleanor some, but he could not get any from her. He was thankful to her for liberating him, though whether that was what *she* had had in mind was another matter.

But she would never forgive him for letting the child see it. Not during the election year. '*Doing* it in front of the child!' That's what she would say. And she'd be right, too.

Nearly right. That's why she should not find out. '*And* with the election just around the corner!' she'd add. And she'd be right, again. Dead right. As always. Nearly always.

'I won't, Daddy,' said Peter, looking anxiously at Philip's anxious face, wondering whether or not to smile.

'Promise?' said Philip.

'Promise,' replied Peter.

'Mummy is the word.' said Philip, relaxing. A bright child-like smile rising from the corners of his generous mouth spread upwards and outwards till it almost touched his temples on either side. Teeth that looked and felt coated with fresh cream flashed in the rapidly advancing sunlight that was breaking in through the window.

'Mummy is the word,' responded Peter: it was a joke they shared when they did or said or ate anything Mummy disapproved of and which was meant to be a secret.

When Peter opened the door to go out into the balcony, the wind brought with it the cries of the strange naked man. Perhaps he should have told his father about him. But it was too late now. Perhaps this. Perhaps that. He should have this. He should have that. Too late this. Too late that. Half his conscious life was taken up with perhaps's and should have's and too late's. If only he could be like his mother, who never regretted anything. At least that's what she said out loud to others. Who knows what she said to herself, silently. When he spoke to himself, he said things he would never dream of saying out loud to others.

The wind continued to bear the cries of the strange naked man.

He pressed the palms of both hands against his ears and prayed to Jesus to look after him; and to help him to help the strange naked man.

He began to look forward to his first breakfast together with both his parents in a long time.

His pulse soared with anticipation at the thought.

Mine took a dive.

6

'Where did you disappear to now, Peter? And after waking me up before the birds could clear their throats for their dawn din! Honestly, you should be tied down with a . . .' Eleanor stopped mid-sentence as she saw Philip's tall figure trailing behind the tiny frame of the boy. 'You didn't go to . . .' she began again with a choking gasp, but Philip interrupted hastily, 'Oh no. I met him in the garden on the way here. He was playing with Trix.'

She looked greatly relieved. 'As long as he's taken the old girl to her room, and not brought her any where near my kitchen,' she said in a matter of fact voice, then added suspiciously, 'Why were you coming here in the first place, Philip? We were to meet at six in the evening to leave for the dinner.'

'I . . . couldn't sleep. Didn't feel like working either. Thought I might listen to some music here. My stereo has been playing up. Or should I say not playing up.' He made a feeble attempt to smile at his feeble joke.

'Honestly. And you bought it only last month. What make was it? You must write to the manufacturers. If you won't I will.'

Philip said nothing, just nodded vaguely.

Eleanor did not pursue the point. 'Tea? Coffee? Orange juice?' she asked, pouring out a glass of milk. She handed the milk to Peter while trying to meet Philip's eyes. Philip looked away and said, 'Is there any pineapple juice?'

Eleanor went to the walk-in-cupboard-sized fridge by the side of the bay window, looked inside, fumbled about. 'I'm sure there was plenty. Natalia must have finished it.'

'Where is she anyway?' said Philip, tapping the kettle, upsetting it and nearly spilling some boiling water over himself.

'Oh do keep your hands to yourself,' Eleanor blurted out, then, embarrassed at her words, brought the subject back to Natalia. 'Where do you expect? In bed. It's hardly seven o'clock on a Sunday morning for heaven's sake. If Peter won't sleep, and because of him, his mother can't sleep, that does not mean that nobody else should be allowed to sleep either,' she said peevishly, forgetting that she herself had asked Peter to wake Natalia up only a short while ago. 'The poor girl works hard enough as it is,' she added more gently.

'I suppose she does.' said Philip without really thinking about it.

'And now, young man,' said Eleanor, finally settling down after pouring herself a cup of coffee. 'Let's hear what you were bursting to tell me.' She smiled at Peter, stretched out her hand and patted his tiny hand across the table; then, shredding the curtains of restraint, she gripped it firmly, squeezed it warmly, and kept holding on to it. Peter couldn't keep anything to himself any longer, not while in the throes of such a rare mystical experience.

'I saw a . . . strange man today, Mummy. He . . . didn't have any . . . any . . . and he was not . . . feeling well. He

34

needed . . . needs help. And . . . and some clothes. He didn't have any of his own. Not any at all. And he wasn't well. He was . . . hurt. Badly. All over. Even there. You know, there, down below . . . there . . .' Peter was trying to choose his words very carefully so as not to break his promise to his father. He should not mention exercising, even the dog; or any naked man; but once he had started he was having difficulties saying all he wanted to say within the prescribed limits.

However he had already said more than enough as far as Mummy was concerned. Daddy was sitting on the hot plate of a cooker about to be switched on.

'Hurt, and swollen?' she asked so softly she was barely audible.

Peter responded with a look which remembered Tom rather than the grey man. That was answer enough for both of them. Both were up from their chairs, Eleanor hastily discarding Peter's hand and Philip spilling his orange juice all over the table, both speaking simultaneously.

'How could you Philip, how could you, in front of the child . . .' came the very soft, very controlled voice of Eleanor.

'Mummy . . . The word,' came the panic-stricken falsetto of Philip.

'How often have I told you NOT to go to Daddy's . . . har —' Eleanor just stopped herself from saying 'harem', turned to Philip and said 'What did you say Philip?' in a mystified voice.

'It was on the beach, Mummy. On the beach I saw the nak . . . naked man.' Might as well say the word now, thought Peter. 'On the beach. Not in Daddy's . . . On the beach.'

'On the beach,' Philip was relieved. 'On the beach. You're misunderstanding.'

'That does not mean I am wrong in principle.' Eleanor was deflated, but unrepentant.

'Of course not.' Philip was almost back to base. 'You are right, as always. Always right. He knows it. I know it. The whole country knows it. The whole world . . .'

'You wait till the whole world finds out about you. At least I can live with myself. Wait till they find out about *you*! That will be the end of you, as well as *me*.'

'Yes. Yes. We all know that. That is all you worry about.'

'I do. I certainly do. I can tell you that. God knows I've seen enough of your boyfrie . . . Oh my God what am I saying! What am I doing! Look what you have made me do now. Behave in this extremely irrational, unforgiveable manner, and in front of –'

'– of the boy. Yes, yes. It's all my fault. Always is. I made you do it. I always do, don't I?'

'I think it's disgusting of men – and women, in case you think I'm being sexist – to wander around naked, showing themselves in front of . . .' Eleanor's voice trailed off into silence.

Philip walked over to the window, Eleanor sat down. Peter rose to his feet as silently as he could – glass of milk still untouched, throat more parched than ever, breathing getting painful – he tried to sneak out, as he always did on such occasions during the first available lull.

'Do not, young sir, do not attempt to wriggle out of your responsibilities by walking out on a crisis. I think it is high time we got to the bottom of all this. Don't you think you have caused enough trouble for the day, without leaving everything up in the air? You owe us all an explanation. At least that's what I think. Don't you?'

'Yes, Mummy. Sorry, Mummy.'

Peter was asked to 'tell all', 'reasonably and patiently'.

Philip held his breath, not knowing what Peter's cross-examination would bring out.

Peter tried his best, but as the encounter itself was somewhat unreasonable, and Peter himself impatient, it had its problems.

'What colour was the man?'

'Grey, Mummy.'

'Grey! Must be black.'

'Why must be black? Why not white?' Philip butted in aggressively.

'Oh do give the chip a rest. A black man is more likely to look . . .'

'More likely a white man, naked and going blue in the morning chill.'

'All right. I'll take your word for it. You are the expert on the subject. Peter, I think you had better leave for now, until we need you again. Go play with Trix for a while.

'As I was saying, I bow to your superior knowledge on the subject of naked men.' Eleanor bowed gracefully.

'Thank you.' He accepted the bow graciously, then added in as caustic a tone as he could muster, 'At least I know something about what I claim to know about. Not just make hollow statements without facts or knowledge or understanding, on the strength of mere prejudice.'

'It is good to see you exercising your mind for a change, instead of your body!'

'At least I have a mind, and not a rule-book.'

'And a cheque book. Don't forget the cheque-book.'

That shut Philip up and Peter was recalled.

The rest of the day was stored in Peter's memory in sharp staccato movements of hyper-charged activity interrupted by equally hyper-charged inactivity; flashes of dialogue, happenings, silences.

When Eleanor started telephoning the police, and Peter grasped that all the grey man would get from his parents was arrest and not help, panic set in. He silently prepared and rehearsed in his mind a new and 'final' statement for the benefit of the police.

The man was 'mixed-brown' – a compromise between his mother's 'black' and father's 'white'. Apart from that and the colour of his hair, the man he described was so much like Tom – he even described his erection in detail, including the big wart which he had seen on his glans – that Philip concluded that Peter had not seen anyone other than Tom at all, and was making the rest up simply because he could neither remain

37

silent nor bring himself to tell the truth. This made him feel both grateful to Peter as well as angry with him; but most of all he was afraid for Tom. What if someone else knew about the wart. Philip was sure someone would. Tom was an active bugger, no matter what he said. Eleanor, on the other hand, was convinced that the boy was telling the truth. He could not possibly make all that up. Philip agreed with that, for reasons of his own.

Peter himself hated every minute of it. He only talked about the 'naughty' bit because the police officer kept asking him about it, repeating and repeating and repeating the same basic question in so many different words and ways, smiling and cajoling and putting his arms round him and patting his cheeks and calling him a brave little boy – it all made him extremely uncomfortable. He'd have said anything to put an end to it. The consequences were much worse and more frightening than his worst expectations.

First they wanted to take him to where he had seen the man. That wasn't too difficult, on the face of it. All he had to do was take them in exactly the opposite direction. But even so, there was always the fear that the grey man could have wandered away, anywhere. Also, out there on the beach you could see a long way, and it was possible that they would still spot the grey man. Then there was Stewart. He hadn't exactly seen which direction Peter had come from, but he had to be careful not to take them anywhere near where Stewart had been looking for him. Stewart would say that neither the man nor Peter had been there.

However, all went well. After more than an hour on the police jeep, circling far away from where Peter had seen the grey man and in bush- and tree-lined areas to prevent distant vision, they returned 'unsuccessful'. Peter was relieved beyond words. Fortunately, when he had taken them to the 'green' cliffs, the police, instead of getting suspicious, had said that that's where they would have searched anyway. Such men preferred to hide behind trees before selecting and pouncing on their intended victims.

The worst part came later. Peter was taken to the police station to be 'examined'. Just in case more had taken place than the boy was willing to admit or talk about.

Philip protested strongly, but Eleanor insisted that the proper procedures must be followed. It was in Peter's own interests, and in the interests of society at large. It was 'men like him' that created 'men like him'. It was an aside, and no one but Philip heard it, but it was enough to put a stop to his protests.

By the time Peter came back, cradled in Natalia's arms – she had insisted in going with him – he had a blank look in his eyes and a new awareness of life – an awareness that made him view growing up and grown-ups with some fear and considerable distaste. An open sexual encounter he might have been able to cope with and accept. Devious probing of mind and body with motives which he could sense but not understand, repelled and scared him.

More than ever he wanted to help his grey man. In helping him, he would help himself. He could feel that in his bones, not quite knowing why. He now only thought of the man as the 'grey man' rather than the 'naked man'. The events of the day had made him loathe even to think the word 'naked', let alone actual nakedness. Certainly not in connection with his grey man, whose nakedness was so clothed in suffering.

He didn't exactly think these words, but he did exactly think these thoughts.

Eleanor was greatly relieved to learn that the boy had not been tampered with. At least not anally. And as long as his anus had not been disturbed, it didn't particularly matter what else of him or in him had been disturbed, and how grossly.

She didn't exactly think these words, but she did more or less think these thoughts. And she was greatly relieved that the boy was anally intacto. She didn't realise that he was not. Not after the police and doctors had finished with him.

Philip thought it was all a bloody farce, a black bloody farce. Just because the boy had to come running in at that moment. It was the first time in a long while, too – because of the elections

– and he had to rush in that day! He felt sorry for the boy as well. The bloody police. The bloody doctors. Poking their dirty noses into . . . fucking everything . . . Why couldn't his bloody oh-so-pristine wife leave bloody well fucking alone? Philip was not allowed to swear openly.

All in all it had been quite a day for the family: Philip Peruva, Eleanor Poacher (she had retained her maiden name), and Peter Paul Poacher-Peruva. And it did not come to a close after darkness set in. Not for Eleanor and Philip, who were attending a very important dinner where the first indications would be given as to who might get overall responsibility for the as-yet-unnamed shanty town development scheme to provide hotels, beaches and entertainment for the tourists. Not for Peter, who had the responsibility to devise his own scheme to provide food, shelter and clothing for the grey man.

7

The long autumn night was getting colder by the heartbeat. Struggling against the rising wind, hoping to beat the rising tide, one bag containing his lunchbox and two flasks (hot soup and hot coffee) slung across his shoulders, another bag with a blanket and some clothes tied to a skateboard which he dragged behind him, Peter forced his aching limbs to carry him towards the cave where he imagined the grey man would be waiting for him.

Peter had slipped out of the house by turning off one of the alarm systems to the left of the building and getting down to the sand garden. Once there, it was just a matter of pushing out the right stone, and he was out. With his bags and skateboard it had been harder than usual, but he had managed. The guards did not often come to that side as the sand garden there was surrounded by a tall stone wall, with barbed wire all round its base and its top covered with broken glass. Besides, whenever his parents were out for a late dinner or a party or business meeting they stayed back for the night in one of their town houses instead of returning home, and therefore the guards tended to be less vigilant, even though they were meant to be more so.

The main problem had been convincing Natalia not to take him to sleep with her in her room. She often risked the displeasure of Eleanor and took Peter to bed with her if he was feeling physically or emotionally low. Peter loved it. Natalia couldn't understand why he had objected tonight. She had even offered to sleep in his room, but he'd strongly resisted that suggestion as well. Natalia felt so sorry for him. He must have had a truly bad experience at the hands of that pervert. That is why he was evading any emotional or body contact. She only hoped it wouldn't leave any permanent scars on his psyche, nor irreparably damage his capacity to touch and form relationships. Natalia was a student of psychology and such things haunted her. For the moment, though she was very concerned for Peter, she felt the best course was to respect his wishes and leave him alone to sort out his problems with himself.

Peter's relief was short-lived: Natalia said she would look in at night just to make sure he was sleeping well and not having nightmares, which he sometimes did. With contracting lungs he made her promise not to do that. He did not give any reason, just said 'please'. He looked so worried that Natalia agreed and promised, but it increased her concern for him much more. *What was going through the poor boy's mind? What had he suffered? Was suffering?* Had she known, she would not have understood. Nothing she had learnt in her psychology lectures had prepared her for that. She would no doubt have found an explanation. It would not have been the right one, but it would have been sought with the right motives.

The night was clear. The stars shone abundantly, undaunted by the light and the might of the full moon, complete with flickering halo. It was well past midnight. Peter was tired, breathless and afraid, getting more tired more breathless and more afraid with each number that he counted. He kept forgetting anyway and had to keep going back to one. The tide and the wind continued to rise: one purposefully, one erratically; one surged and bellowed, one howled and yowled. Both danced in passionate abandon: one naked and on display, one hiding behind trees or coursing through bones; one within progressively defined boundaries, one limitless in its freedom.

The bag across his shoulders was growing in size and weight. Tying the other bag to the skateboard had seemed an excellent idea at the time, but its progress over the yielding sand and the unyielding stones ranged from the difficult to the impossible. His arms hurt, his wrists hurt, his shoulder was coming off. The strain on his calf and thigh muscles was pulling his sinews away from his bones. But still he carried on, determined to get to the grey man. To clothe his nakedness. To wrap him in a warm blanket. To feed him. And most of all, to give him a cup of steaming hot coffee. Whenever his mother felt tired or unwell, she always said, 'Oh, what wouldn't I give for a cup of steaming hot coffee.' What wouldn't he give to give that cup of steaming hot coffee to the grey man! He didn't have much to give, he thought. Everything belonged to Mummy. She had often told that to Daddy. The thought depressed him. He wished with all his might that he had something to give. Something that was his very own and nobody else's. Then he would give that something to give the grey man a cup of coffee.

Peter knew that concomitant area of beach – where land and sea cohabited in a state of constant concupisence – like the palms of his hands. His interest in palmistry, not to mention near obsession with astrology, clairvoyance and related occult 'sciences', had led him to study his palms with greedy fascination. They were small, hardly bigger than those of some babies; pink, as pink as any white boy's, and covered with millions of tiny broken lines criss-crossing one another at all angles. They were lines of worry and suffering and death.

As soon as he learnt to read fluently, shortly after the age of four, he spent most of his spare time with his eyes and mind on books of outlandish character, including those on the mystery of faith. He had first seen the March issue of the magazine *Prediction* at his Grandma's – Philip's mother. March the thirteenth happened to be Peter's birthday, (an embarrassing occasion for all, as it was really his 'abortday' – was there an abort sign, he sometimes wondered – his mother had explained all about his birth reasonably and patiently to him) and he was tempted to see what the magazine had to say about his birth sign, so prominently displayed on the cover. From then on he was trapped.

He bought and borrowed magazines and books of similar substance from whatever source he could. He didn't understand most of what he read, but he understood more than anybody else he knew. Whenever he asked either of his parents or a teacher, or any other grown-up he could vaguely trust, all he got was, 'You should not be reading all that nonsense, and at your age too!' For once Uncle Paul was not much help either. He'd just shrug his shoulders and say, 'Who knows! Certainly not me.' 'I!' Eleanor would call out if within earshot, 'Certainly not *I*.' And the matter would end.

It was to consider these vast – at least for him – issues in the solitude of the vast spaces under the sky, underneath those very stars that governed the destinies of Adam's children, that Peter used to sneak out of his house at all times of the day and night; mostly nights, because it was safer then – safer as far as human beings were concerned, especially those immediately surrounding him. He did not mind the jackals and the foxes and the snakes that roamed free in the night. He knew all the caves and hiding places for miles around. He also knew that some of the largest and most comfortable ones were the most vulnerable to the onslaught of high tides.

Tonight would be one of the highest tides of the year. If his grey man was in one of the caves he reasoned were the most obvious choice for a cold and tired man, then he was in imminent danger. The empirical rationalist in him, inherited from the Poachers, took over smoothly and effectively from the magic- and mystery-obsessed ontologist inherited from the

Peruvas. It was the latter that prevailed most of the time, in spite of his mother's excessive emphasis on the former. A personalised form of pagan Christianity, more scavenged than learnt, bridged the precarious gap. He was more of a true son of the island, once known as Pirdoz by the natives, now called New Heaven, than Eleanor could have dreamed in her worst nightmares.

As Peter's tired feet began to falter and wander in the wrong direction, somewhere in the distance a jackal howled, a sound of fear or pain rather than his normal call. Rumours that wolves were beginning to colonise an area behind the river in front of the ancient Mother Mountain, and were driving the jackals out began to filter through his mind. There were also stories of werewolves, sighted on the night of the full moon, a night such as this. His mother had discarded them as silly superstition, and even his father had agreed; but they had used them to warm him for the nth time that he should not attempt to go out of the house alone, especially at night. It had had the opposite effect on him. Not that he wasn't scared, but fear only added another dimension to his fascination. He would like to meet a werewolf, or at least *see* one. And as for wolves, he'd heard and read that they had been known to adopt human children. Perhaps he was too old, but he was small, and if he curled up and lay down helplessly, maybe they would adopt him. It would be good to have wolves as his adoptive parents. He might be of more use to them than he was to his real parents. They didn't *need* anything. They *had* everything. At least his mother did, and his father didn't seem to be doing too badly either. But wolves! He could bring food and water for them, and keep a look out to see if any bad people were coming to harm them, and discover new caves for them . . . Perhaps even teach them to be vegetarians. Trix loved soya and beans and lentils more than meat.

The thought now, of meeting some wolves, brought new vigour to his bones, but flesh was still unsure and direction still lacking. A snake reluctantly slithered out of some thorny bushes and led the way. Peter followed in a hypnotic, somnambular trance. Eventually the snake crawled into a narrow cave of black rock, to ensure that Peter was left with no doubts as to where to find the grey man.

The cave was lit by a greyish light, a mixture of shadows and moonlight filtering through cracks in the rocks. In a corner smoothed and rounded off by flood tides, lay the grey man. The grey light on his grey body neutralised all colour, and he looked transparent, like a glass fish.

He was on his back, mouth shut, eyes open, arms lifted above his head, legs stretching straight out. His pupils rested on Peter as he came into view, but it could have been an illusion caused by the shifting patterns of light, as his eyes remained unseeing. His mouth appeared to open, but it did not speak. He made no attempt to cover his mutilated shame.

A tombstone fell on Peter's chest. He had come too late. His grey man had died. Died alone and hungry and naked.

His little body began to shake uncontrollably. The bag of food slid down his arms and fell with a liquid thud on the rocky floor. His breathing became more and more strained until a weird squeaky noise, like metal scratching upon metal, began to accompany each breath. His legs lost the pain of the long laborious trek across the sand and the stones, bent with relief, and began to crumple beneath his meagre weight. He tried to steady himself by spreading his feet slightly apart. The right hit the skateboard, which wheeled noisily to one side. Unable to hold himself any more, he allowed his body to take its own course, which it did, ending up on the skateboard. With its cargo of the bag and the boy the skateboard rattled further to the right and came to rest by hitting against the grey man's ribs. Peter meanwhile tried to reduce the impact of the fall and to steady himself by extending his arm and grasping at the nearest wall of the cave which curved crookedly over the man's body. However his fingers were trembling so badly he was unable to press firmly against it. He keeled over and fell half across the man. The cold of the man's body, colder than the cold stone floor, rose and penetrated through the boy's flesh to his blood. He lost all co-ordinating power, his brain and body seemed to go their different ways, his arms and legs flailed about like those of a drowning person. His hips began to jerk sideways, his neck flopped. His breath grated louder and louder. The snake slithered round his contorting body, hissing harmonically.

A hoarse growling added its sound to the boy's breathing and the snake's hissing. Icy fingers moved at the joints, lifted themselves up from the floor, and found the boy's hand. The snake slunk away, its duty done.

Fortunately, the boy's own body had grown so cold that his hand did not find the grey man's flesh quite as painfully freezing as it might have done otherwise. No burn marks. No frostbite.

The same need, the same force, the same will, which had first brought the grey man back to life and made him tear his hood off, again impelled him to sit up and put his arms round the boy.

The boy's strength and co-ordination returned. With manic urgency he began to unzip the food bag in order to take out the flask with the coffee in it. A section of his brain was telling him to get the blanket out first.

8

The grey man took one sip of the coffee, splurted and spat it out. What he really wanted was water.

He saw with shame the shocked look of deep hurt in the boy's eyes and forced himself to drink the rest of the hot sticky liquid from the plastic flask top. He felt much better for it. Not surprising. For all its bitter artificiality, it was made with water and served with love. He could feel his bones stretching to their full capacity, and holding.

The grey man wrapped himself and the boy in the blanket. He looked at the clothes the boy had brought: one T shirt, a pair of blue jeans complete with belt, one pair of briefs, a pullover, socks and a pair of trainers; all that, and the blanket and the food and the drink! He looked again at the puny figure of the boy. He wondered. And he believed.

Both of them ate the food: the man only a little, for his stomach had shrunk and needed time to recover its elasticity;

the boy a lot, for he had been starving himself all day to save up food for the grey man. Eleanor hated waste and Natalia had to keep a close check on the food in the house. Peter didn't want her getting into any trouble – she was already being held responsible – covertly – for the missing pineapple juice. Had it been a weekday it would have been easier to get away with it. At weekends Mummy itemised the larder and the freezer and the fridge very carefully. It did not take much time on the specially programmed computer, and the process was deadly efficient. When the computer did make a mistake, if it did, suspicion wrapped itself round the entire household like a shroud of smog. Nothing was said to anyone in particular. Just a point made. And the point was sharp.

After they had finished eating, the grey man indicated that he wanted to get dressed. The boy modestly turned round, as if he had never seen the man naked before.

A great sleepiness came over him. The fear and fatigue of the day, the anticipation and preparation for the night, the long heavy walk, the pain of believing the man to be dead, the joy of seeing him alive – all united together to benumb his deluged senses, to prevent them from collapsing under the strain of over-exposure. But such release and relief was not to be. Not yet.

A hiss and a swirl penetrated like a white-hot corkscrew through his frozen mind. The snake? Yes. He saw it hurriedly scuttling out of the cave. And no. The hissing and swirling continued after him; if anything, the noise and movement were strengthening.

It was the tide coming in.

If they weren't out of there within seconds, they would be swallowed by the tumescent waters of the moon-lusting sea.

Even outside real safety would not be guaranteed unless they went up the cliffs, or way out to the eastern side of the beach, towards the southern slopes of the Mother Mountain, not far from the delta of the river, where the shanty dwellers lived. Many were the times his mother had warned him never to go over to that side, and never to talk to one of those people.

Philip's people had once lived there. Not so long ago.

Peter jumped up, turned round, shouted, 'The tide! The tide! The tide is coming. Hurry!' and grabbing the grey man's hand he pulled him along behind as he rushed to get out of the cave.

The grey man heard and understood Peter's words. More than that, he understood and felt his urgency. He was in the process of getting into the jeans at the time. He stumbled out of them as he ran to keep up with the boy. Soon they were outside, having left everything in the cave. The man regretted that, but Peter's mind was on one thing only: escape. He pulled the man up towards the cliffs behind the cave. The climb up them was sharp and steep, but it was the quickest way to avoid the spraying waves which were now rolling forth like an army of water molecules hell bent on taking their revenge on the incarcerating shores.

It soon became clear that neither man nor boy had the strength nor the expertise to make the climb at that time of the night, and in their condition. The man had just managed to put on the briefs and nothing else. The sharp flints from the rocks were jabbing his feet and causing pain he had forgotten how to feel. The boy's limbs were both stiff and limp, making a successful onslaught on the cliff face well nigh impossible.

The man panicked, and looked wild-eyed at the boy. What had he done? Caused the boy's destruction in an attempt to save himself! The boy, however, knew an alternative, even though he had never before tried it, at least not to its conclusion. Not right up to the shanty town. But he knew the general direction to follow, and had walked half-way across a few times. That would be enough to get them out of the way of the tide. Pointing in that direction – because the man did not speak, Peter assumed he could not hear either, and therefore did not speak himself, except when he had shouted out about the tide, without thinking – Peter began to run, then turned and beckoned the man to follow. The man did not need any further encouragement and ran after the boy, soon overtaking him. He stopped, turned, picked the boy up in his arms, and started running again, with a speed and strength which amazed both of them. The sea gave chase, but for all its power it had its limits and limitations.

After what seemed an age of running, the soil underneath the man's feet changed character. A variety of vegetation began to appear, ranging from thick fragrant bushes to tall trees, some well spread out and generous, some lean and sparse. Another stretch of water with a different colour and a different music shimmered in the distant moonlight. The land began to rise, not sharply but with gentle undulations. Peter squeezed the man's arm to indicate that they had escaped the area of the tide. The man stopped, but it was too soon. The strength of the wind that night caused the sea to force its way in further, and they had to move on yet again. But by this time the fury of the waters had abated, just the foam and froth remained.

The man picked the trunk of a solid-looking tree to lean against. He let his body slide downwards till his buttocks touched the damp earth below. He spread his legs out and pushed his neck back and rested it against the gnarled living wood. He shut his eyes and waited for his breathing to drop to a regular rhythm. When he opened them again to look at the boy in his arms, he was fast asleep.

The man shut his eyes again and went to sleep himself. A peaceful, dreamless sleep. A peaceful, dreamless sleep from which he was soon to wake up agitated, and as if in a dream.

'Oy, you!'

A sharp voice followed by a sharp light followed by a sharper voice, 'What the Hell . . .' and a heavy bass voice, 'Holy Mother of God!' followed by lots of soft voices hushing and shushing along with a shuffling of feet and jostling of bodies. The light was hastily turned off.

By now the grey man was fully awake and standing up, with Peter, half awake, still in his arms.

'Holy Mother of God!' said the same voice again. A number of hands and fingers crossed themselves against a number of chests.

'Magda was telling you not tonight. Not on Easter Sunday,' said the sharp voice, only not so sharp now.

'Hush. Do you want . . . And keep your fingers off that torch button in Christ's name,' came the sharper voice, still somewhat sharp.

'Don't!' said another voice, hoarse.

'Don't what?'

'You know, do not take the Lord's name . . .'

'Shut up. Shut up all of you,' said the bass voice again. Everybody shut up.

The face behind the voice moved closer to the grey man. It was clear that he was using up every atom of courage in his body to do so.

Peter was wide awake now, had jumped out of the grey man's arms and was standing as close to his legs as possible, holding tightly on to his hand.

THEY are here, he thought to himself. *And they are going to kill us both. Kill us in the most horrible of ways. Starting with pulling our nails out. Then our teeth . . .* His imagination far exceeded what Eleanor had told him about the shanty dwellers.

'Take care, Jonah,' whispered the no-longer sharp voice.

However Jonah continued to advance steadily, nerves in perfect control, but heart missing every other beat. There was nothing on Earth of which he was afraid, but he was here facing something which was not of this Earth. In fact, if it hadn't been for the presence of the very Earthly looking boy, he would have let his reputation take care of itself and made a run for safety. But if a tiny boy could withstand whatever this creature was, then so could Jonah, son of Magda – the mother of the bravest sons of the land, of whom he was the last.

He was now within inches of the grey man. He stopped and surveyed what he saw. The tall figure of the grey man: an emaciated body; an old and agonised face – so old and agonised that the sorrows of centuries were etched on its features with painstaking complexity; the prickly sharp crop of grey stubble on the chin and jaws and head – all clearly visible, as if his transfixing grey eyes radiated a silvery light of their own which made the moonlight redundant. The razor slashes across the grey man's nipples vibrated with a life of their own above his gently heaving chest.

All Jonah's fears dried up, curled and dropped away like leaves of a beech tree in autumn, so quickly and so suddenly he didn't even have time to wonder why.

'Wha . . . Who are you?' He spoke so softly he could hardly hear himself.

The grey man opened his mouth and pointed to his carved-out tongue. A shudder and an anger and a love ran through Jonah's body, the like of which he had not experienced since the death of Ishmael the youngest of his mother's sons, Magda's favourite, and whom he had always hated until after the point of death, when he learnt how much he had always loved him. But it was too late. How could he possibly feel such powerful emotions for this ancient stranger, from who knows where, as he had for his baby brother, not twenty-one on the day of his death. He was afraid again, with a different kind of fear.

'Please sir –' Peter could hold himself silent no longer – 'Please. He won't harm you. He just needs some clothes. And somewhere to live . . . sleep. And some food. And water. He would really like some water.' Peter wasn't in the least surprised to realise that he knew exactly what the man wanted. 'I brought him some coffee, but . . . he drank it. I brought him some clothes as well, but the tide came in. They were too big anyway.' Peter's verbal tide ebbed away as suddenly as it had flowed out. He looked askance at the underwear which was barely clinging to the man's hips. The inadequacy of his help made him feel smaller than he was.

'And who are you, young man?' Jonah said somewhat jauntily, his usual confidence staging a come back.

The question brought some facts about his own life back to the forefront of the boy's mind. Something very akin to terror came into his eyes and his voice.

'I must get home. Mummy will . . . if she finds out . . . Natalia will be in serious trouble. And Stewart. And Tom. And me.' This last in muted tones.

'And where is home?'

Peter told him. There was a hushed silence. 'You mean you are the son of . . . of Peruva? And the other one, what's her name . . . Poacher?'

'Yes, sir.' Peter was trying to be as respectful as possible, resisting any impulse to be 'smart', as he could be when riled or on the defensive. He felt both riled and on the defensive. Yet he was at his politest, not because he felt like it, but because he thought this might make Jonah, and the others, go easy on him, and the grey man. 'Peter. Peter is my name. Sir.'

There was a hum of excitement among the men. One of them moved forward and whispered something in Jonah's ears. Jonah pushed him away quietly.

'Let's first take you home then, young man, Peter,' said Jonah. Peter's relief was beyond words. But along with relief for himself came worry for the grey man. 'And once we've taken you home, we'll find some place for . . . for your friend.' Peter could hardly believe what he was hearing.

Jonah turned to his men, 'Come on, friends, this way.'

'But that's the *opposite* way, Jonah. You can't . . .'

'I can, and I will. So don't waste any more time than we have to.'

'Even if you must,' spoke yet another, 'why must we all go. You know the risk. One of us can take the boy home and the rest can stick to the plan.'

'We are all in this together. Always have been. We stay together. If one takes the risk, all do.'

There was a post-natal silence.

Jonah picked the boy up, to his great consternation, and started walking up the hill in a northerly direction.

'The house is that way,' said Peter in a trembling voice, pointing down the way they had come, now really worried. He could feel his chest beginning to tighten up again.

'If we climb up to the top here, then turn right at the top, we'll get there in half the time.'

Peter tried to think about it rationally. It seemed to make sense. He tried not to think about it any more.

'What do we do about *them*?' said the sharp voice, sharp again.

'They come with us, of course. What a stupid question,' Jonah said irritably, and Peter noticed for the first time that even in the moonlight three of the men looked distinctly different – they wore thick long coats and carried bags, and were very wet indeed.

The party started walking uphill. The ground here was grassy and soft and easy under the feet.

When they reached the top of one edge of the hill, they could see the path they had been on curve and come up to the other side of the hill. There, far below, were a number of men and some cars, clearly visible from up here though on the path itself they would have been hidden behind trees and bushes.

Jonah dropped the boy to the ground with a gentle thud and almost hissed through clenched teeth, 'Holy Mother of God. If we'd taken our usual route, we'd have been had. Good and proper.'

There were similar reactions from the rest of the party. Jonah studied the grey man and the boy with a new look in his eyes.

Peter peered down once more, this time with greater concentration. The men below were policemen. The cars were police cars. His stomach turned within him, and with one silent heave threw out its contents. It had been empty most of the day. It was empty again.

Peter was taken to an agreed point, midway between the wall surrounding the sand garden and the wooden chalet. Beyond that it wouldn't have been safe for Jonah and the others; before that too far for the worn-out boy. Jonah said he'd keep a look out through his binoculars to see that the boy got inside safely. Peter said, 'Thank you, sir.' This time he meant it and felt guilty for having thought bad thoughts about the man and the others. 'Less of the "sir", young man. The name is Jonah.' 'Less of the "young man", Jonah, the name is Peter.' 'Ah, so we are awake and kicking at last. That's what I like to see in a young man, Peter.'

The grey man held the boy's hand and looked at him. Peter said, 'Yes, of course I'll come to see you,' and ran off towards the wall, a new happiness giving strength to his tired bones. Peter didn't have many friends. Today he had made two. One of them like no other in the world.

Jonah kept looking through his powerful binoculars until he could clearly see Peter waving out to them from the balcony on top of the spiral staircase. The grey man extended a hand, took the binoculars from Jonah's hand and looked back at Peter, and waved back. Jonah was astounded, and as speechless as the grey man. No one had ever dared to take the binoculars – or anything else – away from him so unceremoniously before.

The moon was beginning to slide further and further along the horizon to make way for the sun.

Jonah and the grey man and the others began to wind their way back, very stealthily, very carefully. There was mounting swiftness in their cautious steps. They had to get back before the first light of dawn caught them with their human cargo, and whatever else besides.

Bremmin, the capital city, had once been the major port of New Heaven. Now, with the increasing use of air traffic and the installation of new docking facilities at the southern port of Shira, shipping had suffered a major decline. However, some of the 'dead' areas now forming the outlying part of the shanty town were still good for 'certain types' of naval activity, the type that could do without the benefit of customs and other officials. Jonah was aware that it couldn't go on indefinitely. With new schemes for 'development' daily cropping up, everything would change. How drastically, no one knew. Not yet, anyway.

Moonlight and the high tide had their advantages, but they could work against them as well; and tonight was not exactly the best night for the captain to have brought in the men and the parcels. They had all nearly been swept away. And now all this! Magda *had* warned them.

Jonah thanked God for their very narrow escape, and looked again at the grey man. As, indeed, did I.

It hadn't even occurred to Peter to ask how, when and where he would see the grey man again. He just knew he would.

9

Madga believed the world was a camel. It would sit the way it would sit: heaving and humping and leaning and adjusting, raising this and lowering that, grunting and growling and groaning and snorting, curling the lip and hurling the hip, distorting the jowls and contorting the bowels. And it would stand up again the way it would stand: heaving and humping and leaning and adjusting, raising this and lowering that, grunting and growling and groaning and snorting, curling the lip and hurling the hip, distorting the jowl and contorting the bowels. Even though you *could* coax it or force it or induce it either to start standing up or to start sitting down, it would accomplish the act concerned in its own peculiar fashion.

Magda also believed in a living God. If asked how she reconciled her miracle working Creator with her camel world view, she would direct her large black eyes at you and say, 'God made the camel, didn't He?' You might go on to say,

'OK. Fine. But where are the miracles if everything will be as it will be?' Her eyes would grow larger and blacker, 'The camel *is* a miracle. Lord, if the camel is not a miracle I don't know what a miracle is. Do you? So is the world. A miracle. Isn't it? They both go together, don't they?' If you were the sort that is not easily satisfied, you might argue, 'All right, so far as the camel, the world and *a* God is concerned. Surely a *living* God would take a more active role . . .' She wouldn't let you finish your sentence, but would retort, 'If the God wasn't living, the camel would be dead. Wouldn't he?' It wasn't possible to reason with Magda. Her response to reason was like that of a child, a very small child, as yet uncorrupted by the devious complexities and the false verities of logic. You would have also noticed that analytical questions she parried with rhetorical questions. She had learnt that this technique shut her questioners up better than the best arguments.

Clever, you might say. Obvious, Magda would say.

It follows that Magda did not believe in worrying. This did not prevent her from worrying – at least every now and then, but she did not *believe* in worrying, as a matter of principle, if not practice. Her camel approach to the world naturally led her to accept that in the end everything would turn up in the only way it could turn up, usually for the best. The camel could carry more water within it than all other creatures. That made it better fitted to survive than all other creatures. There was still a lot of water left in the world. As long as there was water, there was hope. You just did your best to try and direct the camel to stand up, and then pray. And wait.

You might conclude, from all this, that Magda lacked the energy or the guts to fight the world. You would be wrong. Sixteen years on the streets of Tanira – the most beautiful city in New Heaven and second only to Bremmin in size and population – had taught her to fight, and fight hard. Urging the camel to *start* a manoeuvre, she'd say.

There was not much new in her story. She had run away from home, the shanty town, on her thirteenth birthday, to make a 'better' life for herself and ultimately for her family: grandparents, parents, five brothers, two sisters, two dogs, five and multiplying cats – not to mention sundry cousins and aunts and uncles and family friends. She would 'make it good' and then call them all over to Tanira, to live in comfort and style, even luxury and style. It was she who had to come back to Bremmin, back to the shanty town, seven children, nine lovers, many hundred 'clients', sixteen years and one beloved later. The death of her parents in a mudslide by the river coincided with the death of her beloved in Tanira because of drugs. She returned to be mother and father to the family her mother and father had left behind permanently after she had left it behind temporarily. This part of her story was somewhat unusual. Not many who leave, return. That was twenty years ago. She was still waiting for the camel to stand up. Stand up and get going. Or perhaps to sit down. Sit down and settle down.

At age forty-nine she should at least have been able to make up her mind about the position of the camel, if not the condition of the world, you might say. Camel shit, Magda would say. 'To know whether you want your camel to sit or to stand, you must first know whether it is sitting or standing to begin with, mustn't you?' Then she'd add, 'And nobody knows *that*.' 'If I had a camel I would know whether it was sitting down or standing up,' someone once said. 'Ah! *If* you had a camel. *If* this, *if* that. What good is *if* to anybody. If I had a camel I would be riding it.' I told you it was hopeless to reason with Magda.

In many ways her 'waiting' was similar to Eleanor's patience. As, indeed, her 'urging the camel to *start* a manoeuvre' was similiar to Eleanor's fighting spirit. But they fought for different things, and for different reasons, and with different weapons. They also waited for different things.

Eleanor usually won her battles and got what she waited for.

* * *

As I have told you before, Magda tried not to worry, and often succeeded. She grieved and she cried she laughed she grieved she angered she hurt she grieved she hoped she despaired she grieved she sang she danced she grieved; and of course she loved; but she did not worry. She tried not to. It is hard not to worry when you love, but she tried hard not to, and often succeeded. She was not succeeding very well tonight. Today, really, for it was nearly dawn. It was nearly dawn, and there was no sign of Jonah and the others.

Jonah was the last of her seven children living with her. No one had heard from Joshua for many months now. He hadn't written to Jonah or to Magda. Or to Tamar, the woman he left behind. That was most unlike him. Although he had run away in hate and anger and grief, he had still kept in touch.

The youngest of her sons and the youngest of her children, Ishmael, the baby, was dead. Dead before his twenty-first birthday. Isaac, thirty-one, and Amnon, twenty-nine, were in prison, waiting to be electrocuted for the murder of Ishmael's killer. Yet another final appeal for mercy had been launched on his behalf by CASOM – the Campaign Against State Organised Murder.

Her two daughters had married. Maria died in childbirth. She would have been twenty-six now. Ziba killed herself after the sentence of death was passed on Isaac and Amnon. She had been twenty-two. Magda had the consolation of helping to look after their combined children, along with Jonah's children. She tried to forget how many. She had begun to believe that counting was unlucky. She used to always count her children first when counting her blessings. She took great care not to do so any more.

Joshua had left home one night in anger and grief and hate. He kept writing from Tanira for a few months. Since then, no one had heard from him. Not Tamar, not Jonah, not Magda. He had said he'd never forget his mother for as long as he was alive. Now he had forgotten her. Magda hoped that he had forgotten her. Even though it poisoned every drop of her blood to think Joshua, born to her when she was not fourteen

61

years of age, had forgotten her, after all those years of love and hurt, she hoped with all the power of hope that he had forgotten her. The alternative could not be contemplated.

Jonah, now thirty-four and only one year younger than Joshua, was thus Magda's only child and son living with her. Soon he might be the only one living. And it was nearly dawn and he wasn't back.

Magda was trying hard not to worry. She often succeeded when she tried not to worry. She grieved she cried she laughed she grieved she angered she hurt she grieved she hoped she despaired she grieved she sang she danced she grieved; and of course she loved; but she did not worry. She tried not to. It is hard not to worry when you love, but she tried hard not to, and often succeeded. She was not succeeding very well tonight. Today really, for it was nearly dawn. It was nearly dawn and there was no sign of Jonah and the others.

It was a night very like the night of Ishmael's 'murder' – full tide and full moon, beautiful and terrifying as the heart of God. And most fitting too. After all it had been on the eve of God's birthday. On Christmas Eve.

She found her body melting into prayer; and she fought it. She had promised herself never to pray again. That was three years ago. Since then, Isaac and Amnon had been sentenced, Ziba had killed herself, and Joshua had left home.

Even when she lit candles at the church she didn't pray. She clenched her heart and looked at the size of the candle and wondered who lit it last and what he or she could have asked for, but she did not pray. Not to God. Perhaps an aside to the Virgin. A nod for the Holy Spirit, maybe. But no more. Certainly not to God. Or to Jesus.

She was angry at them both – or them one, whichever way you looked at it. On the one hand she was sure they were one and the same, God and Jesus; on the other hand, if they and the Holy Spirit made three, then they must be two. It troubled her sometimes. Sometimes, but not always. Most of the time she just got on with it and believed. And prayed. At least until three years ago.

She wasn't a very literate Catholic, not even a very devout one in a traditional Catholic environment. The character and mixture of the shanty people had changed so much in the last fifty odd years that it was not an all-Catholic all-believing community any more. Many people had gone back to their ancestral belief in spirits and gods and nature. Many had come from different faiths: some entirely different; some corruptions of the true faith, such as Anglicans and Evangelists who denied the Holy Mother.

She had been angry at them both – God and Jesus – or them one, quite often before, mind you. But never until then with an anger that was greater than her love.

Magda believed that you didn't just pray to a living God. You argued with Him. You fought with Him. You laughed with Him. You shared your secrets with Him. You told Him stories. Magda had done all that. She had done all that all the time. But not any more. It was up to Him to make the first move now. He knew what she wanted. He knew what she needed. What's more, He knew what she deserved. If, in His opinion, what she was suffering was what she deserved, then so be it. She was not going to beg any more. If at any time He felt like changing His mind, then she would change hers. Not before.

Tonight, or rather this morning, for it was morning now, she found her body melting into prayer, against all the might of her will. She was fighting it, but she was losing.

It was a choice between worrying and praying. She would rather worry. Yes, she would rather worry than give Him the satisfaction of denying her yet again.

She found her body melting into prayer. It melted.

She cried out in rage and fury even as she prayed – rage and fury at herself, at God, at Jonah. She had told him not to go tonight. She had had that strange bad feeling all week. It was not altogether a bad feeling. Just a strange feeling. And it frightened her. It had been at its strongest that morning. The holiest of days! Mother of God, what had she let happen! But it wasn't *her* fault. She *had* warned them . . .

What did it matter whose fault it was or was not? What mattered was that Jonah . . . Oh, what was the point of it all! The bloody camel would sit the way it wanted to sit, or stand . . . Oh, Jonah. Oh, Jonah. Please come back, Jonah. Come back safe, Jonah. Lord. My Lord . . . Jesus . . . Please . . . Please . . . Jesus . . . Forgive me . . . Please forgive me . . . Please God . . .

The skies split, the dam broke, the waters rushed. I was engulfed with humility and drowned in shame. You could swim in my lungs.

There was a subdued but insistent knocking on the door. It was not Jonah. It was not Jonah's knock.

Somebody with news of Jonah?

Magda ran down the loudly protesting stairs, five feet ten, thirteen stones of firm flesh throbbing with restrained fear. On the way to the front door she tripped over one of the children sleeping in the main room and nearly fell. Recovering her balance she barely stopped to see if the child was all right, then continued her hurried steps towards the door.

Once at the door, she stopped, smoothed her long black dress, ran the palms of her hands over her straight black hair, breathed slowly and deeply, composed herself, crossed herself, took out a bunch of keys on a string from a little black pouch inside a side pocket of the dress, selected the right one, turned it firmly in the lock and pulled the door fully open.

Magda choked on a gasp, brought her left hand to her mouth to stifle a scream, crossed herself with a trembling right hand and reeled backwards.

Whoever or whatever she had expected to meet on the threshold of her crumbling house, she certainly hadn't expected to meet herself.

For there, standing in front of her, the fading moon behind her, was she, Magda, twenty-odd years ago.

It was not the future she had feared, nor the present that engulfed her; but the past come to visit her, on this fated Easter Monday at that hour of encounter between the blanched full moon and the gory half sun.

Time itself stood at her doorstep. Disguised in her body and wearing her beautiful pale silk dress, the one she had worn the night she was deflowered on the cold concrete of a smelly back alley in Tanira. The night Joshua was conceived. She could still see the bloodstains reaching out to her across and through the mountains. How she had cried that night at the ruining of the dress. It had been her grandmother's, and then her mother's. She had actually stolen it when she ran away from home. It would have come to her anyway; but she had stolen it. She couldn't wait that long, especially as she didn't even know how long that long would be.

'What is the matter with you, Magda? It is not like you to be so frightened!' Magda heard herself speak, but she did not recognise her voice. It was Tamar's voice. And yet it was not Tamar's voice, for there was a strange power in it. A power of strange emotions. But strange voice or not, it was Tamar all right.

Different people had said the same thing with different undertones. *Joshua has chosen Tamar to replace his mother!* For Tamar was so very like Magda. As tall as most women in Magda's family, and though much slimmer than Magda, she had put on weight since Joshua left. And now, dressed in that beautiful pale silk dress, Tamar looked very much as Magda remembered herself all those years ago.

Magda did not look so very different now – not a wrinkle on her moon face, nor a grey hair in her black tresses; no sagging flesh in her strong body – just bigger, and in black. She had give all her good colourful clothes to Tamar after the death of Ziba, and had worn nothing but black since. She was going to burn the silk dress, but Tamar saw it and insisted on taking it – it was still lovely, despite some faint marks which all the laundering in Pirdoz hadn't removed. Magda had vowed she would wear nothing but black until Isaac and

Amnon were freed. They were still in prison and she was still in black.

'What are you doing here? At this time when the moon and the sun are meeting and parting. It is not a time to be out unless one must.'

'Oh, but it is a time of must, Magda. It is a time of must.'

She paused in her speech on her way into the house, her face full of curious conflicting emotions which Magda could not decode. Magda always prided herself in her ability to read people's faces – even the faces of strangers, and certainly of those she knew like she knew herself. Her blood whirlpooled within her veins as she looked at Tamar's face. She could not see what was there, but she could feel its power. And it was powerful, whatever it was.

'There's news of Joshua – ' and before Magda could interpose – 'he's fine. He's fine, Magda, he's fine. He's fine. He's fine. He's fine. He's fine . . . Can't you see, I'm wearing my fine silk dress! *Your* fine silk dress! Would I be wearing it if he weren't fine?' Tamar burst into tears and hit her head against Magda's ample breasts and beat her fists against Magda's ample breasts and wailed like a sick dog howling for death while laughing like a madwoman taunting life.

Magda was infused with silent joy at the news of Joshua's safety and overflowing with silent questions about Tamar's reaction to the same news. Tamar felt Magda's unspoken joy and heard her unspoken questions.

'I am happy too Magda, but he's forgotten us. He's forgotten us. He's forgotten us . . . No! No no no no no. He's not forgotten us. It's worse. It's worse. He's forfeited us.'

There was a long silence after that. A true silence. A silent silence. Magda had run out of unspoken words and Tamar out of tears and cries. They just held each other and shared the joy of Joshua being alive and fine.

The time came for Magda to speak, and she spoke. She spoke slowly, 'I know what you mean, daughter. I think I know what you mean. If he'd forgotten us there'd be no pain in his heart. And that would be good, good for him, and so for him, for us. But I don't know what you mean, daughter. How forfeited? You are not coming up with any of your fancy university talk, are you?'

Tamar started to speak and to explain, but could not. 'He's fine, Magda, he's fine,' was all she said as she rocked in Magda's arms.

There was another anxious knocking on the door. This wasn't Jonah's knock either. Nor was it a knock of peace. Was the long-awaited good news of one son to be followed by bad news about the other? Was she to find one only to lose the other? Would she have to forfeit Jonah after Joshua had forfeited her?

Magda could have killed the living God.

But wasn't she being a bit premature? Hadn't she better find out who it was first before contemplating depriving the living God of life?

For the second time that morning she ran towards the front door and, this time without remembering to compose herself or even to cross herself, unlocked the door and flung it wide open.

For the second time that morning she choked a gasp, suppressed a scream and stepped back into the house.

Against the background light of the rising sun, the nearly naked figure of the grey man shone transparent like a glass fish.

The man next to him, a local lad called Ted, knuckles raised as if to knock again, smiled crookedly and said in a sharpish voice, 'Jonah will be back after he's settled the men, the new men. He wants you to look after . . . him. We found him this side of the shore. Jonah will explain when he gets back.' And he rushed away as if to get out of an awkward situation. A few steps gone, he turned his head back and shouted, 'He can't talk.' He opened his mouth, stuck his tongue out, made a slashing movement across it with his left index finger, then disappeared down the hill.

Magda felt the camel was about to sit, and sit on her.

I had to get her out of there. Out of Magda.

10

The two Easter Pageants – later to merge – had already started from the opposite ends of the shanty town, at their usual pace, which managed to be both relaxed and frantic.

One, carrying the larger-than-life statue of the Virgin, cloaked in black, began from the foot of the Mother Mountain. The black of the Madonna was to mourn the disappearance of Jesus' body from the cave. 'They have taken him. They have taken our Lord . . . We don't know where they have laid him . . . They have taken him. They have taken our Lord . . .' the cries of Mary Magdalene – at least according to the Gospel of St. John – were attributed to, and being chanted, on behalf of Mary, Mother of Jesus. However, in defiance of strict Catholic tradition, a beautiful young girl, meant to be Mary Magdalene, also in black, walked behind the float bearing the Virgin, sobbing hysterically and shedding real tears.

The other, carrying the life-size statue of Jesus, the risen Christ – at least according to legend – was approaching from the delta of the river.

When the two met, 'Mary Magdalene' would pull the black cloak off the Virgin Mary, revealing a pure white robe underneath, then she'd tear away her own black gown and expose the gold-sequined scarlet dress underneath: signs that the risen Christ had been seen and acknowledged by the women. This act of witness would signal the dancers, the musicians and the merry-makers to really take over. The revelries would then last well into the night and often far into the next day, depending upon the state of employment and personal priorities of the participants and organisers.

This had been the tradition in Gulroza – the shanty town – for time beyond memory.

Although Catholics were now in a minority in the area, they were a visible minority, known for their customs and rituals and traditions; generally well-liked, and even well-respected, despite the doubts of some of the newer residents regarding their political loyalties. They, the Catholics, along with some older residents, still referred to the shanty town by its original name of Gulroza, meaning Valley of Flowers. And, indeed, not too long ago, that is what it had been: a valley full of flowers. A valley forged through the Mother Mountain, now called Mount Gretna, by the river, now called New Thames. Then it had been inhabited mainly by reasonably comfortable farmers growing potatoes in small terraces upon the mountain slopes. The houses were small and neat, made from local wood and usually standing on flat land, but occasionally on tall stilts bedded in uneven, slanting ground to form a flat, firm base. The roads and streets were no more than rutted hilly paths, enlarged, cleared and occasionally cobbled with chunks of rock to prevent erosion by the seasons, or freak floods. Such floods had become more frequent and violent in recent years as the mountain slopes were gradually denuded of trees and soil.

More and more people, especially young ones, had left Gulroza over the last thirty-odd years, partly because the soil was becoming thinner and less productive, but mainly because of the lure of the city and industry and the jobs which the colonisers and settlers had brought with them, or introduced for the benefit of the less fortunate native population. This outflow was more than balanced by the influx of 'rejects' from the same cities which the locals had found so tempting; and by immigrants from other countries – some originally lured by the state as cheap labour and then discarded as the labour market contracted and became more competitive; some self-exiled economic outcasts, let down by their own ambitions, often worse off than in their own countries and without the financial wherewithal to return; some genuine political refugees – though not recognised as such by the government since they came from poor, unimportant countries and were the wrong colour, politically as well as literally – who frequently lived in hiding and without legal status.

This state of affairs was at first much improved, and then much worsened, as some 'greatly needed' industries were set up a little further up the river, not many miles from from the nub of Gulroza.

In the early phases of this new era came jobs and relative prosperity for the residents. Then there was an increase in the number of people, somehow both imperceptible and sudden. The newcomers built makeshift living accommodation, corrugated iron or pre-fabricated steel structures which did not look too bad to start with, but were uncomfortable even to start with – too cold in winter, too hot in summer – and soon turned ramshackle and into eyesores of profound magnificence. Various schemes to strengthen and tar the roads would have fulfilled another 'great need' had they had not been abandoned half-way through for no clearly explained reason, except for a vague 'lack of funds'. Rumours that industries were discovering and moving out to more 'advantageous' locations proved correct; and soon, apart from the derelict remains of a few ugly concrete structures and warehouses, the only employer that stayed faithful to the area was the New Heaven Division of the international drug manufacturing company,

Wrotham Laboratories. It transpired that the river, New Thames, provided an excellent dumping facility for unwanted chemical waste which soon disappeared into the sea, leaving no 'proven' harmful substances in the river – a source not only of drinking water, but also of food: fish, directly; and indirectly through providing a source of irrigation for potatoes and other root crops, still the staple diet of the locals.

Once anger and protests had failed, a depression, economic and emotional, succeeded in settling on Gulroza. After the exhaustion of democratic means, simple exhaustion. People lost interest in whatever it was possible to lose interest in. Sex remained an on-and-off source of comfort and consolation, new drugs became a more constant one. Rubbish started piling up in the 'newly-constructed' if half-completed streets, and also under the stilted houses and by the edges of the remaining fields and at the foot of the once sacred mountain and by the banks of the once-cherished river.

The whole place was thus rendered ripe for development by and on behalf of those better able to look after it and support it the way it deserved to be looked after and supported. After all, it was a location of exquisite natural beauty, at the base of a still green mountain, overlooking both the sea and the river. Hotels, golf courses, beaches, luxurious villas and luxury apartments: all the necessities of the good life were awaiting creation for those with developed aesthetic sensibilities, denied to the lower orders. The multi-hued foliage and many coloured flowers which once grew and bloomed in the valley, resplendent in their inimitable loveliness, could be brought back with little effort and great profit, within the confines of very private public parks. A shopping mall or two for the discerning, and Valhalla!

All that was needed was a little push, subtle enough to be totally democratic, strong enough to enforce the rule of the law: the new law, still in its embryonic stage, which would place a compulsory purchase order on all existing properties at current market prices. Of course, recourse to law was only to be considered if other democratic means to persuade the residents to move out into the new proposed developments – modern, sanitary, comfortable and 'adequate' – on the eastern side of the island were unfortunately to fail due to the recalcitrant attitude of some troublemakers. However, the grain-growing communities of the east would first have to be moved out to utilise their fertile land for growing other crops, such as cocoa beans, for lucrative export – vital for making chocolates in the more progressive markets of the world. Successful economic planning is not a simple matter by any means.

The band leading the Madonna's procession was an odd assortment of men and boys, women and girls – all dressed in flamboyantly individual colours and costumes – which somehow managed to look like a unified whole. The same personalised yet harmonised character permeated their music: from the modish basoon playing of the fourteen-year-old to the atmospheric bird songs of the eighty-four-year-old.

Magda had given up joining the mourning revellers since she had given up praying. Today she was back, behind the sobbing Mary of Magdala, a role she had once played herself at the age of thirteen. She had been like a poem on grief: no weeping, no wailing, no hysterics, not even tears, just dumb and dumbing deaf and deafening deep and deepening grief, as if she could either recreate and relive the mythical past or see into her own future. She had played the part to such perfection that she had come to be known as our lady of Magda. The name had stuck, and not many in the town even knew, much less remembered, that she was born Maryam. Since Maryam was the rightful name of both the Marys in the life of Jesus, perhaps it was appropriate for her to take on the title of one.

It was a clear sunny morning with a very slight breeze. It brought with it the lusty smell of meadow flowers which still managed to survive in the rocky slopes and crevices leading down to the river, before the soil turned too brittle and sandy for plant life as it headed towards the sea. Lady's mantle mingled with cat's foot and waved with friendly curiosity to the purple saxifrages in the wetter downs below. Daisies and buttercups and orchids of differing varieties and colours and heights blew into each others' arms with guilt-free rapture.

This sensual and sensuous invasion of *her* present by the sensory regalia of *the* present recreated Magda's past and invited it to become her present again. She was Mary again, Maryam again. A virgin again, like the other virgin, Mary, the other Maryam, whose name she bore, even though she was Magdalene, the whore. Mother of God and lover of God, with both of whom she shared the audacious comedy of the cross. Her foot turned lighter, her head reached higher and a smile spread itself upon her lips, a smile which some Leonardo was to capture in the distant future. Or had he already done so, in anticipation, with the vision of the artist? Or was it a perennial self-existing smile that wandered from face to face, from place to place, from time to timelessness?

The breeze dropped, the scent froze, the mountain closed in, the river slowed down, the sea turned to a sheet of steel. The turbulent stench of rotting chemicals surreptitiously appeared to preside over its republic and its public.

They were nearing the deep dip in the valley where the two halves of the carnival were to meet, close to the town centre. Because of its position it was an ideal point from which to view the snaky lines of both the marches as and when they united: the Virgin and the mourners as if descending from the sun itself, the risen Christ and the justifieds curving up from the bowels of the Earth, bearing the source of light with them and within themselves.

The time of their union was not far off now.

Jonah got home and discovered, to his great surprise and joy, that Magda had gone to join the Easter celebrations. This was

Magda's first sign of active participation in the life of Gulroza for a long time. He also discovered the reason for this change of heart and plan: the news of Joshua's well-being. Tamar told everything to Jonah, all that she had dared not tell Magda, even though she had come fully prepared to do so. Instead, she had ended up by saying no more than that Joshua was in some sort of trouble with the police, and so had chosen to hide away in Brite – which was a fact, but only part of the facts, as she had been told by an old friend. This friend had just returned from Brite and, despite express instructions from Joshua forbidding him to do so, had gone straight to Tamar's house and told all, even though it was late in the night.

After leaving home Joshua had gone to Tanira, and using his 'personal knowledge and expertise', got in with a ring of drug suppliers in Tanira. He soon discovered, as Magda had done years before, that the drug business here was very different from that back home. A severe attack of guilt during a drunken bout of self-pity turned him into an informer which, he realised afterwards, only made him feel worse than ever before. Remorse, however, did not stop him from accepting money and a new identity from the police, which he used to establish himself in the tiny island of Brite off the coast of mainland New Heaven. He did quite well there and built himself a fairly 'respectable' life. However, guilt piled upon guilt, particularly the guilt of conniving with the police, and prevented him from getting in touch back home. 'I can never show Magda my face again after collaborating with Ishmael's murderers.'

And that was not all. What had bled Tamar most was that Joshua had got married, and even had a little daughter. Wife and child – two more reasons he could not dare face Tamar, after all the promises he had made to her, or Magda, for she loved Tamar as her own daughter, more so since the deaths of Maria and Ziba. The only other alternative for him was to lie, and that he just would not do.

Jonah heard all this, but as a brother, a son, and a man, he was only happy that Joshua was well and alive; and that his mother had given up her seclusion and gone to join the rest of their people on this the most important day of the year. The rights and wrongs of what Joshua had done did not bother him much, least of all those which tore Tamar apart. He was half sorry, half pleased that Joshua had finally got himself hitched, and thrilled that he had a little daughter. Fortunately he did not say so to Tamar, not so much out of respect for her feelings, which he did have, but because he was too excited to think about it one way or another. It had been a strange night, and a very lucky one at that. The news about Joshua was the final magical touch.

His tiredness and lack of sleep forgotten, he decided to run out and join his mother. Normally he would have joined the other half of the parade, but today he would be with his mother. He stayed on just long enough to thank Tamar for remaining behind to look after the children. Jonah's wife had left him, saying she could not bear to stay on in a house of 'perpetual mourning', especially as the mourning was borne with 'such utter dignity'. Ranting and raving she could have tolerated, but calm, almost icy grief drove her mad, and out. Tonight there were five extra children in the house, along with Jonah's four, as Maria's and Ziba's husbands had also gone with Jonah, leaving their children with Magda, rather than with their own mothers. This was their custom on such occasions – a custom that was a source of constant but concealed friction among the families. Madga still commanded too much respect for open arguments to be aroused. As a further sign of their respect, the men would not come to collect the children, but would wait till Madga sent for them.

Just as Jonah was about to step out of the house he felt himself called back. He turned round, feeling strangely uncomfortable, to find Ishmael looking down at him from the top of the stairs. His heart jumped out of his mouth and lay convulsing and throbbing on the cold damp floor, which was cracked with moss showing through in places and brown mushrooms sprouting in corners and alongside the walls. He had ceased to notice them until today.

It was only when the figure took a step down the stairs and his face crossed the light – it had been hidden in the shadows above – that Jonah realised it was the grey man. He had nearly forgotten about him. How could he have. And how had the man called him? He had no voice or words. Or was it just that he could not speak?

The grey man was dressed in Ishmael's grey cords, grey pullover and grey moccasins. Surprising indeed. Magda had always devotionally guarded all of Ishmael's possessions, especially his clothes. Jonah was struck by the perfect fit. Ishmael had been very tall and very skinny. Perhaps it was the similarity of their build which had allowed Magda to make that startling gesture; and perhaps the fact that grey was Ishmael's favourite colour, particularly for clothes. The naturally flamboyant Magda thought it much too dreary, but Ishmael always did what he wanted and showed not the least desire to follow all of Magda's dictates – unlike the rest of the family. Maybe that's why he had been the favourite.

As the grey man climbed down the stairs and came towards Jonah, he knew that he had no choice but to take him along.

Jonah indicated to the grey man to follow him and started taking long strides towards the centre of the town. Within a few seconds the grey man was abreast of him, and within a few more, was leading. Was this the man who lay dying only last night? At least according to the boy. And he *had* looked so extremely debilitated and worn out. Jonah's uneasiness about the man became more dense, but strangely it was the unease of love rather than fear. Who could this unearthly creature be? Had he brought his brother back from the land of the dead?

He tried to rid his mind of these unanswerable questions so that he could concentrate on the joy of meeting Magda in the crowd.

11

In spite of the vast numbers of people, and in spite of the many wearing some token item of black – no one except the Virgin and Mary Magdalene were allowed to be in full black – Jonah, looking vertically down from on high at the marchers traversing below, instantly singled out the tall black-clad figure of Magda. So instant had been her decision to join the march, and so immediate her acting upon it, that Magda had not stopped to think that she would be breaking a taboo by being fully in black. In the event, no one objected. They were only too pleased to see her in their midst. It was a good omen.

Despite her run of bad luck, Magda, their very own Magdalene, was supposed to bring good luck to the townspeople. The years of her absence had been some of the worst for the shanty town. There had been considerable improvements since her return, though things were sliding downhill fast again. Maybe her return to community life would reverse the trend. Of course, most of the newcomers to the town did not even know her, and some only as Jonah's mother; among the older residents and their children – and they were the most ardent supporters of the Easter procession – she was almost a legend: what with her past, and then the multiplicity of her children's tragedies. The court case of Isaac and Amnon had provoked even the most taciturn to comment, as had Ziba's suicide; not to mention the dramatic disappearance of Ishmael's dead body and the even more dramatic killing, by Isaac and Amnon, of the policemen allegedly responsible for Ishmael's death while in custody.

Forgetting the potholed road, Jonah started to run downhill over the steep unhewn path, waving wildly, both arms uplifted. With remarkable agility the grey man followed and took the lead once again. What had Magda given him for breakfast?

The stillness that had descended upon the atmosphere like the breath of death began to break. At first ever so slightly: a tender breeze, like the breath of a newborn baby, stirred the soft hair of a child, holding on to the long skirt of Magda after losing his own mother somewhere in the crowd. An unreal silvery globe of light appeared in the west, challenging the sun opposite in its pubescent glory. The globe grew, the breeze strengthened. Within minutes, one was a cancerous mountain of clouds, the other a heaving ocean of wind. In the tall grass below, a bird screamed, a knife-edged scream. It could be heard flying away.

As Jonah and the grey man touched the crowd, a screaming monster, invisible except for its effects, rose out of that ocean and sent one disjointed arm to snatch the black cloak off the statue of the Virgin Mary and cast it across the furthest hill, while another arm tore away the black robe from the very human form of Mary Magdalene. The shiny white of one Mary clashed with the scarlet gold of the other in the eerie mixture of reflected light of the cumulus cloud and the incandescent

78

shadows of the rising and falling slopes at the foot of the Mother Mountain.

The crowd, used to the sudden island storms at this time of year, was undeterred in its enthusiasm. But it mistook the blowing away of the two Mary's black outer garments as the sign that the other half of the pageant carrying the risen Christ had arrived. Shouts and screams of claustrophobic, real-life pains masquerading as devotional cries of unrestrained joy shot up in the air like vocal fireworks. Some at the head of the parade tried to shout back that they had not yet been met by the other half of the procession, but no one was listening; and after a while they stopped trying to explain. It didn't matter anyway. After all, the others would be there in a matter of minutes. They could already be seen only a couple of hundred yards away.

Jonah had joined his mother and put his arms round her in a hug of love. The grey man stood close to both of them, the pain and suffering of his face illuminated with a soft, radiant glow of hope.

Soon the two snakes of the pageant were coiled together. Drums out-thundered the rumbling thunder. A rain of water pellets hurled itself upon the ground below from the skies above, but its force could not match the strength of the tears of exultation at the resurrection of Christ and the promise of eternal life – hopefully not in the shanty town – that rained down the cheeks of the singers, dancers and spectators gathered to celebrate their mass of masses upon the church of the consecrated Earth.

I joined in with them, and sang and danced and danced and sang and sang and danced in wild, wild abandon.

12

The rain continued to fall, getting sharper and weightier with each drop. The wind continued to blow, gaining power and momentum with each blast. The revellers continued to dance, matching their combined force and frenzy with the combined force and frenzy of the wind and the rain: the unthought thought that they may be going back to flooded houses in the immediate future only increasing their enjoyment of the momentous present.

Paul found it difficult to keep up with the others. He was as used to the sudden and powerful autumn storms of Bremmin as they, but he was not used to the hard reality of living with them and through them without the trappings of wealth. Of course, Paul had tried to lead a simple life on many occasions; in communes, with gipsies, and hitch-hiking from place to place and from country to country; but it is easy to be poor when you are not. Or it is more difficult. But it is not the same. It does not prepare you for the real thing, even though it may make you understand it better, and possibly give you an empathetic compassion for those who wear poverty as a second, unsheddable skin and not as a fashionable or ideological designer garment; who are struggling at the centre of, rather than observing from the periphery, the less pleasant varieties of living and dying.

As a result of much-publicised protests, the police had given in and not invaded the area in great hordes this year. Now that the small TV crew covering the carnival, fed up with the stronger-than-usual severity of the storm, were also getting in their van to drive away, Paul felt freer to move around. He had seen Jonah come running down the hill to meet up with Magda, but then lost him in the crowd. He decided to make a more determined effort to look for him. Surging forwards among the crazily dancing shouting screaming trumpetting drumming strumming clarinetting singing chanting mob of colourful overdressed children of the faith, whatever their age or religion, he finally managed to reach near enough Jonah to catch his eye.

Jonah, used to expecting anything and everything from Paul, should not have been surprised; but this morning, groggily amazed at the night's events and crocked up from lack of sleep, he was. Raising thick black eyebrows and distending thick black pupils, he gave him a look which asked a few questions.

Jonah put his arms round Magda, kissed her on the cheek, excused himself, moved towards Paul, grasped him by the arm and started thronging his way out, practically dragging Paul along behind. Magda decided to go back home herself. She did not want Tamar to be burdened with the children for too long. They would all have been awake for some time now, and wanting something or needing something or up to something. Besides, she had to find out what Tamar had not told her about Joshua. Once her first flush of joy was over, the feeling that there was a lot more to it than Tamar had divulged was becoming stronger, and she could not put it off any longer. She too started jostling her way out, beckoning to the grey man to follow. Since quite a few people were wearing masks or make-up, no one noticed anything strange about his appearance. In any case, the stamping feet and swirling dresses were now shooting up and swishing around almost as much water as was flooding down from the skies, making everyone's appearance, and vision, uniformly grey.

Once out on the side of the hill, Jonah and Paul started up along a well-trodden path. Jonah hunched his shoulders and bent his head forwards as defensive gestures against the storm, but Paul, just to show he could rough along with the best, or the worst, walked as upright as the force of the wind and the rain would physically permit.

'Met your tiny nephew last night,' said Jonah, then instantly regretted it. Although he could trust Paul not to get Peter into any trouble, he still wished he had kept the little blighter's not so little secret to himself – at least for the time being; and not until, if at all, the need arose to explain the grey man to Paul.

'What! . . . Where? . . . What?' It was unheard of for Paul to be taken by surprise, unknown for him to express such surprise, unwitnessed for him to be lost for words. The thought of his dear sister Eleanor allowing her son of reduced size but enlarged brain to meet any of the shanty dwellers, particularly one whose brother had allegedly – definitely, as far as she was concerned – died of a heart attack when arrested by the police for smuggling drugs, and whose two others were scheduled to die for killing three policemen – it was enough even to send the coolest of cynics into a fit of mild apoplexy. Jonah, who would have relished the occasion on another occasion, remained putty-faced and tried to lead the conversation astray.

'What a storm!' he muttered. After a hurried pause for thought he added, 'And what brings you here today?' trying two diversionary tactics at the same time.

'Where did you meet Peter?' insisted Paul.

Jonah resigned himself to telling the facts. He should have known trying to distract Paul, when he did not want to be distracted, would be like trying to frighten trees.

'Let's go somewhere peaceful, and dry, and I'll tell you. Not that there is much I know myself.' This would give him time to think, maybe change his mind about telling the little he knew, or concoct a story. Maybe not. Jonah liked to play for time. For all his hard, confident exterior there was a weak little boy inside him that was stronger than the strong man outside. That frightened little boy could always do with some extra time. And why not. After all, Jonah was only a man.

They headed silently for one of the several small and large caves – the many wombs of the Mother Mountain, where snakes, wolves and other outcasts of human society bred, hid and survived. *My broken breads.*

These dark, deep and mostly dry mountain caves, high up above the shanty town, were quite distinct in nature and character from the sandy caves in the cliffs by the beach, such as the one in which the grey man had taken refuge. Although aggressive police surveillance had stopped them being used as smuggler's dens, yet tired travellers, hitch-hikers, not so innocent men, and occasionally innocent women, still found rest, comfort and magic in their silence of the centuries. Despite certain obvious risks, like a scorpion in the crotch or a vigilant police officer demanding his share of ass, they were still quite popular for the odd inspired fuck. Some, like Jonah and Paul today, just went for a quiet talk.

13

Pebbles of rain lapidating his bedroom window woke Peter up. He was immensely relieved to find himself safe in his own bed. He had been dreaming that he and the grey man, along with Jonah and his friends, had been ambushed and were being machine-gunned by mounted police, the galloping hooves of their horses clashing cacophonously with the volley of their gunfire.

He raised himself up on his right elbow and tried to peer through the toughened glass with sleep-swollen eyes. Everything outside was grotesquely out of focus and appeared to be in constant and distorted motion behind the vertical rain-pools of ever-changing shapes that were playing about on the window which stretched across the entire length of the southern wall of the room. Peter normally enjoyed rain, and was fascinated by heavy thunderstorms; but this morning the fascination was mingled with an inexplicable fright.

Perhaps it was due to the lingering memory of the unpleasant dream.

Today was the first day back at school: exactly fifteen days after he had handed over his grey man to Jonah and the shanty men. It had rained very heavily that day as well. This morning it seemed to be even heavier – freak weather conditions, everyone said. Sudden and heavy rains were a feature of the island, but the last couple of times their severity had shocked and worried even the oldest and most diehard inhabitants. The losses of the shanty dwellers in terms of houses and property had been surprisingly minimal, so far. But if these weather conditions persisted, there was every possibility of much greater damage, and even danger to life. Landslides, on at least two previous occasions in living memory – and during less powerful storms – had not only destroyed a proportion of the houses, but caused numerous fatalities. A similar catastrophe now would provide many a tut-tutting politician and heart-broken developer a very sad justification indeed for clearing away the whole area to make room for more sound constructions.

Peter understood few of the ramifications of this political and economic game, and none of the rules governing democratic gamespersonship; but he understood enough about the 'problem'. The development of the shanty town was one of the principal topics of conversation in the Peruva/Poacher household, and one of the very few on which Eleanor and Philip agreed, though for different reasons and perhaps with different objectives. A note of dissent was introduced whenever Uncle Paul was staying with them. He was staying with them now, having appeared from somewhere the day after the appearance of the grey man, and going nowhere. At least not for the present. On the subject of the shanty town and its inhabitants his usually laid-back and non-committal approach to life and its problems became almost aggressively involved.

Peter's own confused opinion on the subject had turned into excessive concern since the night he had handed over his grey man to Jonah, the shanty man. And now he was frightened, frightened of the rain and the thunder and the lightning he had once loved. Autumn rain and thunder and lightning were not the subject or the object of wonder and delight and excitement and magic to the shanty people – even though the winters that followed were mild and green in this part of Pirdoz. He could now begin to see them, the thunder and rain and lightning, as *they* saw them; and he did not like what he saw. Or rather, he still liked it, but was ashamed to like it. Ashamed and frightened.

Worse, he was even more ashamed and frightened for being frightened than he was of the fears behind the shame. It was all very confusing. Men were not supposed to be frightened, so said Grandma Peruva, whom Peter loved very much and respected very much. Men must not be ashamed of being frightened, so said his mother, whom Peter loved very much, and of whom he himself was a bit frightened. Between the two and given his own feelings, he was never quite sure what he, as a man, must do.

In fact he was not even sure whether or not he was a man. Yet. Grandma Peruva said you were a man the moment you were born; that is, if you were born a man to start off with. In fact, you were a man right inside the mother's womb; that is, of course, if you were conceived as a man to start off with. Mother said you were born, whether man or woman, just as a person, and it was society which later cast you into one mould or the other. This made Peter wonder whether the little bits came before or after. Father was no help. He would not say what a man must or must not be or do. Mother wouldn't help him. That is, when they were all together. When alone with his father, which wasn't very often, they were so busy doing something or other that they never had time to talk. Peter often wanted to, but never got round to it. Philip was no help, and never broached any subject touching on these worries. Peter would sometimes shut his eyes tight and WILL for his father to start talking about them, but it never worked.

Following Eleanor's logical approach, if not always capable of following her example or her advice, Peter had made out three lists indicating how men should lead their lives. One according to Grandma Peruva, the other according to Eleanor, and the third based on what he read in the papers, saw on the television, or overheard adults saying in company or other children saying to one another in classes or in the playground. Then he had ticked off the common factors. The result was more confusion. However, there was one surprise conclusion. In spite of all their differences, there was one common factor in his mother's and grandmother's expectations of men: both believed men should do what was right and correct, rather than what they, as men, might like or want. The third list was divided on the issue. The real men were those who did what they, as men, wanted and liked; and then again, the real men were those who did what they had to do, whatever the cost to themselves.

On balance, despite some heavy and very tempting material for the other view, the idea that men must or must not do certain things seemed the more favoured, the one more likely to be the right one. What 'must' was the correct 'must' was now the problem – even if on this subject he were to reject the third list completely as being inconclusive and self-contradictory. Take a simple matter, for instance: men must always rush to open doors for women – Grandma Peruva – no reason given; men must never open doors for women – Mother – reason clearly stated: it assumes women are incapable of performing such a simple act as opening a door for themselves without male help, a typically loathsome example of male arrogance and chauvinism. Or take a more serious case, for instance, the presence of men at the birth of their child: essential – Mother; disastrous – Grandma. And so it went on. The two most important opinions in his life not only differed, but often radically clashed.

Peter thought of getting his lists out to see if he could discover how to act in this particular rainstorm, or at least find out how to react to it, but then decided against the idea. It would, as usual, leave him even more undecided, and worried, than before.

He brought one hand up to his face, stuck his thumb into his mouth, shut his eyes, rolled over to one side, took the other hand down below and grasped the only certain thing he knew about being a man.

He wondered what the grey man was doing. He didn't even have . . . *it* to comfort him! Not really.

And he did not have any money.

Peter worked harder and harder at being a man.

He also decided he would ask his father if he could give him some extra money to take to school today. That is, if he saw him before leaving the house. Peter's school was more than an hour's drive away and he had to leave quite early to be there on time.

He wondered what the grey man was doing.

He tried to picture him in his mind. Tom came in the way and obstructed the view with his huge . . .

And then his father appeared with his . . .

Both his father and Tom began to exercise and sing.

The poor grey man couldn't even talk. But he started to dance.

The whole room began to shake and roll like a great big rocking chair.

14

It fell upon Tom to drive Peter to school that day. They had not seen each other since the rocking-chair encounter, and both avoided each other's eyes. Peter hesitated noticeably before taking the seat next to him in the front of the car, making the uncomfortable Tom much more uncomfortable.

He was grateful to Peter for not telling anyone about him, not even Stewart, the other guard. Stewart knew about 'the affair', but Tom couldn't have borne being the butt of his jokes had he also known that they had been caught out together by Peter, and that Tom had had to run out naked to the nearest bushes and hide. He desperately wanted to thank Peter, to show his appreciation in some way, in some words. But there were no words. Words didn't come easy to Tom. He was good at bouncing people out of places where they were not wanted, worked hard at doing what he was told and could handle, was loyal to his friends and bosses, and was good in bed with man or woman. Other than that he had few talents, and fewer words. A man after Philip's heart. And other parts.

The rain had stopped and a bright warm day was lazily stretching out its territory along the sand, stones and puddles of the beach. Soon they were past the scattered exclusive residences and up on the high road – partly overlooking the shanty town, partly on a level with it, but still at a respectable distance. Any expansion of the shanty area and it would almost be on terms of intimacy with the domain of the ruling classes. Peter strained his eyes and craned his neck and looked out and down and sideways to see if he could catch a glimpse of the grey man, fully aware of the practical impossibility of that happening. A few stilted houses could just be made out from the speedily-moving vehicle, looking quaint and charming from up here instead of diseased and in distress. Like pretty little doll's houses, or like magic cottages made out of crumbly biscuits and crackling cornflakes instead of crumbling timber and cracking concrete.

The unspoken tension in the car began to parch Peter's throat. His tongue started to dry up and curl, the roof of his mouth cracked, and his lips felt like boot leather. If only he could ask Tom to stop somewhere for a canned drink. But he could not. After all, he had seen him stripped naked just that morning. If only in his mind. Which was worse. And enjoyed the sight. Which was the worst of all. If it hadn't been for his mother and the police he would not have known it was wrong. But he did now.

His gullet felt like it had swallowed the sun. He must make an effort to ask Tom to stop by at the next confectioner's. He turned towards him, but avoided looking up at him, and as a result found himself staring at his lap. As he did so he saw a movement there. Or thought he saw a movement. The wart hit him in the eye. His golden face turned orange and he could not speak after all.

It was then that a sudden thought occurred and took hold of him. He would skip school that day and go and see his grey man in the shanty town. He might have heaven to lose for it, but he was sure as hell going to do it. He could not tell whether this was something he *wanted* to do, or *must* do; but he'd do it anyway, anyhow.

Once the first surge of strength that comes with the making of a decision had passed, fears and worries descended upon his soul like fog upon the ocean. It was easy to say 'anyhow', but how?

And what would Mrs Mendoza think? What would Mrs de-la-Hay say. What would Mummy do?

His stomach jerked and without any warning half a bucketful of fiery puke gushed out of his burning mouth and on to his lap; and, with the wind rushing in from the open window on Peter's side, on to Tom's arm, his face, his hair and *his* lap. The car swerved under his surprised hands and just missed a fast-moving lorry pushing in from behind. He straightened up and, as soon as he safely could, pulled over to the side of the road.

'Are you all right? I mean . . . are you . . . all right?' he asked in a thick voice sounding thicker with concern but with no hint of irritation or annoyance at being so summarily baptised with breakfast vomit.

'Yes, thanks . . . I'm sorry . . .' For once Peter seemed lost for words as he fumbled for the handkerchief which Eleanor insisted he always carried. Having found it, he clumsily tried to wipe the sick off Tom, carefully avoiding his lap.

Tom, who up until that point, still not sure how to react or to further the conversation, had been slumped pudding-like in his seat, as useful as a gingerbread man, unmindful of being covered with sick – a not altogether novel experience for someone who had been a bouncer in more than a few eventful nightclubs for five of his twenty-seven years – suddenly galvanised himself into fevered activity, pulled out some assorted rags meant to dust or wipe sections of the car, and started cleaning both Peter and himself simultaneously, muttering, 'There, there, there,' and, 'Here, let me' and so on.

Peter did not object to the lack of intellectual drift in Tom's repetitive pronouncements, and felt quite flushed and pleased at this concern and attention. Flushed and pleased, also embarrassed and uncomfortable. He made a few futile attempts to brush away the strong hands of Tom working away tenderly over parts of his body, then allowed him to make him as tidy as possible in the circumstances.

No one had ever handled him with such firm gentleness before. Not even Uncle Paul, who despite his great love for him always shied away from physical contact. Of course, Natalia was quite tactile in her affections, but in a different, more delicate manner, handling him almost as if he were made of fragile glass – partly because of her naturally sensitive nature, partly because of repeated reminders from Eleanor regarding Peter's 'condition': reduced size, weak body, questionable health. Grandma Peruva, too, hugged and kissed him a lot, but she herself was so weak and so old that even her most passionate embraces, much frowned upon by Eleanor, were no more than spidery in their strength.

And certainly no man . . . except the policeman, and the doctors . . . But that was different. Their image sent a shiver through his body which made Tom think he was cold. He tried to hold Peter close, as if to warm him. Peter, now fully back within himself, pushed him away with all his might and shouted, 'Take your hands off me, you QUEER . . . you.' Then pulled himself back into his seat, shrinking as far away as he could, horrified not at Tom, but at what he had said. The word had rolled off his tongue without any conscious choice. He had heard boys, and girls, use it with a mixture of delight, contempt and disgust, but had never used it himself, nor fully understood it. But it must have impressed itself somewhere upon his subconscious, and now came out of his mouth right on cue, just in the way it was used by the pupils in his school. Was it exercising of sorts? If so, was his father . . .?

Tom recoiled at the abuse, shrinking back himself, blitzed by an unknown fear and a well-known shame. 'I wasn't doing anything . . . I was only . . . I was trying . . .' Tom's mouth kept opening, his lips kept moving, but no further coherent words could be heard.

Peter's horror at himself ballooned and burst at the sight of Tom's stuttering humiliation.

If Tom's state caused an explosion of tears in Peter, Peter's state caused an eruption of panic within Tom. For one flashing instant he could have turned round and broken the boy's neck with a single twist of his forearm. If a police car stopped to investigate what was going on, he'd rather be taken for a killer than a child-molester. No one would believe he wasn't once they found out about . . . One look at the tiny frame of the head-down, sobbing boy, and he could have turned round and broken his own neck at the thought.

There was only one way out. And that was out. He opened the door of the car with one mad jerk and jumped straight into the road and into the path and under the wheels of a fast-approaching lorry.

Fragments of him splattered on to Peter through the open car door. Particles of gristle and bone got into his eyes, but they remained open, watching.

Actually, the lorry missed him. But an oncoming car from the other side did not. It caught him in the flank and tossed him high in the air like a rag doll. He landed on his fleshily muscular backside right in front of the car he had been trying to escape. He sat staring at Peter through the windscreen, the outsides of his shoes touching the road, ankles twisted inwards like an infant's, knees raised and apart, palms resting on the caps. There was no sign of blood, or any injury, and apart from looking slightly dishevelled and more than slightly dazed, he could just have been sitting on the grass of a public park ready to eat a picnic.

Peter had difficulty reconciling the image conjured up by his imagination with the man squatting on the road facing his car. The two realities did not clash, neither did one obliterate the other. Both remained distinct and apart and real; and he sat there staring between the two, more dazed than Tom.

Peter had wanted that day to skip school and go and look for the grey man. The first part of the wish was now as good as granted.

15

Both Philip and Eleanor had to cut short their respective PRMs – Progress Review Meetings, so essential to their election campaigns in their respective areas – as soon as they heard of the accident.

Peter, they discovered to their great relief on returning to the beach-house, was all right and already home. Tom, though apparently unhurt, had been detained in the hospital for observation. His escape was not short of miraculous. Had the car which hit him not tossed him straight up in the air above the stream of traffic, and thrown him into the protective shelter of the car he'd been driving, he would have been crushed to a pulp. There was a constant flow of heavy lorries on that road, toing and froing between the coast, where some commercial vessels still landed, and the industrial centres on the outskirts of the city.

Philip promised to himself that he would light a candle in

the church that night, or as soon as possible to thank the Lord for saving Tom's life. Theirs was not a monogamous relationship, nor was it a serious love affair, but each cared about the other and Philip would have been deeply upset had something happened to Tom. Could something still happen to him? What if in the hospital they discovered the wart on his prick and connected it with the man who had allegedly attacked Peter on the beach? Philip didn't believe that story, but that was not the point. If they saw that big wart, what further exposures might follow? What might it – *would* it – do to his election chances? What would Eleanor say? What would Eleanor do? He almost wished they would find the big wart, and connect it . . .

He very much wanted to go and see Tom in the hospital, but felt he should not. Strange that, for had it been Stewart, or any other of their male employees with whom he did not have a relationship, and there were some, he would not have thought twice and just gone. As, indeed, he would have done if Natalia or any of their female employees had been hurt.

Eleanor's relief at Peter's escape – whatever it was he was supposed to have escaped from, she was still not sure and no amount of questioning brought her any nearer to a satisfactory answer – was heavy with regrets. Philip was glad to be able to get out of the PRM. He hadn't done his homework and was not properly prepared for awkward points and probing questions about policies and tactics. Eleanor was angry and disappointed. If Peter had been hurt – thank God that he wasn't – but had he been hurt, she could have borne the disappointment better. But it was so pointless now. A wonderful opportunity to press home certain issues and make strategic campaign decisions, and to instigate and institute her new Action Directives Initiative Scheme, wasted. The next meeting might take as much as a fortnight to arrange. Still, there was the consolation that the planned afternoon walkabout could go ahead as scheduled. Philip, too, was looking forward to the walkabout. He enjoyed meeting people and having a chat about this and that. What's more, he really did like kissing babies. He had seldom been allowed to kiss his own on the grounds that it was unhygienic.

Peter had been a very delicate baby, and had spent the early months of his life first in an incubator and later in a special unit in the hospital. Somehow Philip could never develop a touch relationship with him after that. It was too late now.

'I bet that carrot-nosed Gomez is rubbing his hands with glee,' said Eleanor standing up after just having sat down on the edge of her favourite armchair in the living room.

'Why should Jerry be pleased that . . . Peter has had an accident? I know he is contesting your seat, but even so.'

'You know perfectly well what I mean, Philip. It's the PRM I am talking about. The fact that I had to . . . Oh, what am I doing trying to explain. You know perfectly well what I mean!'

Philip actually had been thinking about the accident – and had nearly said 'Tom' instead of Peter – but he did not press the point.

'Well, don't you?'

'Don't I what?'

Paul, sensing a marital ding-dong, interrupted: 'What is it about elections that brings out the worst in any man, or indeed woman? Tut, tut.' He knew from experience that the best way to avert a row was to direct Eleanor's wrath towards himself. Peter could do without another of his parents' arguments just then. He may not have been hurt, but he certainly looked ill.

'You keep out of it, Paul.'

'Out of what?'

'The election.'

'I wish you'd take your own advice and keep out of it yourself.'

'You are impossible!' said Eleanor dismissively, but not without a hint of grudging affection.

'If I were impossible, I would not be. If I am, I cannot be impossible. Surely your logical mind should –'

'Oh do shut up, Paul. I have no time for your flippancy. I still have to decide what to wear for this afternoon. White. Yes, white. But what if it rains? Maybe off-white. Something, maybe cream . . .'

'How about studded leather and steel whips,' Philip dared to join in.

'You would like that, wouldn't you! Only not on me, but . . .' Both Paul and Philip held their breath. Eleanor withheld her comment, and both Paul and Philip heaved soundless sighs. 'Honestly, you two are such second-rate chauvinists it isn't even worth arguing with you. I must go and get some coffee. Or something stronger. I am not really looking forward to this walkabout, after all this.'

'I think it will be fun. It's only the first of many this year, so you'd better start with a more positive approach than this. Yes, I *am* looking forward to it.'

'Anything to get out of the house, as far as you are concerned. Besides, you *like* kissing babies. Ugh.'

Peter shuddered involuntarily.

'What's the matter, baby?' Eleanor leaned towards him and patted him on the shoulder. 'Why don't you go up to your room, and lie down for a while? I'll ask Natalia to take up some milk for you.'

'I am all right, Mummy. Thank you. I don't want to go to bed now.'

'It is not always what you want that is good for you. In fact it rarely is.'

'Just let him be for a while, Ellie. I will take him up myself in a minute.' Paul was the only one who called her Ellie.

'I know your minutes, Paul. They are longer than most people's hours. Days even,' retorted Eleanor. 'And when you get him there, do try to find out what really happened. He tells you more than he does anybody else.' This last was muttered resentfully under her breath.

'I wish you wouldn't go on, Eleanor, the boy has told you all he knows,' It was Philip's turn to mutter under his breath.

'Do give me credit for some sense, Peruva. Now why would Tom stop in the middle of a busy dual carriageway to get some water?'

'Peter had been sick, that's –'

'May I be allowed to finish? Now, as I was saying, why would Tom stop in the middle of a busy dual carriage way to get some water. And if so, why not go along the road to look for some? Why run across to be hit by a lorry.'

'By a car, dear. The lorry missed him.'

'Thank you, for correcting me, for once you are right. Not by a lorry, by a car. Still, no doubt not a very pleasant experience. Not one to court, spontaneously and enthusiastically, even if perchance one does have the IQ of a demented chicken, which, I concede, is marginally higher than Tom's. Nonetheless, why get out of the car there to look for a drink when only a few minutes' drive up the road is the Peddingham High Street and, wait for it, shops! Or, failing that, in an emergency they could have taken any side road and knocked on a door.'

Paul, having heard most of it before, was resisting the temptation to mouth Eleanor's words before she uttered them. It would have been too childish, even for him.

'We've been through all this, Eleanor. Just wait until Tom –'

'Who, by all accounts, remembers nothing at all. Or haven't you heard? Don't tell me you haven't . . .' Eleanor paused, as if about to go on speaking, but did not.

'Give him time. It will come back to him. It's just shock.'

'It is just convenient, that is what I say. Convenient! Assuming he is clever enough to think up the I-can't-remember stuff.'

'Only a minute ago he had less brains than a demented chicken.'

'Do stop being so literal. You know perfectly well what I mean.'

'Well anyway, give him time. He'll remember. When he comes back –'

'That is all you are concerned with. When Tom comes back. When Tom comes back. When Tom comes back. That is all I have heard since I came back. That is all you are concerned with. Nothing else matters. I had to abandon my plans for my Action Directives Initiative Scheme.'

'Once. I mentioned Tom getting back once. And that because you started going on about him. Whereas your bloody Action Directive Sod All, whatever it is, we have to listen to every bloody minute –'

'No, you do not. Just watch out what you accuse me of, Peruva. It is a scheme instituted by my party, and you know perfectly well I do not discuss party affairs with you.'

'I think I'd better take Peter up now. He really looks like he could do with some rest.' Paul thought it would be best to make a tactical retreat, somewhat in the manner of a tactical vote, a discussion on which was a part of Eleanor's Action Directives Initiative Scheme.

'Well, that is what I have been saying all along. Thank God somebody listens to me. Sometimes.'

'I always do, don't I, Ellie, love?' said Paul, deadpan, knowing full well she hated no epithet more than 'love'; then seeing that Philip had turned his back on her and was staring out of the window, he crept up to her, leaned forward, and whispered in her ear, 'I will look after the silent brunette, while you two sit here and await the return of the dumb blonde. That is, assuming it is hospital policy to discharge the brain dead.'

He ran out, pulling Peter behind him, before Eleanor could think up a retort.

Poor Tom. He was the butt of everybody's jokes. Easy meat. And easy butt. Paul felt guilty for joining in with Eleanor. At least Philip . . . He changed the subject of his thoughts.

When Paul came down half-an-hour later to get Peter a glass of milk, he could hear Philip: '. . . but everyone is not as cold and calculating and logical as you are. People do things on impulse.'

'Well, I have yet to meet one who runs under lorries on impulse.'

'Of course they do. People run under trains, jump from bridges. I am often tempted to –'

'Oh, so now you are telling me the poor dear was so fed up with just being a plaything of the rich and famous he decided to end it all in one great big stupid gesture, with Peter as the final witness to his Grand Duchess Ninochka tragedy.'

'I don't think Ninochka was the Grand Duchess, dear. Besides, there were no lorries in her time.'

'So we are back to being literal. When all else fails, let's be –'

'I've only learnt it from you, dear. You are the one who insists on everything being one hundred and eighty-three-and-a-quarter percent correct and perfect. Your problem is you may think you are always right, but you don't often get it right.'

'No. I don't get it at all, because you are too busy getting it. And that's your problem, isn't it?'

There was solid silence after that. Paul couldn't make up his mind whether to smile or not. He quietly walked back upstairs.

16

'Hi, Natty. Where have you been keeping yourself?' Paul liked shortening people's names, a habit even his friends found irritating. Natalia didn't mind.

'Where have I been keeping myself! It's you who've been missing for seven months.' And twenty-three days, she added to herself.

'Well I have been here for two weeks, but hardly seen you twice. And when I say seen, I mean seen. You haven't given me the chance to speak to you once.'

This was true. Natalia knew there was no future in it. The more she saw of him, the more she spoke to him, the more she let him speak to her, the more she'd get hurt. To keep out of the way was the best way out. One day out on the river and in the meadows, one evening at the theatre, and one night in bed was not enough to build your life on. Paul, with the blood of the gipsy wanderer, was just the type of man

101

that every woman wants for herself and warns her daughter against.

'Come on. How about a kiss. Just for old times' sake.' This was just the wrong thing to say. Paul always knew just the right things to say to women – unless he wanted to be obnoxious, which he was when he wanted to be – but usually got it wrong with Natalia.

'What old times!' Natalia's black eyes turned amber. 'You . . . take, yes, take a woman once, and you think you own her for life. Well, I am not one of your . . . I am sorry. I have no right. I'm sorry.' With that she tried to walk out as calmly as she could, but Paul stopped her. Gently holding her by the shoulders, making no attempt to kiss or embrace her, he took her to one of the 'sensible' high-backed chairs in the room and sat her down.

They were in a sort of informal enclosure on the second floor with a glass wall overlooking the beach, containing an odd assortment of chairs, sofas and settees, love-seats, *chaises longues*, an extendable oval dining table, an oak writing desk with a typewriter and a word processor, a portable TV set, a music centre and a multi-purpose exercise bench along with other body-building equipment. Nothing matched anything else, though each piece had its own charm or personality or function. This had been Philip's study before he had the chalet built. Eleanor hated the room and never used it. So whenever Paul wanted to be alone he came here. So much so that he more or less adopted it and made it his own whenever he was staying with his sister, which was whenever he was short of money and long on time, and not 'travelling'.

Philip and Eleanor had left to prepare for their respective walkabouts; Peter was asleep in his room; Stewart was basking in the sun by the main door; a couple of other men were loosely hanging about the garden; an old woman, a relative of Philip's, was gardening away in the sand garden; another old woman, another relative of Philip's, was busy 'looking after' the house – in effect, doing nothing in the kitchen garden.

A huge black bumble bee had somehow managed to get trapped in the enclosure and was complaining away noisily, hitting her head against the glass in angry desperation at the deception perpetrated upon her by the treacherous substance. Surely the place was possessed, otherwise why should she not be able to go through nothing?

'It is I who should be sorry. And I am. I didn't think that you . . . I didn't think . . . I just didn't think. I seldom do,' Paul heard himself say.

He waited for Natalia to respond, but she remained silent, neither looking up at him, nor down at her feet, nor staring straight ahead. Her eyes were in a different territory altogether.

'How old are you?' he asked, surrendering after a short battle of silences.

'You should know. You took me . . . We went to see the Follies on my last birthday.' Her face was glowing with anger, embarrassment and more, which made Paul feel better, despite the pain of it.

'So I should. I'm not making it any better, am I? Of course I remember. Nineteen candles! Nineteen flames. Nineteen trembling flames. You looked at them, and there were thousands. Thousands of trembling fires in each fiery eye. The sky lit up with stars long dead and never born. How can I forget! How long ago was that?'

Natalia, who had begun to float away on a magic carpet, came down with a thud at the question. 'You don't even remember that. Eight months, one week, five days and fourteen hours ago, give or take a few minutes.' She hated herself for having said that, for laying her vulnerability so open for his inspection – or even his mockery, for who could tell what was going on in that strange mind of his which worked according to its own laws, invented its own rules and operated in a space of its own.

'I did remember that, Natty. I asked for a special reason. To remind you. I had my nineteen candles, well I didn't have them, but might have done if I hadn't been lost on a Tibetan mountain at the time, that many years ago. I could have a daughter as old as you, or older. I started fathering, if that's the wrong word, a few years earlier than that.'

'Please do not resort to that age-old old-age excuse. It is hollow at the best of times. Coming from you it stin . . . smells of hyp . . . it is really unacceptable. Since when have you followed the conventions of society in any way? You do what you please, when you please, with whom you please, where you please and however you please. Yet when it suits you, you are quite willing to have the judgements of the very society you mock and frown upon as your allies. This is beneath you, Paul.'

'Perhaps you are right. But it is you I am thinking of. If only I was half as free as you paint me to be. Perhaps you are right.' He knew she was right. If he loved her he wouldn't have cared if she was nineteen and he ninety. And yet he did love her; but not enough. Not enough to give up his life for her. And ultimately, he feared, that that was what every woman demanded of a man: his life. Perhaps he had a lot of growing up to do himself, despite his age. Or perhaps he had grown well beyond his years, beyond his manhood, beyond his humanhood, and knew more than any son of man is meant to know.

The buzzing of the bumble bee became more plaintive and more desperate. Natalia got up, walked to the glass wall, slid open a panel at the far end, and began guiding the bee towards freedom, using her body as a shield to prevent the bee from going the wrong way. 'That way. There, there . . .' and when the bee continued to bash her head against the glass or move up and down or away, 'Can't you see, stupid thing. Not that way. There. There. Oh, I give up.' She moved to the other side and stood looking out, nose almost touching the glass.

Paul walked up close to her, pressed one palm against the glass, not caring what Eleanor would say about the print, and stood brushing her body with his own, the afternoon sun hitting him head on and lightening his light brown hair almost to blonde like his sister's.

She avoided looking straight at him – in her heels she was nearly as tall as he – but the image of him standing naked by the edge of the river, elbows just above his hips, forearms raised up in the air, palms opened outwards, fingers spread, repainted itself upon the canvas of her mind. With his burnt brown body he had looked as much like a tree without leaves and roots as a human being. The extra stump sticking up from below his belly, with its own fruits hanging beneath, affirmed the image she had of him as both man and tree.

It was Christmas Eve, their first Christmas together. Their first day together: the Christmas before last – he hadn't been around for the last one – but it could have been as long ago as the first Christmas.

When they had finally got home that day, all covered in scratches and cuts and bruises and insect bites, he had taken his easel and pencils and crayons and paints out of the boot of the car, her car, and started sketching the back of the house against the sunset! She was so furious. He had taken the whole paraphernalia to paint *her* against the rising sun, but didn't even take the sketchbook out, just took her clothes off. He took his own off first, when she was hesitant, to make her feel comfortable, to show her how easy it was and how little it mattered – maybe to him – and then started chasing butterflies. Forgot all about sketching and painting. Didn't fuck either . . . What was the point in going over all that again. As if she hadn't done that hundreds of times before.

That was the first time she had seen him naked, or indeed seen any man naked. And the first time any man had seen her naked. And yet they had not had sexual intercourse. Although they had spent the whole day swimming in the river, naked, and running through tall grasses and wild flowers in the meadow, naked, he in painful erection most of the time – made worse when a stinging nettle caught his cock – they had not had sexual intercourse. Paul had not asked, and she had not asked why not. She had wanted to ask, but she had not asked; whether or not he wanted to ask, she knew not. She had at least wanted to hold him, it, ever so gently, and soothe

105

with her tongue the angry rash on the angry swelling; the soft pulpy swelling caused by the nettle on the hard rocky swelling caused by nothing at all; but she didn't. And he didn't ask her to. When they finally did go to bed, about a month later, it was a never-ending bout of hard sex, without words or apparent love. Just fucking fucking fucking. With Paul it was either all tender love, or fucking. He never seemed to mix the two.

'*Never!*' she thought wryly. How could she say? Once. That was all. The one kind, once; and the other kind, once. The evening at the theatre, birthday candles and dinner notwithstanding, had been neither one nor the other, just a celebration of being alive, and being together.

She moved between him and the light, uncertain as to what to do or say, when the buzzing of the bumble bee abruptly stopped, giving a new music to the silence: the steady chirping of a cricket in the grass below. Natalia turned her head, glad to have somewhere to look, and saw the bee flying out to freedom. Paul turned to look as well, but by that time the bee had disappeared. However, he did catch the movement of a rather elongated shadow of something quite tiny in itself, just behind the outer wall of the garden, stealthily escaping away from the main building of the house, towards the chalet.

Without a word Paul ran out through a sliding door to the right, onto the balcony, down the spiral staircase, into the sand garden, a quick dash across it, through a side door, past a half-squatting half-reclining man looking at a sex magazine and gently manipulating his genitals with his right hand inside his trousers – probably a relative of Philip's employed to guard the east side of the house when not much was going on – and out along the wall, as Natalia looked down in utter amazement, dismay and anger.

When she saw what, or rather who, he was after, she understood. But he could have said something before running out. That wouldn't have taken any time at all. He could have shouted out while on the stairs, or from below, without even having to stop. At the very least he could have waved. Her anger returned. On the other hand, Peter was in *her* charge, and if something happened to him, *she* would be blamed. She ought to be grateful to Paul for spotting him, and for going after him. She was. Still, he could have warned her. He could even have taken her with him. She was a good runner, and jumper. If he could be that athletic at thirty-six, or -eight, or whatever, she could match him stride for stride. Her anger returned.

If only one could switch off one's mind as one can a television repeat. Often one did not even do that.

Peter heard softly-running footsteps behind him, panicked and, unable to make up his mind whether to try and make a run for it or to turn back, stood still and silent, breathing heavily. Attempts to stop himself hyperventilating by counting up to six each time he inhaled or exhaled as per Eleanor's instructions, only made it worse.

'Hi there, PT.' PT was not exactly a shortening, but Paul had to have his own special name for everyone, especially for someone as special to him as Peter.

Peter relaxed immediately. It was just Paul; but the sudden draining out of tension in one swift movement left him tender and wanting to cry. Then pleasure at gradually realising that it was not 'just Paul', but Paul, began to strengthen him, and he managed a smile. He still wanted to cry.

Paul waited for some verbal response, didn't get any, and spoke himself again. 'Now, I've known for some time that you sneak out of the house to who-knows-where at the strangest of hours – and good luck to you. I still keep doing it, and I am a little older than you, believe it or not. But you do have to be careful. It is not always very nice out there, however nice it may seem. Sometimes it is, but not always.' He was playing for words, hoping Peter would say what he was up to without being directly asked. He had come to stand next to him, ready to start walking ahead if Peter chose to walk on; but Peter just stood there, awkward, half-smiling, half-looking like he was about to cry.

In his anxiety and in the face of Peter's silence, he said something he did not really want to say. 'Honestly, Peter, today of all days! Don't you think you have had enough excitement for one day? You still don't look well,' he added lamely. He had not only said exactly what Ellie would have said, but even called him Peter.

Surprisingly, it worked. Peter saw the concern in Paul's eyes and voice, and relented, 'I was only going to see the grey man.'

'Who? And where? And how?' This was the second time Paul had been thrown out of gear by the Peter/grey man combination.

'At the shanty town.'

'The shanty town! And how, may one be permitted to ask, were you going to get there?' Supreme Being! How much like his sister he could be. He had never before thought they had anything in common, except love. 'I'm sorry. I am just, well, surprised. I thought perhaps you had a secret place little children go to hide or sulk or play or fantasize or something, and were going there. Where do you usually go to?'

'I do have a special place. Only it is not one place. It is a lot of places. But I am not going there today. I am going to the shanty town to look for the grey man. Can I still go? Please? Please?'

'How will you get there? Do you know how far it is? It may look close, but –'

'It's . . . It is far only by the proper . . . main roads.'

'You don't have to talk like that with me! I am sorry if I sounded like Mummy, but –'

'If I stick to the paths up and down the hills, through the woods and across the big road, it'll only take me an hour.' The note of certainty in his voice despite the vagueness of his direction, and the sudden confident look in his eyes surprised Paul even more than his aborted venture.

'That so? Just look at your little legs. They are like match-sticks.' Supreme Being twice! This was worse than Ellie's term, 'reduced size'. What was the matter with him today? Had it anything to do with Natty? 'OK, OK, so you get there in a hour, how will you know where to find your grey man?' From the little Jonah had told him, and from what Peter had confided in him later, there was really no way of telling who or what he was, or where he might be at any time, given or not.

'He's staying with Jonah, isn't he?' Peter was getting more and more excited, not in the least bothered by the 'matchstick' simile – as coming from someone else at some other time he might have been. 'And it won't be difficult to find where Jonah lives. Everybody knows where he lives?' There was another question mark in his statement. 'Everybody who was with him that day knew him. They must have known . . . They would know where . . .' He stopped as he realised how illogical he was being. Mummy would be very angry at such slipping up, almost as angry as at his slipping out to go to the shanty town. He brightened up as he sighted another trail of thought. 'Besides, everybody would know the grey man by now. He is . . . *striking* enough.' He was pleased to have found the right argument, and the right word. He had not wanted to say 'strange' or 'peculiar' – the first words that had occurred to him.

He was right. Everybody did know the grey man by then. He was considered by some to be evil, the one who had brought all this excessive rain and the storms with him; others thought him to be the one saving them and the town from being deluged and destroyed by the rains. He was feared by all. Revered by many. Sympathised with by most. Loved by a few. Hated too.

'What if someone picked you up and walked away? You know that can happen. Or handed you over to the police? You only look about five.' As he saw the gold turn pale in Peter's cheeks at the mention of the police, he stopped, bent low, picked him up by the waist, and held him up against his own waist, as some Indian women carry pitchers of water, and started walking away.

'Where are you taking me?' giggled Peter, who was not normally a giggler.

'Home,' said Paul. Then hearing Peter's giggles subside, he added, 'Borrow Natty's car and drive you down to Gulroza to find your grey man. Wouldn't mind a chat with Jonah myself.' Jonah was the one friend whose name Paul hadn't been able to truncate. And Magda. But Magda was an affectionate title anyway, already nicked.

The blood rushed to Peter's face turning him bronze, more so when Paul dangled him upside down still by the waist.

It was then that Peter said a strange thing in a strange voice, 'I know where the grey man is.'

'Yes, and so do I. With Jonah,' retorted Paul, finding nothing strange in what he said, and attributing his strange voice to his upside-down position.

'In a big blue cave with a little brown hedgehog,' said Peter. Now it sounded strange to Paul. It sounded strange even to Peter. He didn't know why he said it. I had not deliberately prompted it, but neither had I done anything to prevent it.

17

Up and down, straight and winding, far then near again, and they were in the shanty town. Natalia had agreed to come along; part reluctantly because she didn't much enjoy going to new places or meeting new people; part annoyed because Paul had taken for granted that he could borrow her car; part pleased just to be included – on the grounds that after all it was she who was ultimately in charge of Peter. She had also agreed to let Paul drive. She was a little embarrassed by her somewhat rust-eaten nine-year-old model; Paul loved it. He was embarrassed by the brand new Westbourne 300 that was always ready and waiting in the garage for 'family or state emergencies'.

Jonah's house, being among the oldest, had no direct road leading up to it and you had to park some way away and then walk up a steep, uneven half-broken cobbled path. Not the best for high heels, especially inexperienced ones: Natalia's got caught twice and she nearly fell over three times. 'You could have warned me. It would have taken me a minute to change my shoes.' 'Sorry, didn't think.' 'You never do, do you!' 'I'm the first to admit it.' 'Nothing to be so terribly proud of.' 'Never said I was.' 'You don't have to say it.' Etcetera. Peter was much too thrilled to hear any of it.

Magda opened the door and was pleased as ever to see Paul. 'What blessed wind blows you here? Come in. Do come in. This your little boy? Can't be. I mean, he could be yours, but not your girl's. She's just a child herself. She is your girl, isn't she? What a beauty! Lucky man, you are!' Magda couldn't have said so many wrong things in one breath for a bet, as far as Natalia was concerned.

'I am nobody's girl, but my own woman. And I am not a child. Neither am I a "beauty". Beauty is a horse or something. I am a person. And whether he is lucky or not has nothing to do with me! And it was not a blessed wind that blew him here, but my wretched car that drove him here.' All her days, and indeed weeks and months of frustration and heartbreak exploded upon the astonished Magda. Had Magda not looked so resplendent in flowing black – her cheeks still glowing from the news of Joshua's wellbeing, her eyes gleaming with the joy of seeing Paul – Natalia might have been kinder. As it was, she could not control the anger that had been building up inside her. She felt used and discarded, needed less than her broken-down old car.

Paul had never seen her like this, or heard her like this. Where was the gentle Natty who had nearly cried when he had pulled a colourful weed out with rather 'too much force', to give to her to wear on her hair when she wasn't wearing anything else?

Natalia herself was shocked at herself, but decided to put on an unrepentant front rather than an apologetic one. She held her head high, to all appearances poised and cool.

Magda, who knew women and men and life better than Paul ever would, slipped out of her initial surprise with remarkable ease, welcomed them inside with a flourish of her long, powerful arms and said, 'It must be a hotter day than I had thought. Do come in. And tell Magda what she can do for you, man, boy and person? Come in.'

By now a host of little children, of both sexes and various ages and curious shapes and designs had gathered round them, staring: from Paul, whom they vaguely knew; to Natalia, of whom they seemed a bit wary; to Peter, whom they found strange. Some were grinning, exposing teeth, or holes where teeth had been and would be again. Others had thoughtful, serious expressions, and at least two were distinctly frowning.

'Thank you, Magda. We will. This is Natt . . . Natalia, Natalia Litvinof. She helps my sister look after her son. PT here. Peter. Peter, say hello to Magda. If you are good she might let you taste her mango delight one of these days. Natalia is also completing her degree in something very important at the Balk University. She hopes to join the government and run our islands a little better than hitherto. Am I right?' He was asking for it, but Natalia didn't give it to him.

'Right,' she said. Then to Magda, 'Pleased to meet you.' The time had come to relent, 'I am sorry if I was a bit abrupt. I . . .'

'Don't let it bother you, Natalia. I spent sixteen years of my life selling myself in the streets of Tanira, the men I loved are all gone, the one I loved most is dead, my youngest son was killed, two others will be hanged, the oldest has gone forfeiting me and clouding Tamar's heart. Maria died giving birth to this little one, and left three other little ones behind. Ziba killed herself and left two more behind. Jonah's wife couldn't take him or me or all of us any longer and left, leaving five behind. You can see most of them here. Nothing upsets me any more.' She was not complaining, nor being ironic or bitter, nor trying to make Natalia feel bad; she was just saying what she knew or thought or believed, as she always did. But you had to know Magda well to know that. Paul did. Just. Natalia did not, and she was horrified. Horrified at herself for having hurt someone who was already so hurt, and horrified at Magda for talking so casually about it all to a complete stranger.

'Hello Magda,' said Peter.

'Jonah's not in, but he'll be back soon. He's only gone to get some milk for the baby,' said Magda, ushering them into the surprisingly spacious room which formed the entire ground floor, except for a small cooking area at the back. Paul looked around at the retinue of children who followed them in, but could not see anyone who could technically lay claim to the title of baby; on the other hand any one of many could have been in need of milk.

'Tea, coffee, or some buttermilk?' continued Magda. 'The boy, Peter, would like some buttermilk, wouldn't you Peter?' Paul had just squeezed Peter's hand as a hint to suppress his questions about the grey man. People here lived by different laws. Or, if you were lucky, without them. You didn't rush to the matter in hand. You waited. Sipped tea, or coffee, or buttermilk. Or, if you were lucky, wine. You savoured the moment that was now. You talked about relatives who were dead. You made the most of the life that had been lived, enjoyed what had happened, however unpleasant. Or, if you were lucky, pleasant. What was over could be looked upon philosophically. Or if you were lucky, romantically. You were not over-anxious about the coming events. Who knew what was in the twinkling eyes of the stars? Best delay the future as long as the present permits. Or, if you were lucky, longer.

Peter misconstrued Paul's tightening grip as meaning 'go for the buttermilk'. He would have done so anyway. He liked trying out new things. 'I'll have some buttermilk, please Ma'am, Magda,' he said softly. So overwhelmed was he by Magda and the brood that he had temporarily put the grey man to the back of his mind of his own accord.

Paul was mildly alarmed. Much though he loved Magda's buttermilk, it could be a little harsh on tender tonsils. If Peter

114

so much as cleared his throat in an unconventional manner in the next fortnight, Eleanor would cross-examine him about all aspects of his dietary intake during the previous weeks with such persistence and assiduousness that he was likely to slip up. He was not very good under pressure from Eleanor. The only way he did manage to keep a lot secret from her was not to let her suspect anything in the first place. Once she did, the facts were out, more often than not.

When the drinks arrived, he quickly pressed the tea into Peter's surprised hands, taking the buttermilk from him with the remark, 'I should have known you'd change your mind. You always do at the last minute.' He winked and patted his knee, hoping Peter would understand. He couldn't have given him a verbal warning, even during Magda's brief disappearance into the kitchen, as they were under the watchful eyes and alert ears of the battalion of children.

'I'm sorry if there isn't enough milk in the tea,' said Magda turning to Peter, 'but there isn't enough milk in the house. That is why Jonah . . .' Peter switched off his ears and looked at the cup of hot milky tea in his hands. He hated tea. But then he hated coffee more. Milk for the coffee was no problem as Natalia preferred hers black. 'Thank you, Magda,' he said, suddenly remembering his manners.

Magda brought a plate of biscuits for the guests, then produced a large polythene bag and took out a bunch of cheap sweets. She passed them round to her family of children, brought a few for Peter, and whispered in his ear, 'This is not all I have for you!' She put the bag away, pulled out a large bandana from somewhere inside her dress and started untying a thick knot to take out some change which was in a sort of pouch formed by the knot. 'I'll send Littloo here,' she said, pointing to the biggest of the lads, about twelve, 'to get you some nice ripe guavas from the corner shop down the road.'

Paul's heart drummed a questioning tune. Would it be worse to offend by refusing, or to let her spend her precious change on guavas for Peter? He was never quite sure how much Jonah made from his 'extra-curricular activities'. He did know that mostly he acted for political and ideological reasons, but also for a way of life, and more than a little for the pleasure of the game, but there had to be some money in it somewhere. He had to live, and had quite a few to support, even discounting the children of the sisters.

'Oh no. Thank you, but no.' Natalia spoke, assessing the situation from Paul's expression, 'Peter is not allowed to eat between meals. Miss Poacher would be very annoyed if she found out.'

Magda raised her arms to the skies. 'No wonder the child is just skin and bone. Look at him. Just look at him. How old is he? Five? Four?'

'I will be ten next birthday, Ma'am.' said Peter proudly.

'Ten! Lord have mercy on my soul. What do these people with all their money think –' Just then Jonah walked in, and an embarrassing time was spared for all. He had a bucket of fresh milk in one hand, a basketful of little green guavas on one arm, and a pleasantly quizzical expression on his face.

'Oh, what a lovely surprise. Where did you get all this from?' exclaimed Magda with the uninhibited excitement of a ten-year-old herself, rushing to help Jonah with his pleasant burdens. 'The Lord must have known we were having guests over,' she bubbled, even though she could see that the guavas were too raw to be served.

'This,' Jonah said holding up the bucket, 'from Jittu's cow. Their calf died yesterday and they have plenty to spare. And these,' he said holding up the basket, 'just right for pickling or for stuffing in a cushion to ripen, from Melanie's tree.'

'Moanie Melanie! But she hates us. A "whore" she called me once. Only once, mind you. I sent her reeling across the road with a hand she'll never forget. Told her she couldn't be a whore if she lit candles in the church every night begging the Lord to make her one. Not with her face. And her legs. Like beer kegs, they are, her legs. Have you seen them? Keeps them well hidden, she does. But lift up her dress one day and have a peep. Look, and remember. Remember the sight next time

116

you can't sleep. You'll sleep soon enough once you remember those fat gnarled legs.'

Jonah, who had heard the story, and the advice, many times, said what he had wanted to say many times, but hadn't; 'Shame on you, Magda. How uncharitable can you get. She has tried several times since then to make up, but you don't forgive, do you! You never used to be like that. You are becoming hard, Magda. Hard. And that is not good. Not for anybody. Not for you.'

'It's bad about Jittu's calf. Bad,' said Magda, trying to change the subject, and clearly shaken by Jonah's censure. Then, unable to restrain her response any longer, she bowed her head and spoke softly: 'I expect you are right. Sad is the day when children have to teach their mother the difference between right and wrong. May the Lord forgive me for not forgiving.' Her references to the Lord had come back ever since the news of Joshua. She had even started mentioning the Mother of God, and was going to church again. She had always wanted to do that anyway. Just needed an excuse. And she got one. One of the best. Second only to . . . She tried not to think of the fate of her two, whose lives were soon to be forced out of them by those meant to look after your lives.

Suddenly Peter wished more than anything else, as only children can wish for anything more than anything else, that Trix was with him. She had not been too well for some time, and was 'resting'. Growing old, that was her problem; and there was no answer to *that* problem. Why did dogs have to grow older quicker than people? Why did anyone have to grow older? Would he be an old man one day? Somehow he could not see himself as an old man. How old was the grey man? Older than Trix, in dog years, or younger?

'He doesn't stay with us any more,' Peter heard Jonah say and all his sense were alerted. He switched on his ears and turned up the brilliance of his mind and sharpened

117

its reception with quick fine tuning. He often thought of his head as a TV set. It helped him make it work better.

'Where is he, then?' asked Paul, puzzled; and concerned, for Peter and the grey man.

'Spends most of his time in some cave or other. Comes down to the town when he gets hungry, or needs something –'

'Caves, did you say?' interrupted Paul, feeling very uneasy; and, in an inexplicable way, frightened. Peter's strange remark came back to him with a curious ringing quality.

'Yes, caves. There are a lot up by the mountains. Real caves, too, some of them centuries old, deep and high, some wet some dry, some with pictures, not shallow ones like down by the beach. Surely you know about them?' he added, suddenly remembering that he and Paul had spent many hours looking around in some of them years before.

'Of course I do. But it was so long ago. Are there any . . . blue ones?' he asked hesitantly, almost afraid of hearing the answer.

'There are one or two at the back. The walls have been smoothed out by erosion, or man, and over the years they've turned a greyish blue colour. When the light falls on them from a certain angle, they almost glow with a sort of bluey aura. It can look quite ghostly. Most people keep well away from them. Why do you ask?'

'I'm not sure. It's just that . . . What do you make of him? What do the others make of him? Who do you think he can be? And from where?' Paul was not just changing the subject – though he was – he was also genuinely curious.

'That's a lot of questions in one. The last is easy. I think. He is bound to be from Pepper, or maybe from Saviore. Those are the two places where all the political killings and tortures take place. Near here, anyway. Most of the people we –' he was choosing his words carefully – 'get are from those countries. They all tell tales of butchery and mutilations such as this man has suffered. The cutting away of the tongue for talking treason. Often the sex organs are hacked away, for retribution, humiliation and excruciating pain – and to prevent further production of filthy rebels. We do not know whether they have done that to him or not. He can't speak and won't show us or try to tell us in any other way. We have seen all the rest when he was with the lad, your nephew. He just had on those underpants which were half off so we could see practically everything, except the groin. He had his hands there too. Some are treated like that, along with other more subtle methods, if they try to write out messages for help. A few are permanently unable to write after that. This man either never learnt to write, or has been subjected to something like that.

'The heat branding and slashing of the buttocks and nipples is typical as well. It used to be the letters C and B, one letter on each buttock and one on each nipple, to indicate communist bastard. But then somebody started the rumour that it meant christian bastard. This could have alienated the Catholic church, which is already getting disaffected and aligning itself more and more with the rebels, as God means it to, so help me God or I denounce Him. Since then they have stopped branding and razoring the letter, just brand and slash.

'As you know, our country won't recognise them as political refugees for they come from Association countries! The Association of Free World Nations as we all know them to be! Ha ha ha. So what can we do? We have to try and save them any way we can. Can't let them be just butchered, hacked away like diseased trees, cut down in little pieces –'

'If there are so many like him,' Paul thought it was time to interrupt Jonah before he got too carried away by his emotions, 'then how come you, or anybody else, has never seen anyone like him before?'

'Ah but we have. Well, not to that extent. And not grey. Not alive. They turn that colour after they have been dead a while. Many who have come here and seen him say they have seen others like him, only they were all dead. How this one comes to be alive, no one knows. That is why he is arousing such strong feelings in so many. There are those who are willing to worship him. And those who would cheerfully get rid of him any way they can, if they dared. Only they are too scared of him.

'The rains haven't helped. Well, in a way, they have helped, because there hasn't been a flood in spite of the rains. I don't know what to do or say.'

'He's a saint,' said Magda, 'a saint. And no doubt about it. He brought news of my Joshua. And he made the blessed Virgin's cloak of mourning fly away. He's a saint. At the very least. I wouldn't be surprised if –'

'Hold your tongue, Magda. Don't blaspheme. We're already in enough trouble as it is.'

Magda held her tongue, but looked unrepentant.

'There is one other thing which is very strange, unusual, that is happening.' For the first time Jonah looked ill at ease. Not angry, not righteous, not concerned, just ill at ease, and unsure of himself.

'And what is that?' asked Paul, more than curious.

'Well, he seems to be growing younger!'

'Is that all?' Paul said, disappointed. 'What do you expect? If you'd escaped from horrific tortures to a life of freedom, wouldn't you get fitter and healthier, and look younger?'

'I know, that is the obvious answer. But it is more than that. You have to see him. You should have seen him as he was then, and now see him as he is now, to know the difference. It is hardly a fortnight. But the difference . . . It is more than that.'

'It is more than that,' said Magda.

'It is more than that,' said Peter.

'Don't talk about things you know nothing of. How many times have I told you that,' said Natalia. 'You always keep doing that. Talking about things you know nothing of.' She was getting quite upset at the conversation, and more than a little shocked that Jonah was talking so in front of the children. She had to reprimand somebody.

★　★　★

'We are just going out to see if we can find Peter's grey man. Be back as soon as we can.' Once outside Jonah shouted back before shutting the door, 'Have something interesting ready for tea, Magda. And everybody, take care of your great Mama, or you'll have me to answer to. And you know what that means!'

In the days when she was hustling, Magda had instructed her children not to call her mother, or mum, or anything like that, nor to call her sister, as some did, nor to call her by her real name, but to call her Magda, same as everybody else. That wouldn't be dishonest, nor would it advertise to the world how many children she had. The custom had persisted after her return to Gulroza and respectability, even though some in the family, and many outside, disapproved.

Natalia had decided to stay behind with Magda and the children, excluding Peter, of course. She was feeling confused and unsettled. Today she had found herself saying things and behaving in a manner she would never have expected of herself, or even thought possible. Was Paul right after all? Was she just a child? Still growing up? In mind and character, if not in body? But then so is everybody. Everybody who is not dead, that is. Still, she was confused and unsettled, and needed time to think. Time to be away from Paul, to be away from Peter even, if only for a short while.

Outside, Jonah and Paul began to take their customary long strides towards where Jonah thought the grey man might be, forgetting the tiny steps of the boy behind them. The moment they remembered him they stopped and turned back to call him. He wasn't there.

Jonah wasn't worried. Paul was.

Jonah often came out with the eleven children of the immediate family, and sometimes with more, and one or the other was always disappearing round a corner or getting left behind or running ahead somewhere. All turned up safe and sound within minutes, if not seconds. All it needed was a sharp eye and strong vocal chords.

Paul knew Peter was a wanderer and a disappearer – same as he – and something more besides – something which Paul couldn't exactly focus upon, but which was out-of-the-ordinary in a simple rather than spectacular sort of way. Perhaps his ill-health in the first few years of his life and general debility now made him spend too much time in bed, by himself, which made him too introspective, too reflective, too other-worldly.

Soon Jonah too was worried. They called out and looked round the bushes and searched behind houses and up and down the various paths. No sign of Peter.

'Where are the blue caves. Let's go to the blue caves!' said Paul breathlessly.

'What! You must be –'

'Don't argue. Let's go.'

'If you wish. But they are a long way from here.' Jonah looked sideways at Paul in a disbelieving manner.

'Would it be quicker by car?'

'I suppose so. We will have to park by the rubbish tip and walk up from there, but it will be very much quicker on the whole.'

'Fuck! I've left the keys in the house. You wait here, I'll get them.' He ran full speed back to the house, rushed in without knocking, picked up the keys from beneath the chair where he had been sitting, said something about taking the car, and rushed out again before the astonished Natalia could say a word. Magda was used to the strange ways of the menfolk and didn't show any surprise.

For the first time in his visits to Gulroza Paul paid scant attention to the juxtaposition of sinking humanity and rising beauty that held the area in a conspiratorial balance. They parked somewhere up on a high road overlooking stinking heaps of rubbish and waste, and then ran down and up again to the other side of it, reaching the base of the Mother Mountain where it began to soar above the river and the sea.

Paul was stunned to hear Peter's voice, carried by the strengthening winds, while still some distance from the blue caves. How on earth could his little legs have brought him here before their car and long sturdy legs?

'I came by the short-cut,' was Peter's simple answer, when asked, and once he had finished having his little chat with the grey man – mostly about the age and state of health of Trix. After all, if it hadn't been for Trix, they would never have met. Or would they have? Who can tell.

The grey man's silvery eyes shone with startling brilliance as he saw Paul. He opened his mouth as if to speak, realised he could not, gulped, opened his mouth again, raised his hand hesitantly, then dropped it again with a sudden jerk and turned away.

Even Jonah, who knew well the ways and byways of Gulroza, did not know anything about this particular short-cut. He looked from the grey man to Peter with a new uneasiness which rose within him along with the rising winds. The grey man had moved back, against a slippery greyish wall, and was staring at another slippery greyish wall in front of him. He was still wearing the clothes of Ishmael, and this made it all the more difficult for Jonah. He had been given other clothes by other people, but he continued to wear these. He looked quite old to Paul, who had not seen him before, and he wondered what the fuss was about him looking younger. He whispered as much to Jonah, who replied, 'I said getting younger, not looking young,' and Paul was left to make of it what he could.

The clouds had gathered again while they were driving up there, and the afternoon had become darker than it should have been at that time. Paul was about to suggest trekking back home when the sun suddenly reappeared. Its slanting rays stole their way into the cave. Slanting rays shimmering with dancing particles that defy form or shape like the light that reveals, and that elude capture or touch like the force that creates; slanting rays which quivered and shivered as terrified captives, yet were straight and strong as conquering heroes;

slanting rays as from the apex of a pyramid; slanting rays that transformed the whole scene from a prosaic reality to a poetic illusion. An aquamarine mist oozed out of the pores of the rocks and the stones and the walls and the ceiling and the floor of the cave and spread itself into a sea fog, engulfing everything and everyone.

Shapes changed, identities merged or submerged or altered or dispersed. Peter was nowhere, nor was the grey man. In their place stood a young man with a haunted appearance, very much like Paul, only thinner and much taller than his six feet one. He tried to speak, but no words came out of his mouth. No words *could* come out of his mouth, for his tongue had been carved out. He stretched his arms out to Paul, pleading imploring begging. There was so much pain in his silent mouth. So much love in his eloquent eyes. So many stories in his beating heart which lay throbbing on the wet floor of the cave. Still alive, still keeping the young man alive, yet pulled from his chest as a baby is pulled from the womb.

The clouds came back to shield the sun. The walls of the cave reverted to their slippery greyish hue. Peter was back, and so was the grey man.

'Let's go home,' Paul heard himself say, even though he was sure he had not spoken, 'it is getting late.'

Jonah crossed himself involuntarily with a shudder, and they slowly walked out under the open sky, leaving the grey man standing in the entrance to the cave. He was certainly younger now than when they had entered the cave only a short while before. Jonah, who was aware of the ageing down, and prepared for it, was shocked nonetheless. He had never seen nor anticipated so much change in so little a time. Even Paul could tell the difference.

As he turned round to take one last look at the strange man, he saw him stoop, and then squat on the grassy slope. Curious. Paul stopped to watch more closely. The man picked up a baby hedgehog that was lying curled among some roots, and lifted it up to caress with his cheek.

18

By the time they got home after depositing Jonah and collecting Natalia, they were just in time for a quick snack and the early evening international news followed by the local news coverage. There was bound to be something about Eleanor and Philip. There was: a specially-produced news report.

Despite his cynicism and his anarchic view of life and politics, or because of it, Paul loved to hate the great and not so great figures of public life as they made fools of the public in public and of themselves in private, and public. There was no better medium than the television for an addicted political voyeur.

And now to the odd couple of New Heaven politics, began the cheerily monotonous voice of the celebrated TV personality Bobby Lodge, rising and falling, chuckling and sniggering, becoming ponderous and portentous, reproachful or plauditory at all the predictable places, head nodding forwards or backwards or sideways at regular intervals of meaningful emphasis. *One black, one white; one a committed socialist or, as some say, a socialist who should be committed, one a lover of the free market economy who would no doubt be highly valuable in a free market if charm and wit and beauty are worth anything these days. I am, of course, speaking of the beautiful Eleanor Poacher and the equally beautiful Philip Peruva.*

Out in their respective constituencies they went walkabout today, in a climate of titillating uncertainty as to the election date, which could be announced by the Prime Minister at virtually any time. It would be difficult to assess who kissed the most number of babies, but I can certainly tell you that Eleanor Poacher certainly scored a point over her husband when she actually managed to help an old lady across the street. Rumours that the poor woman was bound, gagged and dragged are of course absolutely without foundation, nor was Ms Poacher at any time assaulted by the woman's umbrella. But sources close to Mr Peruva say that only moments later the 'unfortunate' – their word not mine – the 'unfortunate' woman was hastily seen crossing back to the other side of the street, the side where she was in the first place. However, we expect all that will be settled later on in their beachside love-nest.

Among the numerous questions raised by local residents was the one concerning the fate of the Delta Valley Development, centering round the controversial area of the shanty town, once a pretty little village, now a crumbling eyesore. The biggest political surprise is that both parties, with the full support of both Mr Peruva and Ms Poacher, the two MPs closest to the shanty area – Mr Peruva's family still has connections with the village – want the development to go ahead. Mr Peruva thinks it is essential for jobs in the area and to reduce poverty and deprivation. Ms Poacher also believes it will reduce unemployment and bring about prosperity, but is more concerned about the additional revenue to the government through increased tourism. She, of course, vehemently denies that that is her prime consideration, while Mr Peruva equally vehemently insists that that is so.

126

The major difference between the two parties and the two MPs centres on the fate of the local residents, some of whom have lived in the shanty town for generations, when it was known as Gulroza, the Valley of Flowers. Ms Poacher's party believes that they should be rehoused and resettled on the eastern side of our islands to help set up new industries and give a much-needed boost to the economy of the area. Mr Peruva insists that the new development should make provision for housing the local residents in a development site as close to the shanty town as possible so as to cause the minimum of upheaval in their lives

Minimum upheaval will mean minimal benefits, retorts Ms Poacher, not only to the country as a whole, but also to the people themselves. Mr Peruva calls it a typically shallow play on words which disguises more sinister motives of profiteering at the expense of human misery. Human misery, says Ms Poacher, is the strength of Mr Peruva and his party. If human misery was eliminated so would the need for his kind of rhetoric. And that is why they are against her proposals. 'I want to end human misery, they want to perpetuate it, and in so doing, perpetuate themselves.' Mr Peruva argues that the Devil preaching, not just quoting but preaching, the scriptures can be so devastatingly convincing that only the light of truth can unmask its hideous, invidious and insidious features and character. However, he announced with disarming directness that if Ms Poacher and her party can eliminate human misery, which in the last six years of government they have actually managed to increase beyond even the worst fears of their own voters, then he would be the first to give up his seat and vote for the candidate of her choice. Ms Poacher refused to comment on the challenge, calling it a childish bluff.

All through the smiling or appropriately sombre narration, excerpts of actual speeches made by Eleanor or Philip, clips from previous interviews, and pictures of the day's walkabouts kept appearing at expected and unexpected intervals.

A commercial break came, and Paul told Natalia and Peter that he was going for a puke and would be back soon. 'If

I watch the greed goaders at work for much longer, I'll do it here.'

He came back in time for a 'new and strange' development in the 'shanty town saga' which happened quite unexpectedly, and live on television, eliciting a genuine expression of surprise even from Mr Bobby Lodge. Peter was open-mouthed and clearly perturbed.

Some of the residents of the shanty town were being interviewed live, as part of the second half of the report, about their reactions to the proposals of the two MPs. All the older residents and a vast majority of the new ones, though not unsurprisingly preferring Mr Peruva's resettlement programme, were against any form of 'development' in the area – except, of course, the development of existing facilities and the existing houses and the creation of new amenities for the residents. For the living to be thrown out of their homes and for the dead to be dug out of their graves – the local cemetery was in a prime area of exceptional beauty – so that rich upstarts could move in and tourists take over was not generally looked upon as a jolly good do.

So far, nothing unusual. But then suddenly one old woman more or less forced her way to the front of the camera and the microphone and shouted, 'You can't take our homes away now. *He* won't let you. That is why *he* has come. To save our Gulroza and to protect our homes and our children.'

The announcement was startling enough to whet the appetite of any TV newshound. Even if it was to be no more than an old woman's fantasy, it could do with a little pursuing. 'And who would you be talking of, love?' came the woman-of-the-people voice of the lady reporter.

'Diamond Eyes, of course, you silly git, who else can have the power.'

The uneasy silence that descended on the local crowd following the statement convinced the reporter that there was indeed someone or something worth talking about. But before she could ask a further question the woman continued, '*He* hasn't let the floods get us, and *he* won't let you get us either.'

Bobby Lodge's face and voice interrupted the sequence, 'And who is this Diamond Eyes, Jenny? Could you try and find out for us, please?'

That is exactly what Jenny tried to do, and although she discovered that the man himself could not be available for comment at that time, the information she heard about him was peculiar enough to warrant further investigative tele-journalism at as early a date as possible.

The wailing notes of the woman's trembling voice began again: 'He came from the dead to save us. He won against death, and now he's winning against old age. He will win against you as well. You wait and see. He will triumph! He always does! I will be young again. I will be a little girl and play with my papa. You wait . . .'

'He never played with you when you *were* a little girl,' interrupted another old voice, and we were quickly returned to the studios.

But the legend of Diamond Eyes was born. Right in front of millions of eyes. And who could ask for a better start?

Not even I.

19

The sun was on the wrong side of the winter solstice, Moanie Melanie's guavas had ripened on the trees in good number despite the ones that had fallen off raw during the autumn storms, the rains had held back, and the election had been scheduled for autumn, on October the thirty-first, almost four months away.

The fate of the shanty town was still in the balance, in theory. And although it was considered a foregone conclusion by polimetricians, public-opinion-pollstering cephalo-hunters and government-morale-bolstering cunnilingussing punters that the current prime minister and cohorts were here to stay, the government itself was wisely reluctant to take chances and was making a concerted effort to rush through the necessary legislation and award the necessary contracts for the DVD – the Delta Valley Development – to go ahead, managed by companies it considered desirable. Even though the opposition was also for the scheme, the government wanted the full credit for its implementation. It would be a great economic scoop, and a peacock feather in the international-sphere-of-influence cap. The more tourists New Heaven attracted, the more money it made, the more its international reputation and status would be enhanced.

However, all such attempts were being met with serious and unexpectedly powerful opposition from the local residents and their friends.

'And all because of that weirdo, Diamond Eyes. Diamond Eyes! My ruby foot!' mused Eleanor. 'Fancy contact lenses, more like.' But he was the force behind it all. Of this there was no doubt in her mind. Without so much as saying a word, or writing a letter, or lifting a finger, he had mobilised the whole community. He was there to protect them, *sent* to protect them from Mammon-worshippers, come to save them from destruction by Gomorrhites, and as long as he was there no harm could come to them. The stupid superstitious peasants! How illogical and irrational can one get. It had nothing to do with 'proper' religion either, which she could accept. After all, she was a Christian, and a better one than most of them – an Anglican. But this, this was just stupid. Plain stupid. An escaped convict comes here, an illegal immigrant most likely – nothing could be proved either way as nothing was known about him, and even though moves to deport him were being considered, no one knew where to deport him – and they turn him into a sort of cut-price mini-saviour! How absolutely, pathetically stupid. Eleanor, normally not one to flounder for words, could not think of any better than 'stupid', and uncharacteristically repeated it to herself.

There *must* be those who mistrusted him, probably far more in number than one suspected. May be even the majority. The silent majority. The problem was how to get them to break their silence. Even if they were against the DVD, as long as they mistrusted the wretched grey man, they could be used to break the strength of the rest. The question was, how? How to get them on her side, on *their* side? If only Philip would do something. After all he had his roots in that God-forsaken place. But he wouldn't, if only to spite her. Anyway, she would think of something. She always did in the end. And if it involved the co-operation of Philip, she would get that too. One way or another, she would get it. And *him*, whoever the charlatan was. And once she had him, she'd have the rest. Destroy the symbol and the edifice falls. The DVD could go ahead smoothly, successfully and perfectly.

That achieved, her place in the cabinet as the new Energy and Environment Minister, or better, would be assured: the first major step towards her ultimate ambition. And the egg on the face of her neighbourhood would be wiped clean, followed by much-needed and attractive cosmetic surgery. Something the whole nation could be justly proud of. Not to speak of the employment and prosperity all that would bring to the people, of course – the real reasons for her crusade.

It was all the fault of the gassed-up media. If they hadn't hyped up this wretched man, the whoever he was, no one would even have heard of him, and those that had wouldn't have given him a third thought!

That semi-detached reporter, Jenny whatever. And all the fully-detached ones who followed after, from the newspapers, the television. A good story. A damn good story at that! The story of how they might well have to kiss goodbye to their new offices overlooking the Mother Mountain. And how the new network might never materialise now. With all those jobs. And all because of their great story, their magnificent scoop, their ignominious own goal.

Even the rains had eased off. Her only hope lay in the floods. That would teach them to put their own and their children's lives at risk by insisting on living in unsafe accommodation. But Eleanor was not without compassion, and did not wish to pursue that line of thought.

It was *him* she wanted, the others she needed. Nullify the god and the temple falls. The devotees are then yours for the taking.

Those who regularly tried to 'interview' Diamond Eyes, or just see him or talk to him or communicate with him in some form or another – the whole issue was still fresh and novel enough not to have lost its appeal, especially with popular tele-journalism and the tabloid press – came back with very different feelings and impressions from those they had anticipated or prepared for. The diamond eyes were a disappointment, at first, more a product of a deranged old woman's imagination than reality – sort of grey, but with a silvery edge to them which could be uncomfortably unnerving. However, with the light hitting them straight in the pupils – the man could look the sun in the eye – they developed a sort of transluscent glitter, not unlike the sparkle of a diamond. But diamonds suggest the ultimate in hardness, while the man's eyes were soft, and strangely moving. And it was this quality of vanquished but not forgotten suffering, which made even the most cynical feel somewhat shaken and disturbed in his presence, their preconceptions in disarray.

He had recovered his health remarkably since his discovery – no one knew the real facts as to where when and how – and his skin, which was believed to have been totally discoloured at one point, had now regained most of its natural colour, especially in the face and neck, though patchy areas of a dark sallow hue could still be seen on his arms and torso and legs, as he sometimes wandered shirtless, barefoot, trouser-legs rolled way up over long thin legs, along the windy side of the mountains, singing to himself, wordlessly and soundlessly, spiky hair silver-grey on top, glistening brown underneath, dancing above him.

Peter, meanwhile, had been going through extensive medical examinations and tests to see if a new, still experimental drug to promote growth could be used to help him overcome the problems of his reduced size. Eleanor had been warned that although 'work' on animals had shown it to be effective and without any dangerous side effects, its efficacy or reactions on human beings were still uncertain. However, Eleanor, aware of the importance of an imposing stature if one wanted

134

to get ahead in life, was willing to have it tried out on Peter, as long as the doctors could be as sure as doctors ever were that it would (a) result in growth and (b) have no – or at least manageable – side effects.

Between school and the doctors Peter was not left with much time, but he still managed to sneak out to see his grey man – even now he thought of him as such and called him that – on a few occasions, with the help of Natalia – even though she didn't entirely approve – or Paul or Jonah.

The summer holidays were here now, and he had plans to spend more time at the shanty town generally. Besides the grey man, he had begun to love being with Magda and Jonah, and the children there, so different to the ones he was used to. Fortunately, with the election just past the bushes, his parents were mostly out, or too busy when indoors, and he had more freedom than he had ever known before. As long as Eleanor kept getting a regular report of his medical progress, she left the rest mostly to Natalia. Natalia was also busy preparing for her thesis, and let Peter do much of what he wanted to do, as long as she was sure he was in safe hands.

Trix had unexpectedly recovered and seemed healthier and bouncier than before. All seemed well with the world. It was turning out to be a happy summer for Peter, doctors notwithstanding. In fact he had got so used to them by now he could forget about them even when actually being treated.

Paul had disappeared for a few weeks to do a commissioned portrait of a wealthy businessman. And for once had done just that, *and* returned on the promised date! Not only that, he had come back with quite a few other paintings, some of which he had either done earlier on and had lain scattered about at the houses of various friends or in his city flat, and some new ones he had managed to do in his spare time. He planned to exhibit these, something he had always threatened to do, but never 'got round to'. This time he had booked a hall, and got the sponsorship of the local Arts Council, not easy to obtain.

Amnon and Isaac were to be strapped to a very expensive chair each, and voltaged out of existence on the twenty-eighth of September. Theirs would be the first public executions since the death penalty had been brought back by popular demand – instigated by the popular press, with support from the popularly-elected government. The efforts of the abolitionist lobby, still continuing on behalf of many others and successful on two previous occasions, had failed this time. Cop-killers could not expect the mercy shown to the killers of ordinary human beings.

Last and least, I . . . But you'll find that out for yourself. And you'll judge it for yourself. And you will judge me yourself. For you can do what I cannot. For you will do what I will not.

20

Eleanor and Philip were staying in their city houses for a few days, to be at hand to attend some important sittings of parliament, which could last late into the night. The House was due to break up for summer recess in a week's time; after that would come the hectic run-up to the election.

Paul had left early in the morning, to 'sketch and paint' up by the river – which could mean anything, from just that, to a marijuana session with Jonah, to a visit to some old friend he had not seen in months, to a complete disappearing act – long or short-term; or he might be hiring a boat further up the river and stretching out in it to watch the other boats sail by; or possibly going to the city's 'handicapped-by-petty-laws' sex district to see what, if anything, was going on, and if some voyeuristic or participatory action could be had. He had taken Natalia's car, which should rule out the disappearing act – even he wouldn't do that – but anything else was possible. As it happened, that day he really had gone to sketch and paint. He seemed to have become quite serious about it, since being commissioned by the businessman and getting funding for his impending exhibition.

Natalia was busy putting together her research conclusions on the psychological aspects of the struggle of French feminists to establish their rights in a male-dominated world.

Peter was bored.

He could not get interested in the books he was supposed to read, and was unable to find one that did appeal. He wasn't even in the mood to try very hard to find one. There was nothing on television but racing, or some other sport which he could neither play nor muster up enough enthusiasm to enjoy or support as a spectator. Radio was annoyingly repetitious and there was no one to play any games with. Eleanor had dismissed Tom – for 'reckless walking', said Philip; for 'gross negligence' of his duties in not attending properly to his charge, Peter, said she. Stewart had also gone. Now there was just Guido, for the time being, but although nice enough, he seemed to avoid Peter, and would just smile a toothy smile, wave and move away every time he saw him. He got on well with the two old women, but they would be half asleep somewhere in the house or gardens.

He wandered around aimlessly in the house, from room to room, balcony to balcony, looking out to sea, peering round corners for no reason at all, and lifting up ornaments from shelves or table-tops here and there and putting them back again. Finally he went up to the roof, half-way up to the sky, at least that is what he had believed when he was very little. He was not allowed to go up there.

Although there were railings all round it, he was small enough to fall out from between them. Eleanor did not want a solid barrier built, as that would obstruct the magnificent views, nor did she want a glass surround, as then it would look too much like an extended version of Philip's ex-study and would also lose its open atmosphere. The whole roof was a cross between a studio apartment and a garden centre. There were two covered areas, for protection from the sun or the rain, like giant umbrellas or enormous inverted lotuses from another planet. Most of the seating was either specially-treated wood, or stone. There were potted plants of all sizes, shapes and varieties. The centre, one corner and some strips near the edges had been grassed over, with enough soil for plants to grow.

Peter walked hesitantly across, towards the corner which gave the clearest view out to the sea, with the least obstruction from tall tropical trees scattered around the house.

It was a beautiful sunny day. Beautiful to look at, if not beautiful to experience – too hot and quite saturated with humidity. It was absolutely still and unnervingly silent. Peter's skin felt greasy and clammy, more like old bronze recovered from the guts of a long-sunk galleon than its usual crisp clean gold. His unruly intense brown hair, which normally stood out from his head at odd angles was damp and downcast.

He looked out, holding on to the railing and pushing his head between two balusters, something which he was expressly forbidden to do.

The skyline stretched out in front of him like the never-ending stomach of a very greedy glass bowl, filled with the never-ending waters of the sea: restless, angry, bursting to break out of the bowl's transparent confines – able to see freedom filling out the air all round, but unable to reach out to it.

Ships made of bleached bones stood suspended in the middle of nothingness; sail boats moved without movement, without progress, without escape; birds cried out sharing the pain of the water. Peter felt helpless. His heart filled with love for all, but there was nothing he could do. Nothing, to put flesh on the ships, or to make the boats sail out to freedom. Or to let the water out of the bowl. He was trapped in the same bowl himself.

A turbulent agitation, like the waters of the rough sea, took hold of his soul, and he stood transfixed. The image reflected and contained within his eyes assumed a reality of its own, and everything he saw became indistinguishable from himself.

If he had a magic boat, he'd sail out to the edge of the world; if he had a magic flute, he'd play a magic note, the magic note would crack the captivating glass bowl and set the water free, cascading down the edge of the world, greater than the greatest waterfall in God's universe; then, if he had a magic plane, he'd fly himself, and all the boats and ships in the water, out and up and away to freedom. But then if he did that, they would all crash against the same glass bowl inverted into a dome.

An uncontrollable urge to see his grey man again, to talk to him and to listen to him, rose within him like the rising tidal waves within the ocean. He was the only one who had experienced what he experienced, and the only one to help him help the trapped waters of the sea and the distorted bones of the ships.

Be still, I warned him, be still, my child. Be still. But he would not listen. Be still, I cried, be still. But he would not listen. Be still. Be still. Be still. But he would not listen. Let the future come to you, don't rush to it. Wait. Be still. But he would not listen.

He had played his part. The grey man was in the shanty town. The time for action was over for now. The time to rest was here. But he would not listen.

Slowly he pulled his head out of the railings, walked backwards to the stairs, way down to the hall, into Trix's room, picked her up, out into the sand garden, and out through the hole in the wall to trek all the way to the shanty town.

He could hear the grey man crying out in agony. 'Let me go. Let me go. Let me go . . .' His voice was as familiar as the beating of his own heart. 'I want to be free,' he said, 'I want to be free.' But that was a long time ago. He was free now. But Peter did not know that.

Peter too, wanted to be free. He too was free. But he did not know that either.

★ ★ ★

Peter looked up cautiously at the glass wall from where he had been spotted the last time, before creeping slowly ahead. He needn't have worried. No one was up there today.

The first few yards were the worst. Soon he was out of sight behind a scattering of bushes, where clifftop turned to open country before being encroached upon by the tentacles of the city.

Putting Trix down he walked along a once well-trodden path, which used to take the locals from Gulroza to the better part of the beach, less rocky and more quiet with deeper water for both fishing and swimming. It was private property now, but signs of the earlier treadway could still be seen. A tree-stump here, a few strategically placed stones there, some sharp corners too sharp to be nature or coincidence, some rounded corners too rounded to be nature or coincidence.

After about a mile or so, he came to a fork. One way seemed to head straight towards the road, the other disappeared into a thicket of trees. He did not particularly want to go towards the road, but he also knew that to get to the shanty town he would have to cross at least two roads, and the sooner he went past them the better. On the other hand the path through the woods might be quicker in the long run, though there was the danger of getting confused and lost. He was still wondering which way to take when Trix made up his mind for him.

Swishing and swirling her tail in enthralled abandon she weaved her way into the woods, sniffing trees and grass and letting out little yelps of joy.

Peter ran after her, alarmed and still unsure, hoping to get her out of there, if necessary by carrying her out, rather than actually wanting to go that way. However, once within the thicket, his apprehensions vanished and were replaced by Trix-like enthusiasm. The path inside the random woods was, if anything, clearer and better defined than the one in the open country, primarily because of tree stumps, cut to clear the way, acting as markers. Not enough sunshine filtered through the trees so not enough vegetation had grown to stifle the path.

They carried on for some time and, despite occasional moments of worry when Trix disappeared behind a tree or ran ahead, the walk was exciting and enjoyable. Peter revelled in the warm and secret feel of being surrounded by rugged and gnarled tree-trunks of different texture and girth and height, those of reduced sizes having their own strength and beauty alongside the taller and thicker ones. The smooth grasses and the prickly grasses, the berried bushes and the thorny bushes, the suddenly-sprouting heads of so many different types of flowers and the shamelessly swaying bodies of so many different varieties of leaves – all left him delirious with sensory and sensual pleasure.

The distinctive notes of diverse birds, calling out to their friends and lovers, or cautioning each other about an alien presence; the fluttering of their wings as some took note of the warning and flew to a safer distance from the uninivited intruder; and other humming buzzing squacking squeaking singing talking slithering walking hopping bustling rustling sounds of life and the living orchestrated through the air, filling the woods with music, and Peter with such an extreme of joy that he began to half-dance half-trot, waving his arms about and letting out strange calls from his throat in a notably faulty imitation of the greatly superior repertoire of the birds, bees, insects and animals that inhabited those enchanted surrounds.

A fluffy-tailed red squirrel zipped up and down a tree chipmunking her message of surprise, or disdain, or amusement, to all who had ears to understand. A bounding rabbit stopped for a while, lifted his forepaws in the air, sniffed meaningfully, spasmodically pinching his nostrils, and then skedaddled out of sight. Birds of multi-coloured magnificence and aerodynamic splendour could be glimpsed sailing through the leafy air or hop-scotching on trees, peering below and around and above with staccato movements of incredible rapidity.

The combined scent of so much life was compellingly destabilising. Peter almost lost his reason for being there.

An open space appeared to his left. He walked towards it without thinking, and only just stopped himself in time. Beyond was a sheer drop down the cliff. Old Trix, however, was not so quick in her response. Down she went. Peter's brain malfunctioned momentarily . . . But soon he could see two little paws clawing away at the edge as she about turned on the stony slope and managed to hang on. He rushed to help her and was able to pull her up safely. They both needed a while to recover after that. He sat down cross-legged on the rough grass and put her on his lap and began running his fingers through her coat, lifting her up every now and then to kiss her.

When they were both breathing normally, he looked out to the view presented from up here.

Beneath him spread the sloping meadows leading to the beach. The ships and boats he had seen earlier on were still there, or others very like them. The sea was the same, and so was the horizon. However, seen from this green and living sacrarium, it evoked a becalming and blissful response, not the fear he had felt on top of that huge, cold, man-made temple. He felt at peace with himself and with the world. Why had he been so restless and agitated only a short while ago? Why rush to see the grey man just now? Surely it could wait till Paul came back. Even if he were late in tonight, tomorrow wasn't that far ahead.

'But now we are out here, we might as well go ahead,' he said to Trix, and off they started again.

They had gone just a few steps when he quite suddenly wanted to urinate. Desperately. One minute he wasn't even aware of the need, the next it became the most urgent requirement. It often happened with him after any sort of a crisis or shock or unexpected situation. Fortunately he had the whole place to himself so there was no problem, except which tree to favour and which bush to avoid.

Just when he had unzipped his jeans and pulled out his little bit and was about to start he saw Trix looking up at him through hair-strewn eyes. 'Off, Trix, off!' he shouted in a peeved voice as his water began to spout uncontrollably.

But Trix stood there wagging her tail furiously, and *looking*. Peter, embarrassed and annoyed, let fly a sideways kick which turned out to be harder than he had anticipated. As it hit her across the belly, the movement also sent a spray of his urine against her eyes. This unexpected double attack sent the old girl trotting off to one side and, though sorry for having hit and sprayed her, he was also glad to be able to relieve himself in peace. He would give her her favourite sweets, a good bath and a rub-down first thing when they got home, he promised himself as a measure of atonement.

He did himself up properly and in a satisfied, leisurely manner, then started walking ahead, looking for Trix as he went along. He called out her name, but there was no response. At first he wasn't worried and thought she'd be just running circles round some tree or doing something equally doggy-sensible. But when minutes went by and he could see or hear nothing which was remotely Trix-like, his worry-button was switched to 'on', and he began calling out to her in a loud, breathless voice and started running back and forth looking under every tree and behind every bush. Nothing.

He had lost all sense of direction by this time. To make a fitting environment for his inner turmoil the elements altered their voice and colour. Rolls of clouds started amassing across the skies, clearing their throats before commencing their thunderous roars; and an unnatural darkness invaded the woods, a darkness illuminated by flashes of brilliant whiteness. In senseless panic Peter ran as straight ahead as the trees would permit, calling out, 'Trix, Trix, come back Trix. Trix, I'll never hurt you again. Please Trix. Trix, Where are you! Trix. Trix. I'm sorry Trix. Please. Please. Please God. Please Jesus. Please. Trix. Please . . . Please . . . Trix . . .'

Suddenly he was out of the woods and beside a road. There, not far from him lay Trix, on a grassy verge by the edge of the tarmac. A passing motorist must have clipped her and knocked her aside.

She was still warm, but dead. There was no doubt about that in Peter's mind, even before he actually reached her and picked her up. There were no signs of injury on her body, except a very slight and thin trickle of blood down one side of her mouth. It was damp to the touch.

Peter's whole body was shaking and his hands could barely keep hold of the lifeless life in his arms. She was so soft and gentle beneath his convulsive fingers. He kept calling out her name, but the sounds that came out of his throat were more like the yelps of Trix herself than words formed by his own voice.

He must bury her here, in the woods, along with all the beautiful creatures of the earth and the trees and the bushes.

He placed her gently on an area of soft tufty grass, and took his shirt off. He wrapped her carefully in the shirt, then walked back into the woods to look for a suitable place to dig, somewhere soft and warm and safe. Somewhere with a conspicuous landmark that would serve as a sort of headstone for her, as well as make it easy for him to find it when he wanted to visit her. His feet were having trouble steering him in any given direction and his eyes were having trouble focusing, but what had to be done, had to be done. That was a man's primary function in life.

The clouds were rolling in and out, darkening the skies, and then splitting suddenly to reveal a sharp angry sun. The thundering of the clouds had started in earnest now, in response to the sun's unwelcoming glare. The wind was gently moaning its way through the leaves, lifting up the ones scattered on the ground, and bringing down the ones high up in the trees.

He found a tree-stump with a sturdy little branch growing out of one side which further sprouted two crooked little green sticks, one of which had even some leaves adorning its tip. Not merely that, there was a big boulder of greyish black rock next to it near a patch of soft-looking earth. And it was along the main path. Ideal.

He placed Trix on top of the tree-stump, and began to look for something to dig with, a strong pointed branch or a longish sharp rock. He found several which looked promising, but when he tried to dig, they were useless. Partly they weren't strong enough, partly he wasn't.

Time went by, he grew more and more tired, his breathing became difficult and he felt invisible hands grasping him by the throat and choking the life out of him. What was life? What had gone out of Trix? She looked exactly the same, felt exactly the same. But she wouldn't after a while. He became sick all over his thin ribbed chest and skimpy bare stomach. It had been hot when he had started, but now the wind was beginning to turn cold. Without his shirt his skin came out in large sandy grains and his spine felt like someone was running ice cubes over it.

After a while, he stopped trying to dig. The heat of exertion brought out sweat which produced more cold. He stood up and looked at the undug grave of his friend. He remembered her, young and energetic, when he was about two, licking his face and practically sitting on it. How could she have grown old while he had not even grown young? But she had not died of old age. She had been killed. Killed by him. There she lay on a tree-stump, half-wrapped in his old shirt, half-naked where the wind had blown the covering off, killed by her own best friend. Her only friend. Nobody else much cared for her now that she was old and a bit of a nuisance, shedding hair all over the place and wetting herself when she oughtn't. Killed. Just for looking up at his willy as he pee'd.

The clapping of thunder got louder, the flashes of lightning whiter. He made another attempt to dig.

Another flash, so white it made everything black. Peter was kicked in the guts by a giant boot and felt himself hurtling headlong towards extinction.

The sensation of intense heat burnt his mind out of shape. If this was hell, he deserved it for killing Trix. The thought of Trix brought movement back to his limbs and he managed to raise himself up from the ground. He was still on all fours when he saw the fire. There was no Trix. He stood up with quick mechanical jerks only a short distance away from burning trees. The dry spell of the last few weeks helped them to splinter and crackle and explode into starry flames. It was a majestic sight. And it was hot.

A heavy squally shower burst through the leafy arena and fire and water fought for supremacy in primitive grandeur.

'Trix!' Peter called out, 'Trix!' He rushed towards the heart of the fire to save her, 'Trix, Trix!' But he stumbled and fell. Had the angry wind not been blowing the fire away from him he would have been badly scorched.

The shower stopped as abruptly as it had begun, and the clouds rolled away again, as if to give Peter enough light to look for his old dog.

'Trix!' shouted Peter, stretching out the 'i' to its ultimate limits, and beyond. 'Trix!' – beginning on a high note and ending on a lower, 'Trix . . .'

The clouds and the shower returned with renewed strength to test their power against the fire.

'Trix . . . Trix . . .'

Paul, seeing that the weather was not conducive to sketching or painting, had packed up his gear and was driving home when he thought he heard Peter's voice calling out from the woods. He drove as near to the source of the voice as he could, then stopped, jumped out of the car, and started yelling. 'Peter. Peter. Is that you Peter?'

The reply came, 'Trix . . . Trix . . .' The voice was not as loud and clear as before.

It was Peter.

'Peter. Peter!' Paul's voice was stronger and more urgent.

'Trix. Trix . . .' The voice was now almost soft, gently calling out, 'Trix. Trix . . .'

The rain was squelching under his running feet when he thought he saw a movement to his left. There, silhouetted against the brilliance of the dancing flames, was Peter, naked torso peppered with ash, looking more grey than

147

golden, staggering and swaying and whispering. 'Trix . . . Trix . . .'

The clouds split once more and the sun shone through bright and clear. Before it could disappear again Paul caught Peter's eyes. He had never realised they were such a light grey colour, with such silvery streaks. For one passing instant, as they hit the sun, they sparkled like diamonds.

21

Paul sent for the doctor as soon as he got Peter home. He had developed a high fever and kept muttering incoherently, suddenly sitting up and calling out to Trix, or repeating Paul's name or saying 'Sorry, Mummy' or screaming to be let out.

By the time the doctor arrived, Natalia and Paul had cleaned and tidied Peter up. They were not sure what to tell the doctor.

It would be terrible if Eleanor found out where Peter had been found. First, Natalia would be questioned as to how she could have let the child leave the house. What it would mean in terms of her future was debatable. In normal circumstances she would have been peremptorily dismissed, without a reference. However, the difficulties they had had in the past in getting good 'persons' – usually female persons were preferred – to look after the boy, and the fact that Natalia was an exceptionally intelligent and well-brought up girl going through University were strong points in her favour.

Then Peter would be asked where he was going, what he was doing in the woods, and, most important, why. His motives would be 'drawn out' by cool, logical and persistent questioning; the dangers, selfishness and thoughtlessness of his actions would be explained to him in detail, and he would be told to write them out, and asked to dispute or contradict them if he felt Mummy was wrong. He would be made to apologise to all concerned, especially Uncle Paul, for the worry and bother, and the doctor, for wasting his time which could have been spent on someone more in need of his services; and so on. Then he would be forbidden ever again to leave the house, even accompanied. Or at least not until and unless Eleanor felt that he had 'learnt his lesson'.

On the other hand it might help the doctor make a proper diagnosis if he knew what had happened. The compromise of telling the doctor but asking him to keep it a secret from Eleanor was a tricky one at best, and a risk. Doctor Cook had been Eleanor's family doctor for a long time, and he would almost certainly want to confide in her.

As it happened the doctor did not show any great curiosity. Peter was probably suffering from delayed shock following the accident in which Tom and he had been involved some time ago, brought on by a nightmare or a sudden flash of memory – a not uncommon occurrence among children – and compounded by exposure. He must have gone out for a walk with the dog, which was why he kept repeating the name of the animal, without being properly wrapped up – Eleanor had often complained to him about that – and got caught in 'one of these blasted spell of rains. Thought we were rid of them.'

The assessment was probably not too far removed from the truth, thought Paul. And where was Trix?

Paul's second shock of the evening came when the doctor casually mentioned on his way out that Peter's 'growth programming' would now have to be delayed till he was fully recovered, which was a pity because all the results of the tests were favourable and as far as he was concerned they were ready to embark upon the treatment.

This was the first Paul had heard of it. Apparently the drug would be administered in carefully-regulated doses at irregular intervals of time, related to the results. The growth-rate was not directly linked to the dosage, and would depend upon the response of the patient. Sometimes there was no development for a considerable period after intake, and then a sudden burst of increased development. Careful monitoring was the key. But all the signs were that Peter would make an admirable subject, and all that was needed now was for him to be fit and well, and 'off we'll go'.

Paul's first response was fury. How could that woman play about with the body, possibly even the life, of her own son like that! But on reflection, he wasn't too sure. Perhaps it was a good idea. If the doctors were sure . . . What he needed was the scent of a joint in his nostrils and the feel of paint between his fingers. Maybe a cunt round his cock. Not Natalia's, though. A complete stranger was who he wanted. Someone he had never seen before and was likely never to see again.

'Boy, do I need a fuck!' he said, walking into the glass-walled study after seeing the doctor out.

Natalia was there, having tucked Peter safely in bed. 'I beg your pardon?' She stopped, turned to face him, fine nostrils flaring.

'Sorry. I was talking to myself. Besides, I didn't mean you. I mean someone I have never set eyes on before, and would never see again.'

'That's comforting. And very flattering. Thank you.'

'Sorry again, dear Natty. I didn't mean it like *that* either. It's just that I want someone who has a need I can fill – sex, money, company – and who can fill the need I have. No commitment, no selling the soul in exchange for a body. No moral blackmail, no sordid demands for faithfulness. No wedding ring round the balls, tightening its grip with every stroke. Just plain, simple, honest-to-goodness fucking.'

'Well then, make the effort. Go out and search for someone. Who knows, you might get lucky.'

'Just look outside. It's raining panthers and wolves. Too wet for a word with four asterisks which rhymes with hunt. If only one could order one at home.' The tease in his voice was ever so slight.

'You mean like take-away food. A pizza or something?'

'Exactly. You got it in one.'

'Forgive my ignorance, but I do believe such places exist.'

'You mean escort agencies and the like? Con factories. Besides only the rich can afford them. Now don't . . . don't interrupt yet. I am not just talking of myself. I mean some neat and simple system, which honest men and women can operate, and afford.'

'Did I hear you say women? I thought they were just the goods on order.'

'Heavens no. Women are entitled to their cock shops. Most emphatically so. Women, and men who prefer the other aspect of God's pleasure dome, should have their orders ready for them, same as me or anybody else.'

'And what about the women, and men who "work" in these . . . establishments? Haven't they got any dignity, or rights?'

'It is for them to choose. I know for myself I'd rather "work" as you so meaningfully articulated, in one, than in any rotten mind-destroying factory, or most of the regular nine-to-five jobs that people are so proud to do. Such as making bullets, testing nerve gas on rats . . .'

'Oh, so we are back riding our moral high horse. Somehow after what you have been saying it just does not seem quite that high any more.'

'Why? You tell me why? Why is a man or a woman allowed to hate as many men or women as he or she likes to hate, but be expected to love only one? You tell me that.'

'You are confusing love with making love. You can love as many people as you want. Brothers, sisters, friends, uncles, aunts, strangers . . .'

'OK. Let's take making love. Why should making love to a lot of different people be worse than making hate to, and for thousands? Why should weapons to propagate hate-making, such as a new long-range missile or a more efficient aircraft carrier or just a gun, be greeted with pride and accolades and contracts, while any instrument for making love, like a hard cock, or even a modest dildo, a quiet anal probe or a rising porn star meet with such appalling horror? Why should you be allowed to hurt, insult, demean, or reduce, even kill, but not fuck with impunity? Not unless you are rich and famous, in which case it is great fun and a tribute to the size of your libido.'

'Since when did you become the poor little boy, dear Pablo.'

'I know you've been dying to bring that up for some time. But it's beside the point.'

'That's a convenient counter point.'

'Anyway, I've hardly any money of my own left any more. I just live off Ellie.'

'How noble of you to be so honest about it.'

'That's just as may be, but I could do with a fuck.'

'Come on, Mr Original, say something new.'

'Only lies are new. Truth is older than life.'

'Then go fuck yourself, Mr Philosopher,' said Natalia, finally out of patience, and walked out.

'And the same to you, Miss Psychologist.' He lifted an imaginary hat.

She went up to her room and shut the door firmly behind her.

'I am not going to cry over . . . that . . . that man,' she said. She sat down, then got up almost immediately, went to Peter's room, paused with her ear against the door, gently opened it, saw him sleeping quietly, was about to return, but stopped, went in and sat down in a chair beside his bed.

Paul started searching the house and the gardens for Trix. He was thoroughly drenched by the time he got back in. No Trix.

He took his wet clothes off by the door, threw them in a laundry basket in one of the closets, and walked naked across the hall and up the stairs. He met Natalia coming out of Peter's room.

'I think I should call the police and report a pervert, but I probably won't bother,' she said, and went into her room. She did not shut the door firmly behind her.

'I think you'd better call the police. I can't find Trix anywhere,' he shouted from outside her door.

'You think you are such an anal expulsive, don't you? And the last few weeks you have turned worse than ever. Well you are not!' Natalia replied, opening the door slightly and poking her head out, but not looking at his naked body. She spoke quite calmly, very sure of her thoughts and her words; not so sure of the order or arrangement of either thought or word.

'If you don't wish to telephone why don't you just say so! I'll ring them myself,' he said, knowing full well that that was not what she meant.

And she knew that he knew.

22

The evening was fading out and Paul was making use of the dying light to paint the pouring rain as seen through the glass against the background of the artificial sand garden from Philip's ex-study. This room he had once again more or less taken over – he often slept here as well – calling it, rather unoriginally, 'his retreat'. He was a comparatively neat painter, in as much as he kept all his paints and brushes and any other relevant materials – palettes, brushes, boxes of crayons and pastels, bottles of turps or oils, sketch pads and pencils, hardboards, canvasses, anything – tidily put away or stacked or lined up, in noticeable contrast to the disorganisation of his life generally.

Of course this tidiness was mainly observed when he was here with Eleanor. He had a comfortable and spacious and more chaotic flat in the city, but he was away so much that it was now permanently inhabited by friends, some of whom he did not even know, and he spent less and less time there.

Paul's commissioned painting had been quite an experience; in a sense it had set him on the path to being a serious artist.

He had long been searching for a metaphor, a way of painting the world, when he went to meet the man who had asked him to come and do his portrait.

The man, when he finally appeared after Paul had been looked over and frisked by two hefty characters, took him up the stairs of his interminable house, without a word, to a grand, high-ceilinged room. It was pink and white and decadently rich, full of mirrors and furnished with all sorts of shudderingly modern luxuries and conveniences, such as a jacuzzi in the centre of it and a cinema-screen-sized television screen along one wall. There, still without a word, he began taking off his clothes. He was very old and fat and very tall. His enormous piles of flesh and yards of skin were richly pink and white, like the room; and over-full, like the room, in his case with bulges and lolls and pulps.

Paul had detected a certain amount of campness in his walk and demeanour from the very start, and he now began to get guiltily nervous. He had always believed in offering his sexual services to anyone who was needy enough or bold enough to ask for them, but he would really have to work himself up awfully hard to get ready for this man. Besides, he was rich enough to get his pleasures easily, and it would have been misplaced sexual generosity to give in to him. But, then again, wasn't such reasoning a cop-out, given his own belief that the one who asks is also the one who needs, as against the one who makes or takes or acquires? However, he also knew that asking could sometimes be just another way of taking. Was this man asking, or simply wanting to take? Take him. Take him for granted. Paul was steeling himself for some sort of a response when the man, now completely naked, started throwing large fluffy cushions from the seats over to the carpet, underneath an arched alcove near the farthest, sunniest corner of the room. Still in absolute silence, he lay down on the cushions and beckoned to Paul.

'Would you please push that,' he said in a grating voice which seemed to choke on its own words, pointing to a black button next to a dimmer switch. Still unsure of his eventual response, Paul did as he was asked. Immediately two thick thongy ropes, black with thick, well-padded loops, lowered themselves from the ornate golden arch. Paul's heart gave a short sharp shudder, not of disapproval or disgust, merely of cowardice and inadequacy. He was getting less and less sure of the situation, of the man, of himself.

The man forced his pink podgy feet through the loops, rested the backs of his ankles in each, and pulled at some sort of a pulley system till his heels were almost at a level with his lumpy shoulders. A couple more tugs, and his knee-caps were at a level with his shoulders. Then he removed two cushions from under his head and placed them beneath the crumpled arcs of his ageing buttocks, making an offering of the opening between them as of a maiden's virginity at some glittering pagan altar. Above the greasily-gaping orifice, his upside down balls hung heavily, covering the base of his penis. The member itself, though large, unwrinkled and well-formed, was flaccid, its naked circumcised head pointing downwards towards his many-layered belly. This lack of penile excitement on the man's part was no consolation for Paul. It was always easier to be done by a male you did not like, than to do it to him.

'Would you please pass me my pipe, it is there, sitting on top of my loving wife.'

It turned out to be on top of a very large photograph of a very small woman, placed flat, face up, half hidden beneath a blue vase of Chinese origin; all collectively rested on a cheap-looking glass-topped coffee table.

'There is also a lighter somewhere on her face, please bring that along as well.' Paul could not see the lighter on the woman's face. In fact he could not see the woman's face. It was hidden beneath the bottom of the vase. Under normal circumstances Paul would have understood, but today he had to be told that the lighter was in the vase.

'Thank you. Thank you very much indeed,' said the man after Paul handed him the lighter, and the rather curious pipe with a nearly twelve-inch long, rough and sturdy stem, expanding grotesquely along its length and crowned by a huge bulbous cup. 'Would you now please light the pipe for me.' He added a further 'Please?' when he saw a slight hesitancy in Paul's eyes. There was a real note of appeal in his harshly-creaking voice, and Paul was getting more and more uncomfortable. One arrogant note in the man's words, one sharp glint in his intricately veined eyes, and he would have gone. As it was, he felt himself being subtly sucked into a situation over which he seemed to be losing the little control he had had at the start.

After the pipe had been successfully lit, the man threw his shockingly white head between his rolling thighs, shut his eyes and puffed at it with deep slow satisfaction. The ropes were now tautly pulling at his toes on the carpet, well behind his hugely rounded shoulders.

'Get your stuff ready and paint away now,' he said, suddenly opening his eyes. 'I hope you are as good as Eleanor says you are. Do not worry about any mess you might make. I want the best portrait that you can create of my asshole. It has been my only faithful friend through the vicissitudes of a long life.

'It has seen the world go by and not uttered a word of complaint. It has been buggered by the biggest black slaves that money can buy, and the hugest whitest ones that money can buy. It has been fisted by the wildest proudest boys money can tame, and dildoed by the prettiest gentlest girls money can win.' He paused, a long pause interrupted by puffs of smoke, then added in so surprisingly soft a tone that he could hardly be heard: 'It has also been loved by those money would not have lured . . . I hope.'

He lay silently puffing again for some time, then a childishly

158

gleeful expression appeared quirkily on his redly-swollen face. 'I want *this* painted, framed and hung, to be adored, admired and adulated for and by generations.

'The prints of the portrait will go to my beloved children and other sundry relatives. That is all *they* are getting from me. Everything else will be turned into cash and go towards feeding and housing the hungry and the homeless. It will be put to good use, I can assure you.'

Suddenly Paul burst into life. He had found his metaphor for the world: the man's hole disappearing up his mind, his soul emerging from out the opening.

He set to work.

Prior to that painting, painting for Paul had never been more than an erratic but passionate encounter, his search for a metaphor notwithstanding. Travelling, or to put it in his words, wandering aimlessly through life was his style and his way. He liked to refer to himself as a never-born gipsy, or a no mad nomad, or a mad nomad. He had, to use words carefully chosen to irritate his sister (tantalize her brain is what he would have asserted), wandered in life from an anarcho-situationist revolutionary place to an anarcho-universalist-cum-anarcho-pacifist position, having passed through stations of tyrannical to benign dictatorships, capitalist havens, communistic to monastic and communalistic enclaves, through democratic ways, by-ways and territories.

Although he had his overalls and aprons and paint-splattered jeans, he often painted without any clothes on and took a good soak in the bath afterwards, which was easy as his 'retreat' had a bathroom adjacent to it and he did not have to go through the house naked – expressly forbidden when Eleanor was about. In spite of their disagreements and incompatible views on life, living and politics, Paul respected some of Eleanor's rules and regulations; especially on literally, her home ground. She had stood by him during many difficult times, financial embarrassments, troubles with the law, problems with law-breakers; and, uncharacteristically, taken a lot of slagging from friends and enemies on his behalf. Paul was grateful. Now. He wasn't always.

She and he were twins, but he had been given away to a childless aunt almost immediately after birth and brought up under a very different set of rules, or lack of rules. As a child and as a grown man, until quite recently, he had not been able to forgive his mother for what he saw as abandoning him; and the more his adoptive mother lavished love and gifts on him, the more he resented his own mother, without too much respecting his aunt, whom he insisted on calling 'Auntie' and not 'Mother' as she very much wanted. Although he did love her he tried his best not to show it, and although he longed for his mother, he tried his best to disguise his longing as hate. The situation was made worse by the fact that the two families lived quite near each other and in constant contact. Paul's mother had thought it would be an advantage; it turned out to be the opposite. He did everything he could to besmirch the name of both families, and often succeeded.

Eleanor, although she would never admit to it, felt guilty about Paul's plight from a very early age, and assumed self-allocated responsibility for him when they were a little older. At first it angered Paul even more, and he got worse, stealing large sums from his real father, embezzling funds from his adoptive father's business, breaking into both their houses, fucking anything on two legs, taking drugs, mixing with the shanty town people and other undesirables; and later on taking an aggressively active part in any movement or cause or organisation which could in some way rattle the exclusive cages of society, the more gilded the better. However, as he grew older, and after he had travelled round half the world, seeing and living with all kinds of people in all sorts of circumstances, he changed his responses. His responses and his attitudes, but not his beliefs. In a more powerful way than ever before, he was convinced that he had been right in defying society and the social orders.

But his feelings for the individuals involved in those set-ups, set-ups that he loathed and feared, did begin to alter. Hate and anger began to give way to a sort of sorrow which hovered dangerously close to love. It certainly turned to open and unashamed love for the family that he had tried his best to humiliate all his early life. A love mingled with a special kind of gratitude for Eleanor, who had been the most forward in keeping him out of serious trouble whenever he was in it, and in pleading his case with the family – even though he feared most of her beliefs, opinions and yearnings. This disassociation of the deed from the doer, separating the dogmas and creeds and beliefs from the beings of those who held or cherished those dogmas and creeds and beliefs, was the process of growing up that he had achieved in the wilds and deserts and jungles of this world, and which he might never have managed had he remained a child of its 'civilised' parts, whether enjoying them or fighting them. Or so he believed.

He learnt that a person is not what a person does, or what a person thinks, or what a person believes; nor all three, nor anything more. A person just is. Like a cat is, or a mountain is, or a grain of sand is. Each deserved respect for its identity for its own sake. No other reason was needed, and certainly not required. Once everyone realised that, there was no necessity to cheat or kill or hurt anyone else. For all that cheating and killing and hurting was nothing more than the by-product of the desire to earn that respect for one's identity which was one's right as a created being. If it was offered, as it was meant to be, without ruse or pressure or bondage, without the accoutrements of wealth, or the trappings of intellect or success or achievement, or the approval of him or her or the next – then the struggle to force respect out of others would cease, and with it would cease all that was violent and vicious and ugly. The more competitive and demanding the society, the worse it would get.

Paul couldn't always, if ever, live up to what he believed to be the truth, and until recently it made him feel worse about himself, more judgemental, than towards anyone else.

He should do better because he should know better! But he was beginning to realise that this was only a form of vanity; and that he too deserved acceptance of his weaknesses, as he believed others did of theirs. Because he thought he knew better did not mean he was better; just as someone who did not know better was not worse. He just was. And that was all there was to it. With this acceptance all the rest would fall into place, would right itself, would become good. It might take time, but it would.

The thundery mood of the day was making the darkness enhance its density at a faster pace than the passage of the hours warranted. Paul was wondering whether to use it to his advantage, to evoke an empathetic feel in the painting, create an ambience in keeping with the atmosphere of the day, or to pack away till tomorrow and wait for another similar day. By the looks of it that day could well *be* tomorrow. Perhaps he could paint from emotional memory at a later date altogether. Just then the music flowing out of his radio stopped for the on-the-hour news. He enjoyed classical music, most music in fact, without understanding it or knowing much about it, being musically illiterate. He swivelled round to turn the radio off as he could not bear the news while he was painting, but he stopped in mid-step as he heard the first item. It was about a fire in the woods –

. . . in the no-man's-land between the slums of the shanty town and the elegant beaches to the east. The fire was quickly brought under control, thanks to the heavy rains, but firemen fighting the blaze saw something suspicious beneath some of the underbushes on the rocks below the woods, which took much longer to bring under control. It turned out to be the body of a young boy from the shanty town, who had been missing from home for two weeks. There were clear indications of a sexual assault, as the body was naked and there were injuries surrounding the sexual parts. A source close to the police said that there could be a link with two other sexual attacks, one on a girl aged twelve and another on a boy aged ten, and one indecent assault on a girl aged

eleven. Two of the three children involved were also from the shanty town.

Paul paid no attention to the news that followed. His concern for Peter, already great, turned to serious worry. What had he been doing there on his own? Had he been on his own? He must get answers to a few questions. Perhaps Natalia could help.

He was out of the study and on his way to Natalia's room when he thought he heard Eleanor's voice downstairs in the kitchen.

What can she be doing here? he thought to himself. She can't possibly have found out about Peter and the woods and the fire. But you can never tell what Ellie can manage to find out once Ellie sets her mind to it! Not so soon, though. Even if that stupid doctor did manage to inform her of Peter's fever, somehow, somewhere – he was toadyish enough to do that in the hope of getting a commendation point from her – he didn't know any details himself about what had actually happened. Thank God.

He changed direction and headed downstairs, glad that he had on his jeans and a T-shirt. As he barefooted his way into the kitchen, he saw Eleanor standing beside the long window, cup of coffee in one hand, telephone receiver in the other, talking in a calm but firm voice to someone on the line. She suddenly became aware of another presence in the room and stopped in mid-sentence with a tense gasp, then realised it was Paul.

'What are you doing creeping about the house like that? Gave me the fright of my life. Not you! How can you be creeping about my house if you are in your own home! It's my prodigal brother . . . Who else. I'll call you later.' She put the phone down and turned towards Paul with quizzically raised eyebrows.

Paul responded by raising his own eyebrows even higher. 'What are you doing here? I live here, remember. At least as long as you are willing to put up with me.'

'Don't be silly. It is you who keep disappearing, not I who send you away. This is your house as much as it is mine. And you know that.'

'As long as I am decent!'

'As long as you are decent. Right.' The smile in her voice went as she continued, 'The OAM at the Rommel Park had to be cancelled, thanks to this rain. I thought I might get in and catch up on some paperwork.' The OAM was the well-publicised Open Air Meeting. She seemed a little peeved, but no more.

There was something not quite right. Eleanor should have been white with rage and red with fury and purple with frustration at not being able to have her well-rehearsed and painstakingly-prepared say. Paul tried to imagine her in all those colours on the canvas, but the picture looked as wrong there to his eyes as it did here to his mind. Perhaps she did have a lot of written work to catch up on. But then again, it would not be at all like her to let a backlog pile up.

The real reason for her philosophic acceptance of the situation emerged from her casually-thrown next remark: 'I can imagine the Gulroza lobby will be having something to think about if this rain continues. When the crumbling shacks start crumbling further, then they might begin to appreciate the value of safe, comfortable, new houses.'

Paul had difficulty controlling his temper. 'How would you like a new house to move out of here?' The moment the words were out of his mouth he realised how silly they were.

'Don't be stupid, Paul. There is no comparison. My house is not falling to bits in a stinking dump-heap!'

'You are right. It isn't.'

'And if it was, I'd be sensible enough to jump at the chance of a new one, and a new life to go with it.'

'Perhaps. If you were sure you would get even the first, much less the second.'

'Are you suggesting we won't keep our promises?'

'It wouldn't be the first time. And as yet there are no promises, either, just plans. And the first priority, and the only certainty, of the plan is to redevelop the area by acquiring the land and the properties. The rest is about as clear as the chemical components of a diabetic's piss are to the naked eye.'

'I refuse to sink to that level of conversation with you, thank you Paul. Now, if you'll excuse me, I have work to do.'

It was only when Eleanor was out of sight that something she had said began to tease his brain. What was it? Something that should be, but wasn't; or the other way round. It was not just her reaction to the rain, that had been explained. Something else was niggling. Something else, but closely related to it . . . The cancellation of her meeting . . . The meeting. The UGM! That was it.

Jonah was holding his – it had been theirs, once – UGM tonight. And he had forgotten all about it.

How times had changed. Or rather, how he had changed. Once, when there had been meetings like this, and over less important issues, he would have prepared for it days before. Prepare, think, plan, virtually live it, long before it actually came to being. And now, over the critically important issue of the shanty town development, he had not even remembered that it was taking place that very night. And he had the gall to be caustic to Eleanor about it! At least she was doing something about it, according to her beliefs and visions for the future.

Still, it was just seven o'clock, much earlier than the darkness outside suggested. Nobody would even start gathering until eight; and Jonah himself, always preferring to make an entrance, never went in before nine-thirty. At least, that is how it used to be. He hadn't been to one for years. But then, he wasn't often around now, nor had there been so charged an issue at stake for many years. He rushed upstairs with the intention of putting on his shoes, grabbing a raincoat, rushing back down, and going out. He met Eleanor coming out of Peter's room. She was about to speak when Paul put his arms round her, lifted her off her feet, twirled her around, kissed her on both cheeks and said 'Thank you. Thank you so much, dear sister, for reminding me.' He went running on, leaving a resigned-looking Eleanor staring at his receding backside.

'I suppose I will have to ask Natalia,' she muttered to herself and went over to the door of her room and knocked. She knew Paul well enough by now to know that she would never know him well enough to know what went on in his mind, or why he behaved the way he behaved on any given occasion. She also knew that it would be pointless to ask him anything when he was in that sort of a mood.

Two minutes later Paul was about to knock on Natalia's door to ask for her car when he heard Eleanor's voice inside. After a moment's hesitation he moved away, quietly walked downstairs, lifted Natalia's car keys from the key rack by the door and ran outside. He'd apologise to her when he next saw her. He must get a car of his own. He had owned one, but used it so seldom, being away most of the time – usually on trains, or hitch-hiking, or buying a junk motor here and there and then dumping it when it had fulfilled its purpose or conked out completely – that he had given it away to a friend who needed one. Now that he was here, and hoping to stay on for a while, he must get another one, and soon.

He had the choice of going direct to the UGM – Underground meeting, and underground not just in the political sense, but literally, as it was held in a series of subterranean caves – which might at some point in prehistory have been used for some sort of ritual worship – helping with the arrangements, as he had done in his early youth; or of going to see Jonah, and accompanying him to the meeting whenever he decided to leave.

He chose the latter course, mainly because he was not sure if any of the new helpers would know him. He might even be considered an unwelcome and possibly suspicious intruder: the UGMs had always been targeted by interests ranging from right-wing activists to law-enforcement agencies, not to mention general troublemakers and troublelovers of varied political views or no views at all. It might prove difficult or embarrassing to explain his presence.

These meetings were often more than mere political occasions. They were boisterous social gatherings, with drinking, smoking, music, dancing; poetry and other readings by hopeful and successful writers; songs from blossoming, blossomed and wilting pop stars – jolly uproarious get-togethers of the disaffected, revolutionaries, communists, democrats, anarchists, world-changers of all colours, even the occasional watery blue, not to speak of other assorted greats of the future in a wide variety of fields.

And, of course, your average common man or woman, however you may choose to define 'average' and 'common'.

Age was no barrier. Tiny toddlers could be seen wearily falling asleep, bent awkwardly at all different angles in the strangest of places and in the arms of total strangers, along with those who might be called to meet their maker at pretty short notice.

Paul could see it all as if it was around him now.

23

'So you've turned up. I thought you had given up life for art.' Jonah tried to disguise his pleasure at seeing Paul by adding an extra edge to his genuine resentment at Paul's recent lack of participation in politics in general, and the affairs of Gulroza in particular.

Of course, Paul had not taken much active part in local politics for a long time, but that was chiefly because he had been away, and Jonah accepted that. His lack of apparent enthusiasm while in Bremmin, and at a period in the history of Gulroza when its very existence was at stake, was another matter. Jonah was angry, even as he was pleased to see his old friend and comrade.

'One is meaningless without the other,' retorted Paul, sticking strictly to the spoken words of Jonah and carefully avoiding the obvious accusations implicit in his voice and manner.

'Art may have its problems without life. Life can carry on quite well without it, ta.'

'Ah, but what is life if not an art, and what is art if without life?'

'I have greater respect for the creator of one than I have for the marketers of the other.'

'Then how come you are more selective in your love, your concern for other human beings than I am? After all, they are all made by God, if what you say is true. It seems I practise what you preach. Judge not lest ye be judged and all that sort of thing.'

'Because you *cannot* separate the deed from the doer, as you keep so glibly suggesting. I mean, how do you do that? Even Christ separated the sheep from the goats.'

'Poor goats. I'd like to know what was their sin. Apart from being born goats. Personally, I love goats, in the tradition of the same man who said, "For if you love only those who love you, what credit is it to you . . . And if you do good only to those who do good to you, what credit . . ." '

'Stop bringing your . . . You are a mass of contradictions. You weren't before, but you are now. I mean, you want to change the world and you suddenly want people to remain as they are. Tell me how that is possible!' Jonah raised his voice, and his arms.

'Of course I want to change people. I just don't want to condemn them. How can you ask someone whom you have rejected to change? And speaking of contradictions, being a high-minded Catholic and –'

'Oh, all right, all right. There is no need to . . .'

'I was only going to say that being a true Christian and a communist is not always an easy combination.'

'I don't know about true Christians, but us Roman Catholics and communists can manage,' said Jonah with a smile in his silky black eyes. 'Anyway, let's go. I have to get early to the meeting today. It is the launch of our DVC.' Jonah was more relaxed now that he had vented some of his anger at Paul.

The Don't Vote Crusade. Paul had almost forgotten about it. And to think, that all those years ago, he and Jonah together had germinated the idea. Only they had called it the Don't Vote Movement then. Paul still thought that was a better name, but Jonah wanted it to sound like, clash with and confuse the supporters of DVD, the Delta Valley Development. Some suggested DVP for that reason, the Don't Vote Party, but that was turned down since the whole purpose of the exercise was to reject the election process and the parties that subscribed to it. To form a party of one's own to break the hold of the party system was at the very least hypocritical and politically counter-productive. Paul felt that the flavour of religious fervour about the word crusade might put some people off, but Jonah believed that it was a plus point. And it was his baby now. So DVC it was.

The idea had been shelved in those early days as being too radical and unlikely to achieve much. Times and attitudes and people had changed since then. Or had they? It was about to be put to the test.

Suddenly Paul was aware of a pounding expectancy within him. He could feel his blood race inside his veins with a pace and a purpose he had almost forgotten how to feel. Even his bones pulsed with the old familiar beat. It was good.

24

The meeting started off as something of a disappointment. Paul was old enough and seasoned enough to be aware that experiences once experienced are seldom repeatable, and that the past can never be recreated. Even so, it was a let-down. It was the rain which kept most people away. It had been dry for some weeks previously so there had been no attempt to change the venue, and now it was too late. There was always the danger of being trapped in a flood: a frightening prospect in those deep, winding caves. The exits were clearly marked, but the openings were narrow; and although voluntary hard work by the dedicated had brought electricity within the passages and the main cave hall, the lighting was still dim and would probably fail in such an emergency. A single short-circuit – which was more than likely to happen if water filtered through to the main installation points – could blow up the whole wiring system.

Moreover, the discovery of Abe's sexually-assaulted body had cast a pall over the whole community, reducing attendances even further.

However, quite a few outsiders, mostly young but many older, had travelled on buses and shared a few broken-down cars to make it to the meeting, and that was very encouraging. There was even a brand new Darria 4000 parked at the foot of a little hillock.

Fortunately the rain eased off and the thinning clouds began to disappear behind the Mother Mountain. Nonetheless, the old merry-festival feel and family-gathering atmosphere, as well as the political passion, were lacking. Instead, there seemed a certain hollowness about it all.

Things began to improve after a few drinks and an aggressively soulful song about the plight of the working poor:

The poor work harder when unemployed
Work harder to live
Work harder to die
Work harder to give
Their children but a lie
That there's a bright future in the present's dark void
The poor work harder when unemployed.

It was followed by a sad dirge on the loss of communities forced to leave their homes under economic and political duress:

We shall be here no more my friends, we shall be here no more
The eye of the sun
The face of the moon
Will search around for us
Hoping we'll be back soon
The cries of the gulls
The roar of the waves
Will call out to us
Across the sea of days
But no one will see us cross the threshold of our door
For we shall be here no more, my friends, we shall be here no more
The rocks will be cold

Without the touch of our hands
The rich'll all prosper
On the poor man's lands
The flowers in the meadows
The birds in the air
Will mourn old friends
But no one will care
The good earth'll be buried under polished floors
When we shall be here no more my friends, we shall be here no
more.

There was nothing new in all that, but that was the point and, ironically, the charm of it. The fact that for once, or rather once again, the words of the song were threateningly real gave an added immediacy and strength to their music.

Paul looked around and marvelled, as he had marvelled before, at the size and space of this underground shrine. How many seasons of labour, how much dedication and faith, how many lives must have gone to create it? Or was it natural? The labour of the present day was evident in the unconcealed wiring, the few scattered lights along the ancient walls carved with ancient images, and the stone blocks serving as both tables and chairs. Everything was sparse and simple, giving the powerful rock walls and corridors, the roughly-hewn floor and the clipped, cup-cut ceiling an added dignity and a sense of common purpose. The constant half-light that pervaded this subterranean mountain temple lent it a strange aura of mystery and magic. Remove the puny electric lights, replace them with torches of dancing flames, and it would be easy to imagine a people falling on their knees to worship a power greater than their own.

When Jonah began his speech, things really took off. In the centre of the hall, standing on a huge rock slab under a strong naked light, huge black eyes shining with a strong naked light, waving his arms about like some half-demented Old Testament prophet, he declared his purpose, gave his message, and called for action. It was not like old days. It was better.

Jonah's big booming voice resounded round the cave hall, echoing back and forth, filling out the gaps and the holes and the alcoves and the cavelets and the outlets that surprised you by their presence at the most unexpected corners of this inverted citadel.

Jonah's speeches, if written down, would make poor reading. His arguments, frequently tatty and patchy, were at times downright untenable, and the main focus was on sentiment and emotional appeal. But when delivered in his hypnotically powerful voice, his tall handsome figure swaying rhythmically to the music of his words; his large dark eyes flashing around in his face; his thick dark hair jumping about over his head; his arms describing magic circles in the air; his hands and fingers clenching and unclenching themselves, now opening out in a supplicating gesture of appeal, now tightening up in resolve, now pounding up and down with uncontrolled and uncontrollable passions – when he spoke like this, the impact on his listeners, often already converted, was very strong indeed.

Tonight he outperformed himself, even though for once most of his audience were not already converted. Some were openly sceptical, many openly opposed. And despite the fact that all were united in their desire to save Gulroza, the vast majority were still committed to the democratic processes of New Heaven. Even those disillusioned with it seemed content to be merely apathetic, and although they often did not vote themselves, they were not prepared to help transform such apathy into a campaign of the same volatile nature as those which had evoked their indifference in the first place. They considered this an unacceptably ironic twist to the situation.

And yet they listened: silent, still and hushed. Inexplicably, their numbers seemed to have increased beyond expectation or even possibility. When Paul looked around at the amazingly attentive faces of the audience, he was amazed himself to see every seat taken, and yet more people standing around, some with their hands on little children's mouths to stop them from making any irreverent noises.

This time even the text of Jonah's speech was better structured and better argued. Its substance, passed round in photocopied leaflets, went like this:

DVC
THE DON'T VOTE CRUSADE

JOIN US IN DEFEATING THE PRESENT SYSTEM, BEATING ITS PERPETUATORS AT THEIR OWN GAME. DON'T VOTE FOR ANY OF THEM!

NO VOTE IS THE MOST POWERFUL VOTE OF ALL! IT IS A VOTE OF NO CONFIDENCE. A VOTE OF NO CONFIDENCE IN ALL OF THEM, AND THEIR SYSTEM CAST IT BY CASTING NO VOTE AT ALL

VOTE AGAINST THEM ALL DON'T VOTE AT ALL

As we are all only too aware, in all systems inequities exist, in some they are even rampant. But at least they are recognised as such by the people, and loathed as such. In the democracy of New Heaven they are sugar-coated, honey-sprayed and marketed with such nerve, verve and style that even the best-intentioned among us mistake them for what they are not. And not only do we do nothing to destroy them, we actually join the powers that be in selling them. To ourselves!

Before they inflict the worst indignities upon our fellow human beings, they manage to make the rest of us believe that this is the 'best they can do in the circumstances'. They not only commit the most awful and the most stupid acts, but make them lawful, with our consent. These acts are further made to appear good and right, in order to convince the 'vast majority', with the help of the 'free press' and the highly-placed, highly-paid actors at the centre stage of the 'freedom of speech theatre', that they are good and right. And if you do not like them, you are free: free to disagree, free to starve, free to be homeless, free to shout about or against them. Nobody will even consider you important enough to try and shut you up. But if someone did, and THAT someone happened to be important enough, then that someone would know how to shut you up, and when to shut you up, acceptably and democratically, with the consent and the approval of the people!

This consent and approval is obtained by distorting people's minds and visions and ideals to suit the rulers. This is done with the three Ms: Money, the Media, and the capitalist Moghuls. And YOUR VOTE. Simple.

THE OPPRESSED ARE MADE PARTIES TO THEIR OWN OPPRESSION. People are made to come willingly to the slaughterhouse, the ballot papers stuffed so high up their ***** that it chokes the throats that can voice dissent; or makes the voice that does come out of grated throats appear out of tune and discordant and ridiculous. You are made to condemn yourself with you own voices. AND YOUR OWN VOTES!

> DON'T LET THAT HAPPEN TO YOU
> DON'T VOTE
> JOIN THE DVC
> THE DON'T VOTE CRUSADE

When he had finished speaking Jonah stepped down from the slab and perched somewhat uncomfortably on its edge. Now was the time for Paul to get worried – the time for open questions.

Jonah was a natural master of the art of public speaking, especially when addressing people motivated and swayed primarily by emotion rather than intellect. And he was excellent at giving orders and being obeyed. These, in marked contrast to his speeches, were in terse sentences, saying or stating or demanding no more than the bare minimum, and were meant for his 'business associates' rather than for social and political compatriots.

When it came to answering in-depth questions, or filling out his propositions with detail, or arguing out the finer points of a proposal or a course of action, he was marginally above being utterly hopeless. He was either so keen to achieve his ends that he had not thought out the means properly, or he got so emotionally involved that he forgot to put forward plans and logistical details which he had thought out and worked at. Or he simply lost his temper and with it the argument.

These were the times when Paul came to his assistance. They had been a regular double-act once upon a time: Jonah the orator and the rebel-rouser; Paul the debater and the rationality counter. Even though his actions may have been and often were most irrational, he was even better at being reasonable in conversation, when he wanted to, than his dreaded twin sister herself.

Paul strongly resisted the urge to join Jonah on the slab today. He knew that he had been away for so long that he had forfeited the right to do so. That is why Jonah hadn't asked him, as he always had before. Paul did not blame him. On the other hand he would hate it if Jonah mucked it up now after such a brilliant opening speech.

The questions started, and with them came Jonah's usual initial humming and hawing, not too serious in itself, but a prelude to the ebbing of his confidence and the disruption of his cool. This inevitably led to damaging blunders of tactics or dialectics.

His anger at injustice and his passion for the cause often misdirected themselves at his questioners, alienating those very people he had set out to woo, most of whom happened to be sympathetic towards him in the first place. The possibility, under these circumstances, of changing the opinions of those not on his side was then slight indeed.

Paul was seriously considering taking the floor even at the risk of greatly angering him. He would apologise profusely afterwards, even on his knees if necessary, saying that he had done so in all innocence, genuinely believing that they were still a team.

Paul was about to walk up to the centre slab where Jonah sat and make a tactful takeover bid, when he detected an almost imperceptible change in Jonah's gruff responding-to-questions voice. Others must have noticed it too, for the slight rustling restlessness which had started to permeate the meeting since Jonah had finished his speech began to die down once again, and an appreciative calm descended on the atmosphere.

Heavy, strong-smelling smoke was clouding the soft lighting in the caves and blurring the vision, in spite of the adequate natural and man-made ventilation. In the sleepy haze Paul sensed another ancient presence in these ancient halls, the presence of the grey man – looking like neither an old man nor a young man, but just like a man, and leaning gently against the centre slab. So calm, so possessed; so different from the vomitting pissing screaming wreck of a creature who had found himself naked and mutilated on a part of a beach in a part of a world of which he had no recollection whatever.

Jonah spoke clearly and effectively once again, answering questions, parrying criticism, advancing arguments, making impassioned but restrained pleas.

He didn't need Paul any more. He had found a new partner for his double-act, a partner who allowed him the use of his own voice.

'We don't just want everybody to have the *freedom* to own a house, we want everybody to *have* a house.

'We don't just want freedom of speech, we want our voices to be heard – not just the voices of the press barons with the government in their pockets, voices which get shoved down our throats so consistently and so strongly and so cleverly that ultimately we cannot distinguish them from our own and begin believing in them ourselves. That is the worst and most insidious form of brainwashing, carried out in the name of freedom of speech.

'We don't just want the *freedom* to work where we want to, we want *work*.

'We don't want to run like idiots with our pants hanging between our knees in search of abstract concepts such as life, liberty and the pursuit of happiness. We want concrete assurances about the business of living, and we want the wherewithal necessary to make it a successful business.

'Of what use are freedoms without the means to achieve those freedoms?'

All this flowed out in response to a long question, near the tail-end of the discussion, about fundamental freedoms in a democracy. And to make a final point for the Catholics in his audience, Jonah recited: ' "If a brother and sister be naked, and destitute of daily food. And one of you say unto them, be ye warmed and filled; notwithstanding ye give them not those things which are needful to the body: what doth it profit?" James 2, 15–16.'

The impressive silence that followed this calm outburst seemed to signal his final victory, at least in moral terms. But then an old woman stood up from a table facing Jonah and spoke in a quavering voice: 'You know where I come from, for you helped me get here. That one, the one standing behind you, is probably a name on a missing list from the same country, or one very like it. We are dying out there for the right to vote. For those very freedoms you chose to mock. What do you say to that?'

There was a great wave of approval for her words, and cries of 'Hear, hear', clappings and other approbatory noises rose from all sides. Even Jonah's greatest supporters in the crowd could not boo or hiss the woman, but waited breathless for Jonah's reply. For a moment it looked as if he was going to lose control, or worse, his temper. Even the grey man was seen to bow his head.

'You won't be allowed to vote here either, good lady. In fact, if any of those for whom you may be tempted to vote were to know of your presence here, they would promptly make preparations for your send-off to the same glorious land you have escaped from. It is a friendly power, and don't you forget that. It does not matter to them what is done, and to whom, or how. All they care about is, *by* whom it is done. If it is a "friend", they can rip out your tongue, or cut off your prick, or burn up your ass, like my friend here —' he didn't even know the grey man's prick had been cut off and he didn't know why he said it — 'or use chemical warfare on your children, it is fine. All they would do is try their level best to cover it up. That is their freedom for you.'

Although there was much clapping and whistling approval for this answer, some were still not satisfied, 'Clever. And true, I'm afraid. But it still does not fully answer the woman's question,' said a young man from well behind her to further approving noises.

'I don't think I can give a full answer to her question, except to remind her, and others, that when *people* ask for *the* vote, it is a very different situation to when *politicians* ask for *your* vote. By fooling, cajoling or plain buying of a few they can rule and bully the rest with as great a lust for power as any despot you care to name.'

'But at least you have a choice,' said a young woman from one end of the hall.

'What choice do I have in an essentially two-party system where both say much the same things? No matter who you vote for, they will destroy Gulroza.

'The only real choice you have is either vote them into power, or refuse to vote them into power. I strongly urge the latter, the Don't Vote Crusade. Follow it, and learn to live with your conscience in peace. Follow it, and don't allow yourself to be abused. Remember, in their own law, the one who aids and abets is as guilty as the one who commits the actual crime. Stop aiding and abetting those who commit unmentionable crimes against humanity in the name of freedom. Do not allow yourself to be fooled and gulled, again and again. Not again. DVC. DVC. DVC . . .'

180

Soon the whole hall was on its feet, chanting DVC. DVC. DVC . . .

Those who had not made up their minds joined in the chorus under the hypnotic trance of the occasion, chanting DVC. DVC. DVC . . .

Those against it started echoing the words for the sheer heck of it, chanting DVC. DVC. DVC . . .

Those who knew nothing of what was going on shouted the loudest. Little children's high voices could be heard, distinct from all the others, chanting DVC. DVC. DVC . . .

25

The big storm hit the shanty town in the first week of September, some six weeks after the official launch of the Don't Vote Crusade and a further six weeks before the elections. Two people were killed; five were missing. Most of the houses were damaged, some severely; a few were completely destroyed. Telephone lines were broken and electricity and gas supplies were badly disrupted, causing additional suffering to all the residents. Perhaps worst of all, sanitation services stopped completely, and piles of rubbish collected everywhere, with all the attendant risks of infestation and disease. Since the roads leading up to the mountain base were blocked by fallen trees or mud slides, the only means of access was by helicopter, and the problem of getting victims of the disaster to medical care units was getting more acute by the hour. If a serious epidemic broke out, the condition of those afflicted would be intolerable.

Both the political parties, though deeply shocked and grieved, were now more convinced than ever that the Delta Valley Development project was the best solution for the shanty-town dwellers.

For the government the catastrophe carried two definite pluses, one negative, and one doubtful element.

The negative was of course the tragedy itself, and its cost in human and economic terms. The problem of re-housing some of the shanty people would become an urgent imperative for the immediate present, rather than something to be dealt with at some uncertain date in the uncertain future. The funds involved might well exceed the original estimates based on the development proceeding along normal, slower lines. However, there was also the possibility that some sort of emergency housing rigged up now might work out cheaper in the long run than having to build new and better-equipped housing estates later on – even though most of the cost of these could be gradually recovered from the tenant-buyers.

The two pluses lay in the near certainty that, with a little bit of well-played concern, the government might now be able to purchase the properties in the shanty town at market prices, which given the present state of most of the houses, and the fact that residents would not be in a position to undertake the necessary extensive repairs, would be very reasonable indeed. This would not only enable the Conservatives to lay the foundations of the DVD, but to do so in the lifetime of their current tenure – a great achievement indeed, by any political standards.

The doubtful element lay in the fate of the Don't Vote Crusade. Its sudden and quite remarkable success – which had taken it beyond the shanty town to all sorts of other areas, due in part to some bright spark reporter from a mass circulation daily who had happened to be present at its launch – was certainly in the interests of the Conservatives, in the short term, possibly up to the election and perhaps even beyond. But damage to its base might well destroy it, leaving its adherents and advocates to return to the welcoming fold of the Socialists. That was bad. On the other hand, in the long term, it might turn out to be a good thing. The success of such a subversive movement was eventually going to start gnawing at the roots of democracy, at the roots of the Conservatives – the newly-gained working-class support, won after many a hard-fought year, might well be in jeopardy by the time the next election came round.

The opposition found some comfort in the storm, barring the pain of the tragedy, of course, but only some. The Socialists did want the Delta Valley Development to go ahead, but under their auspices, not offered to the Conservatives on a platter. However, it might sound the death knell of the Don't Vote Crusade, and that should bring in a few extra votes. Thank God for small mercies. Also, the government might well now be pushed to house the shanty-town people immediately somewhere close to their well-loved Gulroza, rather than hundreds of miles away on the other and barren side of the islands, where their votes would be completely wasted, lost in that Conservative preserve. No doubt that was why it was planned to rehabilitate them there in the first place.

Both sides were pleased that it would finally discredit the weird Diamond Eyes. His exalted status as some sort of a living, breathing patron saint of Gulroza and the protector of its people could hardly be sustained any longer.

Recently he had become an even greater force, making regular appearances on the television, in the newspapers, at public meetings – always appearing with Jonah wherever Jonah went. And although it was Jonah who did all the talking, for obvious reasons, the still, silent presence of Diamond Eyes, standing – always standing – just behind him was the real focus of attention, and the real source of power. His presence could somehow even be sensed on the radio. At least that is how the people felt. Certainly the people of the shanty town.

Attempts by the government to try and deport him somewhere or other badly misfired, sending whole sections of the country into paroxysms of indignant rage, increasing his hypnotic appeal, and giving massive free publicity to the Don't

184

Voters – ironically riding high on the crest of the same kind of wave of political publicity that they were out to contain. But this was in the short term. 'Democracy always works for a short time and for limited purposes,' was Jonah's response when tackled on the issue. 'We are not here to destroy it, simply to ensure that its usurpers, the politicians, do not take it, and us, for granted. For those who have put them there, people like us, won't always be at their beck and call. Not unless we get some long-term guarantees from those running this circus. We are sick of being bullied into submission by a minority disguised as a majority by the present electoral system. What we really want is consensus politics.' As Jonah spoke these well-publicised words 'consensus politics', which, along with the DVC, were to play a significant role in the somewhat distant future of the country, Diamond Eyes stood behind him, silent and still as usual, but closer than usual.

He had not been seen for three days following the night of the flood. That was a good start for his slide down the hill of fame, thought Eleanor to herself as she decided on the most suitable items to wear for her second helicopter visit to Gulroza. Philip had been there yesterday, so even though she had gone the day before, she was on her way again today.

'After all, what are neighbours for?' she had said when one of the ardent reporters at her tail had remarked how good it was of her to come rushing to the scene of 'this great tragedy'.

When the same reporter asked Philip the next day how it felt to be back in the place where he 'hadn't been for so many years', Philip was too upset to think up a proper retort. Most of the papers commented on his lack of real concern as opposed to the genuine caring attitude of his better half. The television networks showed suitably edited clips to the viewers, allowing them to make up their own minds.

26

Eleanor's helicopter, and another one following with camera crew and reporters, hovered over the shanty town, circling round, looking for a suitable place to descend, like a pair of giant bumble bees engaged in a courtship dance.

Just as they seemed to have decided on a landing point Eleanor happened to see something which made her cry out, 'Look! Just look down there!'

The pilot did just that and was sufficiently impressed by what he saw to allow the helicopter to whirl its way towards the sight. By that time the second helicopter pilot had also seen the reason for the swerve in the course of the first and moved alongside as close as was safely possible.

Down below, one side of Mount Gretna had caved in, the steep side facing the New Thames which cut through its guts. The collapse had taken place in a face of the mountain slightly turned away from the streets and houses spread up and down along the curve of the valley. Under normal circumstances, despite its position, the locals couldn't have failed to notice it, but with most people engaged in a fight for survival it was either not seen or just not reported. Huge boulders from the cracked, ancient mountain walls had tumbled down into the river causing a partial block in its flow, which might soon result in flooding up-river near the centre of the city of Bremmin itself.

'Is there anywhere there we can safely land?' asked Eleanor with increasing concern in her voice. 'This looks terrible.' Then, conscious that all her words could be reported, she added, 'An avalanche could come down on the poor people and that would be just terrible.'

'It might be dangerous, if there is still any movement among the rocks,' said the official minder by her side.

The thought of danger gave further strength to her determination to be the first at the spot and 'risk her own life to warn the poor beleagured locals, and initiate measures to save Bremmin from sure catastrophe'. She could almost see the headlines. The opportunity was much too good to miss. If there was any real danger, she would certainly be taken out of there in safety. There was no doubt in her mind about the professionalism of her companion and crew. A sniper's bullet can sometimes not be stopped. Only fools would allow a boulder to roll over somebody's head. She was not in the company of fools.

'One cannot go through life without running into danger,' she said, 'Please, I must go down and see the extent of the slide, and judge what possible dangers it can pose for the poor people of the . . . of Gulroza. They must be warned as soon as possible.'

'We can warn them just the same. There is no need to take risks.' To the minder it was not only Eleanor's life at risk, it was also his job. If the least little thing went wrong . . . There were no second chances in his line of work.

'My mind is made up,' Eleanor declared. 'Can we land somewhere as close as possible to the site, please.' And that was final. The message was relayed to the reporters in the second helicopter who were absolutely delighted to be in on the scoop. Suitable spots were selected for touchdowns.

Even before the whirling blades could come to a rest Eleanor was stepping out and down, followed by her security guard and the band of reporters and camera crew. Eleanor was becoming more and more popular with both press and public: her striking blonde beauty and effervescent personality, her controversial marriage, her well-reasoned and well-articulated speeches and equally impressive published articles, often deliberately provocative but always measured, precise and with substance; her well-chosen words in interviews and when answering questions anywhere, delivered with a brilliantly disarming smile or a moving air of concern – depending on what the moment or the occasion demanded – all combined to make her a much more sought-after and publicised figure than her position in the government demanded. People liked to look at her and to read about her, and she sold newspapers and magazines. She pulled in good ratings when on television. In fact, she was tipped for *the* job in the not-too-distant a future, and she made no attempts to hide her ambitions in that direction. Now was her opportunity to take another right step on that road and confirm her position, not only as a woman of merit but also as a woman of the people – a quality not often enough associated with her, and which she desperately wanted to affirm.

They were in the middle of a patch of grassland where some scouts, guides or campers had left the remains of a fire. Other evidences of human presence were also scattered about, much to Eleanor's disgust. The tall, strong-legged minder had to increase the pace and the length of his strides to keep up with her as she skilfully avoided obstacles and raced round towards the edge of the mountain which appeared to have collapsed, amid shouts and warnings of caution.

The sight which appeared in front of all their eyes, with the force of a sudden hallucination, was the most majestic which she or any one of the party had ever witnessed.

Way down below them the old river sliced its path through a winding gorge, part muddy and browny-green, part clear and bluey-green; high up above them rose the old mountain, part rocky and uncompromisingly barren, part earthy and rampant with life. Straight in front of them, beyond the maddening splendour of many-coloured flowers and grasses, almost within touch, almost white, spread the gentlest looking sky this side of Eden, bespeckled with the wings of a thousand butterflies. Just behind them lay a sea made of roughly-blown glass, decorated with dots and lines and strokes of bold and random gloriousness. They could have been waves or lines of surf or boats and ships and sails, or else the toy alphabet of the petulant child of some god who had tired of playing with them and strewn them about in a tantrum born of frustrated dreams. For one brief moment Eleanor became somebody else: she knew that if her seed had germinated within the wetness of the earth here, she too would never want to leave this place. But then she was herself again, and realised what potential lay in this place and how cruelly it was being wasted, and how badly and urgently it needed development.

The side of the mountain had not avalanched down, as they had expected, but opened out. There was a gaping hole in the rock, an archway high and grandiose enough to compare favourably with that of the most ambitious of cathedrals. A huge tonnage of stones and rocks appeared to have been vomited out by the mountain, as if in some great inner turmoil she had been unable to hold on to her guts; or as if in orgiastic fury the ancient Mother had opened her mouth to spit out rocks like angry words of rage.

For once the camera crew and reporters were overawed by a presence greater than that of Eleanor and they rushed forward, cameras clicking, ejaculating into their microphones, and to each other. For once Eleanor followed rather than led.

Once inside they were met by complete blackness, which, coming as they had from under the brash light of the hot sun, looked blacker than blackness ever looked. Flashlights flashed, momentarily illuminating the entrails of the ancient Mother, and then plunging them back into primordial darkness. Hoarse cries of warning were again directed at Eleanor, and she felt the strong arms of a man take hold of her arms with the words, 'Sorry, Ma'am, but you cannot be sure of what or who may –' His words were left unsaid as he stopped mid-sentence, open-mouthed and motionless. As, indeed, did everyone else present. Even Eleanor, not prone to wonder and marvel, wondered and marvelled, for the second time that day.

The womb of the Mother lit itself up with a golden irridescent light, coming from a source or sources not plainly obvious, but presumably from concealed openings somewhere higher up in the vault-like ceiling of the chamber the size of a sports arena that opened itself out in front of their disbelieving eyes.

The edges of the floor along the perfect circle of the walls, the walls themselves, and the centre of the chamber – all were covered with bones. The pile in the centre was as large and as high as a pile of wood built for a gigantic bonfire-night celebration, or as a pile of wood stacked up in a cone to burn heretics in the name of the Lord. They looked like human bones, though it was quite possible that the bones of other animals may have been mixed in with the human bones. Though there was no complete skeleton, at the far end of the chamber a set of bones had been wedged into the wall to form the shape of a human being, legs dangling, arms spread out, as if in crucifixion. The arms were not arm bones, the legs not leg bones, but the head was indeed a skull. Skulls had also been used to mark the hands, the feet and the genitals. Clearly there was a purpose in the arrangement, and in the choice of bones. As to what that purpose was, there were no obvious clues.

Standing next to this strange crucifix of assorted bones, silently looking at the intruders, was the grey man. His eyes sparkled and shone with the cutting edge of a diamond as they encountered the eyes of Eleanor.

It was a cutting edge that was not just sharp, but smooth and soft and gentle, the edge that pares away cancerous cells from healthy flesh with compassionate skill.

After a long moment of petrification, cameras went wild with flashlights. Even in her state of unaccustomed and therefore frightening awe, Eleanor didn't fail to realise what she had done: handed the best possible publicity scoop to this unnatural man who stood looking at her with so much love in his unnatural eyes.

No matter what she did now, she would never be able to compete with what *he* had achieved. And through *her* efforts! She stood where she stood, ignored and forgotten, as the cameras clicked insanely round the bones and upon the grey man.

She would have to get even with him some day. She did not know how. She did not know when. But she knew she would. She would have to.

And why did he keep looking at her like that. Looking only at her. And why is there so much . . . it couldn't be . . . love in his God-damned eyes? Surely it couldn't be . . .

And why was she getting so upset about it. Even . . . hurt? How could that be? Why should she be . . . *hurt*?

Suddenly she wanted to go up to him, to talk to him, to put her arms round him.

How could this possibly be. This was not reasonable. It was completely irrational. This should not happen. It could not happen. It must not be allowed to happen. It was not happening.

She must destroy him. Destroy him before he destroyed her.

She could not possibly allow herself to *love* this man. Love! What on earth was she talking about? What had happened to her? This living mass of bones, standing next to these dead masses of bones. How could he? How could she?

Somewhere in the heart of the old Mother she could hear a strange music, the gurgling music of a child's voice, the music of the gently-bubbling waters of a mountain spring.

She had to destroy him. There was no other alternative. *He* left her with no alternative.

I tried to hold her hands, but she moved away. I tried to enter her eyes, but she locked her eyelids. I tried to seep into her blood, but she turned her skin to steel.

I stood unheard, ignored and helpless.

27

A week had gone by since the storm. Most of the roads had been cleared and traffic to and from Gulroza had returned to normal, or as normal as possible given the circumstances. Power cables were still in shambles and there was no electricity, and no hope of it for another few days yet. Worse, there was no water from the taps. Either the storage reservoir had burst or it was polluted and had been disconnected. Perhaps this too was due to lack of power. Nothing was known for certain – information was scarce, with no television, a limited supply of newspapers and only battery-operated radios working. All they revealed was that the authorities 'were trying their best' to restore supplies. The villagers were angry and suspected conspiracy: no electricity and no water, damaged houses – that should force them out!

Four of the five missing, all adults, had been found.

Two, out for a walk, had rushed towards the Mother

Mountain to escape from the sudden storm and to seek the shelter of a cave. There they had been met by a boulder not so keen on the shelter of the cave and on its way out to enjoy the storm. The result had not been entirely in their favour, but in the words of the eternal optimist, it could have been worse. Extremely foolish of them, said their wives, but then what else could be expected from two foolish men who went out for foolish walks no matter what the weather.

One was discovered naked up a tree. No one knew how he had got there, and he certainly wasn't telling. Who would, in his position? He was in the habit of showing his love towards his neighbour by giving it to his neighbour's wife in the mid-section of a sturdy old tree which overlooked the wife's garden shed where they could see him doing it to their boy's maths teacher, who so loved the child that she came to their house to give free lessons to him whenever the child happened to be away. When the storm burst, the woman had had the good sense to dust down her skirts, clamber down the tree and enter her house. The man was not respectable. His trousers had blown away by the first gust of strong wind, and his erection took a long time to subside: a great boon in normal circumstances and much appreciated by those who came in contact with it, but a bit, and what a bit, of an embarrassment while naked in a storm. He had been in too much of a panic to move at first, and then some branches had fallen on him, trapping him inside their powerful bends and curves.

The fourth had been asleep in his house when the roof fell on him, and he had been cleared away along with the rubble. Although his wife swore she knew nothing of it, there were those who had their doubts. Moanie Melanie was not known for her love for her dear spouse. But then again, Moanie Melanie was not known for her love for anybody. This did not mean she was getting rid of them by the cartload. Anyway, since the man had suffered no more than a few broken limbs and was his usual grumpy self, there was not much harm done; and Moanie Melanie's grief, or joy, was short-lived, fortunately, or unfortunately.

The fifth, a ten-year-old girl, was still missing. Her parents were frightened and worried, but still hopeful. The villagers shared their concern, but not their hope. There was a general fear, first expressed by the police and shared by most, that her disappearance might have more to do with the child molester than with the storm.

Magda looked at the water buckets. Two were empty and although there was still enough in the other three to last them for the evening, she thought it best to fetch some more from the stream now while it was still light. A municipal lorry had started bringing water to the community once every morning, but residents were suspicious. There were rumours that the water was deliberately contaminated, and wherever possible people fetched their water from the many streams that tumbled down the face of the mountain. They were strong as small rivers now, so there was no dearth of natural water. The government, in its turn, was warning the residents of the danger of the spring and stream water, saying that the possibility of 'unfriendly' viruses and bacteria could not be ruled out after storms and flooding. The locals said that was just to provide themselves with an excuse in case of any spread of disease.

For once Jonah tended to agree with the authorities and warned Magda against stream water, but Magda trusted the Mother Mountain and her water far more than she did the local authorities and their water.

The discovery of the bones in the sacred womb of the Mother Mountain, a miracle wrought by the old gods and the new God with the help of the storm (working for the old gods) and Diamond Eyes (working for the new God), had strengthened the people's resolve to stay in the valley where their ancestors had lived and died – the ancestors of the whole nation, not just of the locals, a theory which united the 'newcomers' from other parts with the old families. The result was more suspicion and ill-will between them and the agents of the state. And as in all cases of suspicion and mistrust, rumours of the wildest nature circulated freely and were treated with the respect given to proven fact. Even allies and leaders with a good ration of common sense had a hard struggle discrediting them. So much so, that Jonah couldn't convince Magda that there was no necessity to drink stream water. However this ironic twist to the tale was not half as ironic or half as twisted as the effect of the storm on the DVD scheme. Eleanor could not stop blaming herself for the major role she played in bringing that about.

Magda wrapped a shawl round her shoulders – the winter chill still lingered in the air – picked up the two empty buckets, stepped out of the house and headed towards the nearest stream.

After she had gone a few steps she turned back to look at the house, thankful that it was safe and undamaged. It had been built of solid stone, and was perched on a rocky slope which let the rain water trail downwards without soaking into the foundations. The houses lower down on more earthy soil had fared much worse. Many of the newer houses, constructed of wood and set on tall poles, had also been damaged. The stilts had proved a mixed blessing. In some cases the water had flowed under them leaving the houses undamaged; in others they had been washed away, taking the entire structure with them. Magda said a little prayer for those who were suffering and asked God's love to take them into its folds, thanked the same love for the safety of her own home, and continued her walk to fetch water.

Half-way on, Magda changed direction and decided to go to a tiny spring a little further away, slightly uphill, hidden behind a cluster of trees and known only to those who knew about it. She had played there as a child, and had sometimes had to fetch water from there. Whenever her mother had wanted to cook 'something special', she had said, 'Go Maryam, my sweet child, get God's sweet water from the sweet spring by the fallen tree. I want to make you something special today. None of this tasteless muck from the tap for that!' She always said 'something special' without saying what it was, wanting it to be a surprise; but mostly the children knew beforehand, having been sent to the shops to buy this, or to the meadows to pluck that.

Loaded with memories of a time long before her first-born was born, which incongruously seemed after her last-born was dead; of a time when capital punishment was just a cumbersome topic for a school essay, not the destiny of two strong young men who were once her unborn children; of a time when sex was a delightful vision of heaven, not just a trek up through the guilt of hell and back again, legs-up exercise bringing worry that another miserable life might result from it, another miserable life being no more than another miserable death; filled with such memories of a time before, she started up towards the spring of her childhood.

Once there, she began to feel like a child again. A mischievious smile appeared on her lips digging dimples in her smooth cheeks, her tall, firm body began to sway to the rhythm of the breeze, her steps became light and wanton and she foolishly skipped to the edge of the spring, not caring who saw her. She put the buckets down on a firm, level piece of ground and began to hum to herself. Soon her hum turned into a full-blown song and her light frisky steps into an effortless dance. She spread her arms out like the branches of the fallen tree which marked the secret spring – fallen but still green and growing – and began to twist and turn and swirl to the memory of the music of her first love.

She could still see him naked in her mind's eyes, even though she never saw him naked. He was rather small, very black with very white eyes and very white teeth. She never knew his name nor did she ever find out why she loved him with such a painful love. She was only ten then, and he was sixteen. He reminded her so of Ishmael's father, very black with very white eyes and very white teeth, though perhaps not as small. Ismael was very like him, only taller; so tall he could touch the sky whenever he chose to touch the sky.

Jonah's father was fair-skinned. Fair-skinned but dark-haired with flashing dark eyes. Her own eyes were dark and flashing too. That was why Jonah's eyes were so very dark and so very flashing.

Joshua's father was big and blonde and blue-eyed. She could never forget his deep blue eyes as he lay above her and took her, so violently, in the dark end of a dark alley on the darker side of Tanira. But Joshua was not a bit like him. He was pale, like her, with rich brown eyes, like his grandmother's. She had never ceased to be grateful to him for not being like his father. But now he had disappeared, like his father. Amnon was blonde, and very white, well, pink. Nobody is really white, she always said to everybody whenever she could force it into the conversation. I should know, I have seen hundreds. They are all coloured, the whole blessed lot of them, and no two quite the same colour or shade.

She was not sure who had fathered Amnon. She had had more than her share of white blondes at the time, tourists and Pirdozians alike. Nor was she sure about the fathers of Maria or Ziba or Isaac.

And now Maria and Ziba were gone. Dead. Dead forever without ever knowing who their father was. And without ever forgiving her for that.

Soon Isaac and Amnon would go too. Die. It was strange to think of someone who was alive as being dead. Especially if that someone was someone to whom you yourself had given life.

She had always been taught that there was one thing in life of which you could never be sure: the hour of anyone's death. One could be 'called up' the next minute, or go on 'to the end of one's term' – whatever that meant. But she knew the hour of death of not just one but two human beings: her sons. The hour and the minute. Nineteen days from now. On the twenty-eighth of September. At twenty minutes past thirteen hours, after the lunchbreak. It had been pointed out that it might put those involved off their food if it took place before lunch. Very early in the morning could be inconvenient for visitors and relatives. Later in the afternoon would not leave enough time for medical certificates, other paperwork and the handing over of the body to relatives. A lot of thought had gone into the decision, and consideration shown for all concerned: the civil employees, the press and the relatives.

Somehow the thought that they would die without knowing who their father was disturbed her more than the thought of their death. How unnatural of her. But then she was an unnatural mother, even though she had natural sons. The pun amused her and she let out a little girlish giggle before the reality of the situation hit her and she stopped breathing as well as ceasing to giggle.

It was all her fault. She was a slut and a two-bit whore. Any decent woman, a real mother, would at the very least be able to tell her dying children who their father was. Ziba and Maria had gone, died, without knowing and without forgiving. And now Isaac and Amnon would go. Die. They had forgiven her, though. A long time ago. That did not make it better. It made it worse.

At least Ishmael had known who his father was when he died; and when he was alive, always knew. And was proud of it, proud, for his father was the one his mother had loved when she took him to bed. How Jonah had hated him for that when he was alive. And how Jonah loved him for that now he was dead.

A two-bit whore. That's what she was. A two-bit whore, who would not be able to tell her dying sons who their father was. Who had not been able to tell her dead little girls who their father was. But they knew who their mother was. They all knew who their mother was. A two-bit whore.

But she had not been a two-bit whore when she had come here to this bubbling spring to fetch some sweet water for her mother who was going to make something special for them for dinner.

She became that child again as she began to dance and sing to herself, swaying gently or swirling wildly, the mood and the momentum changing with the mood and the momentum.

Almost without thinking her steps directed themselves towards the densely-scented interior of the trees surrounding the spring. Her feet remembered a clearing within the copse which was always covered with seasonal wild flowers. She had used to pick and adorn her hair with them, as well as take some to her mother. As her tall figure, heavy with time, danced its way inside the trees she heard a scuffling movement just in front of her. It took a while to register, and by the time she became aware enough of herself and where she was, she could hear the thumping of fast-retreating footsteps. She missed the sight of a shock of blond hair behind the bushes, but caught a flighty glimpse of a colourful shirt, the type often worn at beaches, with an unnaturally strong neck sticking out of its top end and tanned bubbly buttocks peering from its bottom end. The legs looked strong, lithe and very young. At the same time she heard another set of much fainter steps, accompanied by a whimpering noise.

She was back to the world of the mundane present.

'Who is there?' she shouted in a clear, fearless voice. The effect of her words was instantaneous and unexpected.

'Magda. Magda,' cried a little voice as the body accompanying the words dashed towards her. It was Sunny, wearing a blindfold and not much else. Sunny, the one Maria had died giving birth to. 'Maria died because of him,' Jose, her husband, had said at the time, and he never could love him the way he loved the others. Magda loved him all the more as he was Maria's last gift to the world.

Magda pulled the blindfold off the boy's face. There was uncertainty in his eyes, and his steps were unsteady.

'Oh Sunny, Sunny, my poor child. Whatever is the matter?' But even as she said these words, Magda knew what the matter was.

She was about to leave the boy there and run in wild rage after the unnaturally strong neck and the tanned bubbly buttocks, but the ancient wisdom of the mountain advised her differently.

She took the shawl off her shoulders, went to the boy, wrapped it round his body, lifted him up in her arms and walked up to the point where she had seen the legs run away. The boy's shorts and T-shirt and a pair of trousers and underpants were lying neatly folded to one side, one on top of the other. There was also a box of chocolates and a small penknife next to the clothes.

Magda looked down at the dark earth for courage, and more advice. It was there, waiting for her. She hugged the well-wrapped child to her bosom and rocked him back and forth repeating, 'It's all right, honey. There's nothing to worry. Magda is here now.'

Soon the boy was trying to get out of her tight embrace. She let go of him, fetched his clothes and put them on him. 'That's a good boy now.' She smiled and patted his behind. 'Does it hurt?' she asked quite directly.

'A little,' said the boy.

Another surge of anger was quelled by the breeze blowing over the quiet spring.

'Never mind. It will be all right in no time. No worse than tumbling down the rock face, or getting a beating from that bully down the road, what's his name, Ronny?' She rolled the box of chocolates, the blindfold and the underpants in the trousers, and after a slight hesitation and a grimace tucked them inside the thick waist band of her dress.

'Donny,' said Sunny, managing a half-smile. 'You always get names mixed up, Magda.'

'Not always, you little rascal. Only sometimes. The unimportant ones. Come on, let's go home now. Come on.'

She was about to pick the boy up, but he stood his ground and said he wanted to walk on his own.

'Suit yourself. You are a big boy now and can make your own mind up.'

As they walked, Magda opened her mouth once or twice as if to say something, then could not. When they reached the spring she made another effort to speak, and this time succeeded. 'Don't say anything about this to your dad just yet. You know how upset he gets at little things. Don't tell anyone else, either. Not just yet. But if you want to talk about it, come to me, and you can talk as much as you like. I'll tell you what. You can sleep with me tonight, and we'll talk. How's that?'

'Can I? Can I really?'

'Of course you can. In fact I'll ask, no – *tell* your dad myself in a little while, so you won't even have to ask.'

The boy's strides became more confident. He smiled more openly, showing rather crooked teeth. His eyes were still confused, but not frightened.

'I'll make you your favourite marzipan cookies. What d'you say to that now?'

The boy's crooked teeth grew larger. 'I bet Lister will be jealous.'

'You can take some for him, too, and for your sister. No need to be selfish. I have got a large enough pot, I can tell you that for sure.'

They were by the edge of the spring now.

She picked up one of the buckets she had left behind, knelt beside the spring and pushed the bucket down into the silently watchful water, determined to carry on as normal. It was only when she tried to pull the bucket out of the water that she realised her hands were shaking and all her strength drained out.

'Here, let me help,' said the boy; and soon they had filled both the buckets up to the brim with the cool sweet water and set them down on an even part of the ground.

After resting a while they were about to start walking homewards, Magda carrying one bucket in her right hand and Sunny 'helping' her to carry the other – in reality making it all the more difficult for her – when they saw Jonah come running from the other side of the spring. He was as surprised to see them as they were to see him.

'What are you doing here?' said Jonah at the same time as Magda said, 'What are you doing here?'

'I'm just getting some water. What are you doing here?'

'The police. A whole load of police in an unmarked van were seen tearing down the Logan Road going towards our house. I was just going to the house to see if everything was all right with you.'

'Oh, I am fine. Don't worry about me. The police are probably here . . . something to do with . . . some emergency or something. Perhaps someone trapped in a mudslide.' Magda found it hard to say anything good about the police, and each word was dragged out reluctantly. But recently they had helped the villagers by bringing in food supplies and searching for the missing people.

'Where did you find Sunny. Daniel was looking all over for him. Said he had gone out to play and – oh, that reminds me. They found little Tara. She says she had gone to stay with a schoolfriend, swears she had told her parents. She had even sent a postcard, she says, but it never got here. The post hasn't been coming through anyway. Her mother says she had heard something about going to a friend, but thought it wasn't till next week. In fact she had forgotten all about it. I was almost sure she had been got by that sex –'

'I think we had best be going home now. The children must be getting restless on their own.'

On their way down, Jonah carrying both the buckets of water despite Magda's protests, they heard the sound of sirens, two of them, each pitching its fluctuating screams and clashing notes at the other, both together playing a sinister, life-threatening duet. They definitely seemed to be heading towards their road.

'The police. It is the police coming our way!'

'Police, and an ambulance,' said Jonah, dropping the buckets and starting to run downhill, calling out to Magda, 'I'll hurry down and see what's going on, you bring Sunny. Forget about the buckets. I'll fetch them later.'

'Don't go, Jonah. Please. You stay here with Sunny and I'll

203

go . . .' Magda remembered what had happened the last time her sons had encountered the joint care offered by the police and an ambulance. 'Don't, Jonah. Come, you take Sunny to his home and I . . .'

But Jonah was way down already, 'Don't worry, Magda. I can take care of myself,' he shouted, without looking up.

'Men,' said Magda to herself, 'they all think they can take care of themselves! They are all children. That's what they are. Little children.' She crossed herself, looked up to God, and started running down herself, as fast as she could, carrying Sunny in her arms despite his protests.

28

Living stench from dying matter, piled and shaped like a craggy hill – an offensive child prodigy challenging the scented authority of the ancient Mother – leaped up like a gravity-defying waterfall and sprayed and deluged Magda's senses with obscene vigour, destroying the memory which still lingered in her mind of the aromatic foliage surrounding the unsullied spring of her childhood. Pressing a part of her shawl against her nose, and another part against Sunny's nose, she increased her speed, rolling downhill like a powerful, water-smoothed rock off the Mother herself. Her progress came to a sudden and unplanned halt. Hard rubble from a shattered house mixed inextricably with soft mud brought down by the flood from the new terraces blocked her way. Magda's attempt to take the short-cut to her house was aborted. She had to go back up again and turn into Rapier Street to come down the way approved by the survey map of the town.

By the time she was in her street she could see that the path leading up to her house had been roped off by the police. The people gathered round the cordon seemed to be in a shocked state of agitated torpor and frozen activity. One white, unmarked van and one blue police car stood nose to nose against the door of her house, their roofs shimmering in distorted, liquid reflections beneath the oblique rays of the angry sun, daring anyone to doubt his powers, now that the earth was once again turning towards him as a part of its seasonal pattern.

A sudden scream, like a rogue violin in a symphony of silence, tore through the stagnant atmosphere heavy with apprehension. It was the first of many, emanating from an ambulance that forced its way out from within the crowd and drove away with the speed of fear.

A dark dread landslided itself upon Magda's soul. In spite of all the people in front of her, she felt like a lone spectator in an open-air cinema with a motionless picture screen playing the story of her life in white and white. Or was it the sun getting in her eyes and blinding her with light?

The explanation behind all the drama was quite simple.

The drug squad had raided Jonah's house with their sniffer dogs. Oscar, the newly acquired family kitten, in an act of foolish bravery, hissed and spat and actually attacked one of the dogs, with raised front paws and scythe-like claws stretched out to their tiny maximum. The dog, unprepared for this sudden assault upon his person, responded with defensive ferocity and within trained seconds had ripped the kitten apart like a cushion full of cocaine. With perfectly synchronised simultaneity Tommo, the youngest child of Jonah, leaped in to defend the kitten whose guts and entrails were by now either a bloodied mess on the floor or splattered in abstract patterns of gory loveliness on the time-tinted walls. The young dog, still overflowing with adrenalin-stimulated nervous energy, rooted in the instinct of self-preservation and compounded by the urge to function in the presence of his two-legged masters, turned its frightened fury upon the child.

As the more mature officers tried to use their muscle and technique to separate the dog from the boy, one of their colleagues, no older than the young dog in human terms, panicked wildly at the sight of the child's blood and flesh and gristle mixing freely with that of the kitten, opened fire aimlessly in the hope of frightening the animal away from its prey. One of the bullets hit Ruth, who was hiding paralysed behind a newly-washed and restitched curtain which separated the living area downstairs from the cooking area. Fortunately she was killed there and then, without any suffering or consciousness of pain. By then Tommo had been rescued from the dog, badly savaged, but alive.

With mercurial speed one of the officers radioed for an ambulance, another for the regular police. You can now see for yourself that the explanation for the presence of the police and the ambulance was quite simple, once the facts were known.

All in all it turned out to be a disastrous day for the forces of law and order. They had taken a calculated gamble in the hope of at last finding some drugs in Jonah's house. Previous attempts had shown that he was not foolish enough to store them there normally, but the rains might well have forced him to retrieve them from their usual hiding places. Had they succeeded, the timing could not have been better. The discovery of drugs and the ensuing well-planned media coverage would have prevented any possible flow of public sympathy for Jonah and Magda in the wake of the executions of Isaac and Amnon. The whole family would have stood exposed and condemned as a menace to all respectable, clean-living citizens of New Heaven, indeed of the entire free world. It would have also done incalculable and enormously desirable damage to the Don't Vote Crusade. So great would have been the overall benefits of this find that one of the squad had come quietly prepared with an interesting little packet, in case of a disappointing lack of developments of the right nature.

In the event, the whole operation misfired miasmally. But then, God is not best known for favouring the righteous.

29

It had been a hard day for Peter: first to school, then to the doctor for his final growth injection of the current phase of the treatment, followed by a session at the physiotherapist.

By the time he got home he felt tired, disorientated and fragile. Eleanor and Philip were out, so was Paul; and although Natalia was there to greet him, she said she had to go up to her room to work on her thesis. She wanted him to come up and sit with her for a while, but he said he'd rather wait for Eleanor in the living room. Natalia had made some pasta with mushroom sauce, Peter's favourite, but he said he was too hungry to eat. His best shirt had got blotted with some viscous yellow disinfectant and the smell of the hospital still lingered in the stain.

Philip came in shortly afterwards, ruffled Peter's hair and asked him about school, clearly having forgotten about his appointment with the doctor. Normally he spent some time with his son, but that day he retired almost immediately to his study as he had a friend with him and together they had a lot of work to do.

Peter felt himself dozing off in front of the television, and as there was no sign of Eleanor returning, no phone-call or message, he decided to go up to his room and crash into bed.

He climbed up the stairs, each foot heavy as a ship's anchor, eyes barely able to see the next step. Nonetheless he managed to haul himself up to the top and drag his body along the corridor to the front of his room. He turned the handle slowly, pushed the door open and walked straight into a field of white lilies beneath a sky decorated with fragmented rainbows. The walls of his room were still there but pushed outwards and beyond, across the limits of the finite world. He was standing on water, but his legs were steady. The day's fatigue drained out of his head and his eyes and his limbs, through his feet, and into the cool still waters carpeted with the green leaves of the healing lilies.

The white lilies reflected the colours of the rainbow, being all colours at once and each colour in turn, like prisms of silk appearing to shift from place to place in changing hues, while remaining perfectly motionless in themselves. The moisture vapours rising from the surface of the water-field formed swirling rainbows of their own and filled the universe-sized room with a luminous mist of shimmering reds and greens and blues and yellows, like a rain of radiant fireflies glowing with multi-tinted refulgence. Or like incandescent mobiles of lucent particles in constant chaotic activity, electrons in the heart of an atom: an atom we call the world.

Through the haze of this aurorean painting of water molecules in perpetual motion, emerged the tall figure of the naked grey man: unblemished, unscarred, whole, beautiful and serene. Beneath his weight the water did not so much as ripple; only the lilies acknowledged his approach by gently swaying in the breeze stirred by his moving presence. In poetic slow motion he stretched out his hand towards Peter, the love in his eyes demanding that Peter do the same towards him.

Responding with radiant irises and a vibrant heart, Peter joyously stretched his own arm out to grasp the grey man's hand. But his arm was still by his side. It had refused to obey the command of his brain. He tried again. Still no movement in his arms; nor in any other part of his body for that matter. It was as if he was sculpted in wrought iron from the neck downwards. But that was a preposterous proposition. It could not be. It would be against all laws of nature. He looked down at his body as if to confirm his flesh, blood and bone construction. And he was right too. It was as he had expected. He was made of flesh, alive with blood, and held together by bones. The unexpected lay in the fact that he was naked and mutilated, and grey; even as the grey man had once been.

He wanted to cry out in horror and shame, but could not. No words nor sound would issue from his mouth. It was as if he had misplaced his tongue and forgotten where.

His head turned within itself, and without itself, like the multiple wheel of fate, and he fainted.

When he regained consciousness he was deep within the transluscent waters of the lake-field, held gently in the arms of the grey man. Beneath the surface of the water the roots of the lilies were lilies themselves, and the floor of the lake was also the sky, and what was above was below and what was without was within.

A strong belief oozed out from every pore of his skin, like the protective oils of perpetual youth, that no matter what his physical condition he would be perfectly safe and protected, surrounded by the life-giving waters of the lake of lilies and enveloped by the arms and the love of the grey man.

He had seen the underwater world in TV documentaries and films and it was always a source of fantasy and fascination for him. A great curiosity and expectancy took hold of his senses as he looked around in this subaquatic space, so richly illumined by the glistening rainbow lights that seemed to penetrate its depths with natural ease. But the world he saw beneath this lake, which was at once his room and the habitat of all life on earth, was very different from the underwater world that he knew and remembered. There were no fish for a start. No life at all, at least none that was within range of his senses. Nothing, in fact, but rocky caves, and bones.

And then it struck him with miraculous suddenness that that was how it should be, and indeed how it was. Once he got over this most difficult hurdle of all, the hurdle of simplicity, it was an unbelievably uncomplicated and effortless experience to break free of the illusion of facts and arrive at the soul of truth. This achieved, he revelled in his discovery to a degree of intensity which could only be quantified by a complete lack of comprehension and only be qualified by an utter absence of qualifications.

30

Eleanor returned home after a day's campaigning. She had been looking forward to the day as it involved visiting a car-component factory – always a good supply source of ballot-paper crosses in the right space – and then a tour through a deprived and semi-derelict housing estate in the outskirts of her constituency, which she was once again promising to revamp and was consequently hoping to attract a significant number of voters from the disaffected residents. However her efforts to impress had been marred by a silent protest of marchers following her wherever she went. The wordless, banner-less demonstration was led by Jonah, with the grey man in attendance; or rather, led by the grey man with Jonah in attendance, for the total speechlessness of the protesters, more eloquent than any slogan-shouting, was an acknowledgment of his power.

The day had not been a rewarding one, and Eleanor was tired, depressed and angry. Very angry indeed.

She decided to go straight up to bed. It was one of those nights, rare but significant, when she would almost have been willing to give up her career if she could have had some way of ensuring that Philip would be there waiting for her.

On the way up she stopped by Peter's room, knocked briefly, and then pushed the door open. A quick kiss on the sleeping boy's cheek would not damage his chances of growing up to be a self-reliant individual.

In the soft pale moonlight which had stolen its way in through the long window and spread itself unceremoniously across the floor of the room, Eleanor saw the slight figure of Peter lying face down on the shaggy beige carpet at the foot of his bed. With an involuntary gasp Eleanor rushed in, and without wasting time to turn on the light kneeled beside Peter's prone body and tried to turn him over.

He was unconscious, and dripping wet.

Eleanor pushed the 'panic button' by Peter's bed, turned on the light and started dialling for the doctor.

Natalia was the first to come rushing in from the next room as soon as the bell sounded. Paul followed within seconds. He took one look at Peter. 'It's those . . . those injections of yours,' he said in a rare flash of anger.

'Don't move him,' shouted Eleanor, diverting her attention from the telephone.

'Why not! He's not the victim of an accident. More like premeditated crime . . .'

'Oh don't be ridiculous, Paul,' said Eleanor putting her hand on the receiver. She spoke to the doctor again. 'Yes. Yes, please.'

Paul lifted Peter up in his arms. There was a pool of wet beneath him.

'He looks as if he's just walked out of water,' said Natalia looking both puzzled and worried as she rushed to the bathroom to fetch a towel. 'The doctor had warned against cold sweats, but this . . .'

'Where is the grey man, Paul?' said Peter, bringing all activity to a halt.

'Thank God he's all right,' said Natalia.

'What did he say?' said Eleanor.

'How are you feeling? What happened?' said Paul.

'What did he say?' said Eleanor.

'I am all right,' said Peter, struggling to get out of Paul's arms. He liked being with Paul, liked being held by him, but it was embarrassing being *carried* by him, especially in front of his mother and Natalia. 'I am all right. Just a little tired, swimming with the grey man.'

'Swimming! What in heaven's name are you talking about, Peter?' Eleanor put the phone down telling Doctor Lock that she'd ring back, and went up to Peter, who had managed to get down on the floor and was standing between Paul and Natalia. She ran her fingers through his hair, more relieved than she would have been prepared to admit. 'Now don't be a silly boy and tell Mummy what you have been up to. And who is this grey man?' A strong note of suspicion had crept into her voice.

'That's just Peter's name for Diamond Eyes,' blurted Paul before he could stop himself.

'Diamond . . . Him! How does Peter know . . . *him*. Grey man . . . grey man . . . I am sure I've heard it –'

Philip came heavy-footed into the room. 'What's the matter? Is Peter –'

'So you've managed to get here at last.'

'I came as soon as I could.'

'Spare us the details. The grey man. I am sure . . .'

'What are these bones doing here?' said Philip, partly to distract Eleanor's attention, but genuinely bemused as well at the sight of quite a few bones scattered near the foot of the bed.

214

'God. He must have let Trix store bones under the bed. Really, Peter!'

'Don't look the sort of bones Trix would have had,' said Paul picking one up. 'Look like human bones to me.' Although his artist's knowledge of human anatomy certainly suggested that conclusion, there was worried doubt in his voice.

'Oh don't be ridiculous, Paul,' Eleanor said for the second time that day

'I am not being ridiculous, Eleanor. I know what I am –'

'Now I know! He was the man who assaulted Peter on the beach. The nerve!' Realisation and recognition quickly gave way to anger and fury; and then as quickly to triumph and the scent of victory. 'I have it now. I have *him* now. At last, I have him.'

'You can't let your suspicions run away with you,' Philip began nervously, afraid at the thought of the incident on the beach being raked up. He was still convinced it was all Peter's imagination superimposed on the naked reality of Tom.

'It won't be just my suspicions when Peter has been made to refresh his memory. Honestly, I don't understand it. I don't understand it at all.'

For once Philip couldn't help agreeing with her.

'At last I have him,' repeated Eleanor.

Peter was sick all over the shaggy beige carpet.

September was in its last week and the first flowers of spring were waking up to find some of their favourite landscapes in distress, some of their choice houses in rubble, and some of their best people nowhere to be seen. Their inability to protest against this violence to their expectations by ceasing to be themselves enriched their beauty with the colour of suffering.

Normally in this part of Pirdoz, the transition from a mild verdurous winter resplendent with its own flora to a wildly hectic spring went all but unnoticed, except by the most ardent of nature-lovers. This year even the most insensitive commented on the brilliant excesses of the changing season. The scent in the meadows and valleys got so heavy your head swam in its heady density. In the shanty town itself, mixed with the fetor of festering matter and the putrid wrecks of broken lives, its natural chemistry was so altered that it invited revulsion rather than admiration.

However, the atmosphere of Gulroza was burdened with more than the mere combination of the sweet smell of a new beginning and the bitter stench of a not-so-new decay. Omens and portents, doubts and misgivings, certainties and inevitabilities combined together to form an explosive compound which threatened the very existence of the place and its people.

Jonah's son, savaged by the dog, had survived after losing an eye and a hand. The girl had been buried next to the empty grave of Ishmael; close by two new places were being prepared for Isaac and Amnon.

The growing rumour that Diamond Eyes was about to be framed for child-molesting and child-murder was given added urgency by the growing certainty that Gulroza was about to be bulldozed.

The colour of the sky was more pink than blue; the thorn berries were larger than anyone ever remembered, and the wind moved without moving the grasses.

The crickets had stopped singing at night and butterflies were heard to scream.

31

Joshua came home on the eve of Isaac's and Amnon's executions.

Isaac was strong, with a thick neck, thick thighs, and a chest as large as a pirate's chest. The chair could hardly contain him. The steel straps round his ankles and throat and arms were stretched to the limit.

Amnon was slight – even slighter since his arrest. Extra care had to be taken to ensure that he was safely locked in. Magda was grateful to the designers that the head cage was so built that it could be tightened sufficiently to prevent the neck from juddering too much at the time of the passage of the current.

Electrodes sat perfectly and without any problems on each head and each left leg.

To spare the family the repeat of a traumatic experience, arrangements had been made – at great expense and through the generosity of the greatest ally of the free world – for a simultaneous execution. One chair had been specially flown in, as part of a special aid deal, and an annexe erected and specially wired to the main chamber to accommodate it. The fact that the cost of the trial and the specially-arranged executions could have renovated most of Gulroza showed how seriously the government took its commitment to justice.

The family met the boys and returned to the corridor beside the main hall – which had been shined and polished to the point of being slippery for this special occasion – to wait for the final announcement. One man, tall with thin firm eyes, a fine strong chin and thick short hair, elegantly dressed in an expensive three-piece suit, looked straight towards them all and said, 'Mothers of murderers are murderers too. And so are their brothers.' Two police officers appeared unseen, held him by each arm and escorted him out of the main door. He went without any trouble or any further remarks. One young woman with red hair and a blue dress with white flowers burst into hysterical giggles and had to be dragged away by a male companion of indeterminate age.

When the time came, Magda insisted on going along to the closely-guarded gallery reserved for the press and special guests to witness the execution. Jonah and Joshua were appalled, but Tamar took her side and said it was best for her to deal with it in her own way. Besides, once her mind was made up, no one could have stopped her anyway.

Joshua began crying, without making any attempt to cover his face or wipe away his tears. His nose was running into his open mouth. It tasted of sea-salt and butter-oil. Jonah held Tamar's hand and stared at a fixed spot on the wall in front of him. It looked like a fly dropping. How could it be, in such a hygienic place? Someone ought to complain. He might even do so himself. Once it was all over. Once what was all over?

He wished he had stayed home to look after all the children instead of Daniel and . . . He couldn't remember the name of the other one, Maria's husband. Or maybe he should have accepted Paul's offer to be present. It might have helped. But how?

218

32

Magda saw with unprecedented pride her two beautiful men of flesh turn into two beautiful flowers of fire. Leaping petals of flame engulfed their pollen-filled faces like wind-blown sunflowers. Perhaps that was not what happened, but that was certainly what Magda saw. It was the most singularly beautiful sight she had ever seen in anybody's whole life.

Her body was released of a great weight. She felt light and wispy, as if made of pure oxygen. An exhilarating sense of wellbeing rose from somewhere within her now-defunct, once-fertile womb and spread upwards towards her head and arms, downwards towards her legs and feet. She brushed aside the two policemen, and the lawyer who had tried ever so hard to save her sons, as they attempted to support her when she got up from her seat and walked steadily out into the main corridor.

It was only when she was half-way down that she remembered her promise to herself, to her sons, and to God. She had promised to cast away her black garments the moment her sons were free. They were free now.

With balletically graceful upsweeping movements of her arms, she lifted her dress up over her head and flung it aside. Before the startled eyes of the press and photographers she unhooked her bra and let it drop to the floor even as she slipped out of her panties with girlish skips and jumps. Bulbs flashed and cameras clicked once again as they had done when her sons were being metamorphosed into a new species of floral engineering that transcended the prosaic laws of man-observed nature: the consummation, without consumption or chemical transformation, of fire and matter.

Flushed with attention, Magda's dance-like movements turned into a dance. Her tall body, pale as the full moon, powerful as the full tide, pirouetted on bare feet as she kicked her shoes off, spread her arms out, and let her long black hair fly around her timeless face.

The mesmerised police finally galvanised themselves into action. One officer began gathering her clothes. Two others ran up to her and tried to hold her down. They underestimated the strength of her great body and were sent hurtling back against the wall with the passionate force of a hurricane.

Jonah and Joshua and Tamar heard the scuffle and came running. They had difficulty adjusting their minds to their eyes and froze into inactivity for a long second. Their arrival caused an instant distraction in the same second for the police officers trying to contain Magda. That second was enough for Magda to regain her freedom. With long strides she made her way down the corridor and would have run out, pushing the two surprised guards by the door aside, but three young men and a woman, probably visitors, had the agility and the nerve to step in her way and bar her progress and her exit.

As Magda started to struggle past them, Jonah and Tamar and Joshua from the left of the corridor, and the two police officers from the right, converged on the spot. The two guards tried to shove the young men and the woman to one side, while the police officers, resolving to use their full strength this time, jumped upon Magda. One officer used his thick naked forearms covered with thick black hair to make a stranglehold round Magda's neck, while one of the guards shouted something which sounded like 'Bind the bloody whore!' but which he later maintained was 'Mind the ruddy door!' Jonah saw blood. The blank restraint of the past hour broke out through his veins. Cursing and shouting and crying, burning tears running down his cheeks, he jumped on the officer like a wild bull whose body has been used as a pin-cushion for daggers. This unexpected onslaught caught everyone by surprise. The other officer tried to move out of his way and tripped one of the two young men, who fell heavily to the floor. He and one of the guards trying to help him up were in their turn felled to the floor by Joshua and Tamar rushing past them to get to Magda and Jonah. In the confusion Jonah managed to free Magda from the officer's stranglehold, wound his arms round her naked body and began rocking her back and forth, running his fingers through her hair, his fury spent, the role of mother and child reversed.

Just then the rattle of a gun and the bold voice of a man tore through the atmosphere and Jonah's flesh. 'Mothers of murderers are murderers too. And so are their brothers.'

Magda's naked body, pale as the full moon, but unlike the full moon smooth and unblemished, was no longer naked nor pale nor smooth and unblemished. It was covered with the warm blood of Jonah and red with the warm blood of Jonah and blemished and roughened with the bits of soft flesh and hard gristle of Jonah that accompanied the warm blood of Jonah that poured out of his bullet-torn flesh as through a wide-holed sieve. The blood that once throbbed within her womb, now slithered down her breasts, across her stomach and between her thighs, forging its way back into her womb.

After a moment's stupefied petrification and dense silence came heightened activity and sharp voices. Some more officers came running in at the sound of the shot. Three together jumped on and grabbed the elegantly-suited man who stood calmly, emptied gun in hand. He made no effort to escape and offered himself to the officers, head erect and smiling, his civic duty done. Tamar and Joshua moved to catch hold of Jonah, who hung slumped to Magda's body. She stood at an unnatural angle, a once-brave tree at last bent by a wind stronger than itself, supporting the dead weight of her heavily-built son. Before Tamar and Joshua could get hold of Jonah, his body slithered off Magda and hit the floor with a fleshy thud.

Magda let out one long high-pitched scream, her body on liquid fire like red hot steel.

She mobilised herself. As if charged with a high-voltage current, she charged out of the door, through the portals of the grand modern courthouse built with grand ancient stone, down the steps, past the cordon, through the crowds that had gathered on the vast lawns outside to be as close to the historic event as possible, and out on the road against the fast-moving traffic on the busy motorway, screaming all the while, Jonah's now cold blood coagulating on her strong naked body. Joshua ran after her, out of the door, through the portals of the grand modern courthouse built with grand ancient stone, down the steps, past the cordon, through the crowds that had gathered on the vast lawns outside to be as close to the historic event as possible, and out on the road against the fast-moving traffic of the busy motorway.

Some people dropped their ice-cream cones, some spilled their tins of cool soft drinks, one accidentally stubbed out her cigarette on her husband's bare thigh, as all rushed after mother and son to follow the chase, with their feet as far as safety permitted and with their eyes afterwards. The entire spectacle far exceeded their fondest expectations. The long journey – the courthouse had wisely been constructed well away from the main heart of the city – had been well worth the trouble. The jounalists were clicking their cameras wildly while talking delightedly to their little boxes, eyes sparkling with unspeakable excitement while fixed firmly on their futures. The TV crew could barely keep up with the pace of developments. Live broadcasting is not an easy task at the best of times.

It was a day of miracles. Despite several cars running into each other and many minor and not-so-minor casualties, no one was killed, or even seriously injured.

Magda and Joshua were finally caught and taken to the hospital, unhurt.

Even Jonah survived: in intensive care and in a dangerous condition, but alive; and given his ox-like body, with a better-than-good chance of making it.

All six bullets had missed the heart. It was indeed a day of miracles.

As the nurse adjusted his pillow, of which act he had no consciousness, he suddenly remembered the name of Maria's husband: Dureya. He desperately wanted to tell it to someone, but he could not. He had never felt so helpless in all his life. And all because he could not tell anyone the name of Maria's husband. Dureya. Why wouldn't anybody listen to what he had to say?

33

A week went by peacefully. Tamar insisted on taking Magda home, promising the mostly unconscious Jonah to look after her properly and to marry him when he was fit and well and help him care for his children. Jonah was in no position to protest. Or to rejoice. He had loved Tamar for some time now, and Tamar knew it. Joshua now belonged to someone else, and she had to learn to forget him. Whether or not Jonah wanted to carry the yoke of matrimony was a decision which, like for most men, was made for him and not by him. His function, like that of most men, would be to abide by it.

Joshua returned home. He had a job to keep, and a wife, and a new-born baby: their first, a girl called Magda.

Paul had bought a camper and parked next to Jonah's house and took turns with Tamar to nurse Magda. Not that she needed any nursing, at least not in any physical sense. Except for planning an extension to the house for when Amnon and

Isaac would return, bringing Ishmael back with them, she seemed normal enough, and well enough. She did, however, believe that Jonah was dead; and nothing, not even taking her to see him, would convince her that he was not. The camel had sat on Jonah, she said, but Isaac, Amnon and Ishmael were sitting on the camel. And they were heading this way at a camel gallop. It was pointless to argue with Magda at the best of times; it would now be heartless and artless as well. So it wasn't done any more. The doctors were split in their views. One said it was best to humour her and to go along with whatever she said or believed; her dream world was at least as real as the real. Another said that she should be made to face the facts – the sooner the better; her dream world was an extended nightmare. The first held Jung as his master; the second was a disciple of Freud. Both interpreted their deceased mentors creatively.

Magda had her own views about her dream world and her real world and her nightmares: they were all the same to her, and all unimportant. What was important was her own plan. And that included me – at least a visit to where she believed I lived. She should have known better, and on occasions did; but it was a difficult time for her. So the least that I could do was to be there when the time came.

It must have been about eleven o'clock at night. Paul had been with Magda during the afternoon and the evening, when Tamar had gone to visit Jonah. She came back at about nine, and after snugly tucking Magda in her bed, went to bed herself. Paul did the same. It had been another tiring day of a tiring week. Isaac and Amnon were to receive a delayed burial the next day and everyone needed rest.

Magda lifted her head off the bed and looked up to her right where Tamar slept, then to the bottom of her bed where two of Jonah's remaining children slept, then back again to Tamar. She moved her head and eyes with curious jerky movements, strangely bird-like for one with such strong neck muscles. When she had made sure that all were asleep, she moved her legs quietly from beneath the covers and landed her feet softly on the floor. She stood up, looked again at the sleeping faces of Tamar and the children, smiled at little Ruth, her favourite grand-daughter – not caring that she had been dead and buried for over a week – and then walked on her toes between beds to a small box-room where Littloo slept alongside stacks of broken-down old suitcases and piled-up boxes of this and that. Previously all the children had slept downstairs, but since the rains and the danger of flooding they all slept together upstairs.

Very quietly Magda pulled at one box at the bottom of the pile and somehow managed to get it out without toppling the rest. The box was surprisingly light for its size, and she carried it easily downstairs, walking carefully so as not to make any noise.

Once in the main room below, she moved softly to the farthest corner, where a table lamp stood on the floor. She sat herself and the box down on the wooden floor alongside the lamp, turned it on, and opened the lid of the box. A large fluffy mound of wispy white, turned slightly off-colour with time and age, breathed inside it, peeping out at the outside world through lace-holed eyes.

It was her mother's wedding dress, carefully saved up for *her* wedding. She had never worn it, the cause of her mother's greatest death-bed regret. She had never worn it because she had never needed to wear it. She had never needed to wear it, but she had always wanted to wear it. She could not think of a better occasion to do so than tonight.

She got out of the house, thankful for a black, moonless night. Even though she had a dark brown shawl over the white dress – she would not touch black now that Isaac and Amnon were free – she would have to walk in the shadow of the remaining trees to get unnoticed to the church. It was a bride's prerogative to be late, but she did not wish to take advantage of that, and walked as fast as the full-length billowing wedding dress

226

permitted. She skirted carefully round the house in order to avoid Paul's camper. Who knew what that crazy man might be up to at any time of day or night? She liked him and liked meeting him; but not tonight. Tonight was her night, and her night alone.

By the time she got to the church, her feet were hurting and twitching painfully at the arches. Not that she wasn't used to walking long distances, but she was certainly not used to wearing high heels. Over-conscious of her height – it hadn't been fashionable for a girl to be that tall during her youth – she had almost always worn flat or low shoes, and now her ankles felt as if they had been strung up on a rack. But tonight she was going to be the height of fashion: and these days the taller the girl, the more fashionable.

She climbed reverently up the stone steps, pushed the heavy wooden door ajar, then lightly stepped in, quite forgetting the acute discomfort she had been experiencing in walking only moments before.

I stood just inside the door, just as she had expected, both to give the bride away, and to take the bride. She took my proffered arm shyly, like a little girl, and together we walked down the aisle.

Everything was just as she had expected.

The choirboys were singing, the Wedding March was playing, the guests were all there, the congregation was seated, the sermon was in progress and holy silence reigned – all at the same time. God was there, in person, presiding over his dominion and its ceremonials.

Brilliant sunlight, all the more brilliant for shining in the middle of the night, fired its rays through the stained-glass windows, setting the whole place ablaze with the living, moving experiences of prophets and saints and apostles, and of the Man Himself. Now He was by her side, and up on the ceiling, and higher up in Heaven, and all around in New Heaven, and on the walls in front, and walking upon those blazing windows along with Simon Peter the Rock and Andrew, and James the Elder and Jude, and James the Less and Philip, and Bartholomew and Matthew and Thomas and Simon and John the Beloved. And Judas, all on his own, alone and lonely, hanging from a tree like the first Christmas decoration. Only they did not have Christmas trees in and around the Potter's Field. They did not have Christmas. They did not have blonde-haired, blue-eyed Christs. But they had all this, and more, here. And to her it was real and true. And so it was, whether it was or was not.

His, my, magnificent voice rang out, from and in and through every recess, every corner, every pillar, echoing and resounding, challenging and comforting, uniting and separating. Mary, Maryam, wife of Joseph, Mother of God, spread her cloak of white and pale blue and blessed all the children of her Son, no less for being unbegotten. The Good Samaritan did his good deed to become the eternal neighbour who never came for the sons of Magda and the like. The fatted calf was brought out for the Prodigal Son, wonder in his large white eyes at the sin or crime or misdemeanour for which he was being slaughtered. Abel gloated over his brother's humiliated love, who stood with wonder in his large black eyes at the sin or crime or misdemeanour for which his whole year's hard work and offering had been rejected in preference to a moment's blade swishing upon a wondering lamb.

Seraphim and cherubim sang and danced round the Lord's throne to the music of the Supreme Angel of the Lord. Mary Magdalene joined in the dance, and so, naturally, did Magda. I had no option but to; not that I did not want to anyway. Successful politicians couldn't have stopped me, wild camels stood no chance. But they were there: successful politicians frowning and disciplining and pontificating and legislating against all that was holy and natural and loving; wild camels, curling their lips and sneering and belching and groaning. But Magda tamed them all. The camels began grudgingly to dance with awkward, unwilling grace, as the politicians, suddenly naked, formed a circle round them, kicking their legs up in the air like knickerless can-can girls.

The Daughter of Sion came, and she beheld the coming of the King, meek and sitting upon an ass; strong and riding a camel; and she feared not. Magda led the foal and announced the coming of the Lord, and she feared, as a child fears its first appearance on a stage.

No sooner had she made her announcement than absolute and utter silence prevailed, drowning all sounds of revelry and merry-making. The light of the sun mellowed and mingled discretely with the hallowed darkness that descended upon the tabernacle. With serene quiescence and solidified shadows came perfect solitude.

There was no one there but Magda. Even I poured myself into her and became one with her. It was she alone who stood in front of the larger-than-life ornate cross with the figure of Christ wound round it, in sacrificial coyness below the waist, in all-embracing suffering above. No one but Magda in her ill-fitting gown. Like her mother she was tall, and had once been slim as well. But now the mature Magda had had to struggle into the dress. It bulged here a little, popped out at that spot and dug in at this, held her in where it shouldn't and let her hang out where it shouldn't. But Magda did not care. To her this was the most beautiful dress in the world on this most beautiful day in the world – even if the day was set in the middle of the night and the dress was on the wronged body.

Suddenly she remembered she had forgotten something. Forgotten what she should have remembered. Forgotten to light a candle. But it didn't matter if she had forgotten, for she had remembered.

She went to the sculptured oak pillar, varnished black and covered with carved figures from biblical times. Round it, on a thick wooden ledge encircling the circumference of the great pillar, stood numerous candles, some lit, some burnt out. Perhaps it was meant to be an act of faith to burn candles round the only wooden pillar in the church.

Magda picked up a brand new candle from a barrel-like basket next to the pillar. She did not have any money with her to offer. But it did not worry her. She was offering herself.

229

She lit the candle and heated the wax left over from another candle to fix it on the wooden surface. After a moment's hesitation she took another candle and lit it. Then another, and another. They all looked so beautiful, each flame blossoming into a reckless flower. Like her sons.

Her face lit up with the light of the candles, began to burn with their joy. It was all too glorious, too wondrous, too generous.

She began to hum to herself and sway to the rhythm of her own music. She held out her hand, and I reached out from within her and grasped the offered hand. She put her arms around me, and I around her. I lifted her up and we floated about in the sacred auditorium, singing, shouting, laughing, consummating our love in this final dance of death and rebirth.

Magda's swirling dress, raised up above and around her, swished and hissed, flirting with the arches of the ceiling, caressing the texture of the walls, kissing the flames of the candles. Soon it was ablaze itself, its fine layers of lace and silk shooting forth little stars of fire in all directions as they circled round and round in this dance of release. Magda's voice, both plaintive and rejoicing, rose above the sizzling fizzling spitting crepitating frenzied yellow snakes, and reverberated in the empty halls of empty adoration.

It started to rain outside. It came down in a torrent of fury, lashing against the church walls, hurtling against the church roof, rattling the stained-glass windows. But not all the water in the good God's good Earth could have quelled the fire that raged within Magda. Still, the awesome music of the rain provided a fitting accompaniment to Magda's song of final emancipation.

She continued to sing and dance in a wild ecstasy of abandoned hopes and grasped certainties, long after her charred remains ceased even to smoulder upon the centre of the elevated altar.

I continued to sing and dance with her. We both continued to sing and dance, the culmination of a life-long and on-and-off courtship.

34

To the surprise of many and the great delight of the government, public opinion swayed heavily in favour of the ruling party after the execution of Isaac and Amnon and the lewd behaviour displayed by Magda on national television. Newspapers devoted pages to the event, discovering highly interesting new facts about the case and the criminals and their families. The fact that the new facts were already well known only added to their piquancy. After all, it is the duty of every honest journalist in a democracy to satisfy the people's right to know what goes on – and if they already know, to remind them – even if it has never gone on, nor is ever likely to go on. In that case, especially so. Through facts substantiated by percentages and statistics and equations; or by thorough researches into the nature and vulnerability of public opinion, and the democratic manipulation thereof.

Pictures of the naked Magda scuffling with the police and the guards and subsequently endangering public life and safety by running shamefully yet shamelessly on the wrong side of the motorway – built with taxpayer's money – appeared for days after, along with a full exposé of her life as a prostitute on the streets of Tanira. Her sensational death by fire took the excremental excitement of the dailies and the Sunday specials to new pitches of multi-orgasmic delight. Freedom of speech was in full flow, and who could argue with the merits of that, except a traitor or a communist.

The end product was a vividly pictorial essay in easy English on the triumph of the forces of good, represented by the state and its loyal servants such as the police and the judiciary, against its enemies such as smugglers, murderers and their handpersons, supporters, friends, neighbours and so on. Justice was victorious, evil was overcome or destroyed itself; order reigned supreme over anarchical elements.

The moral to be drawn from all this was that wishy-washy socialist policies engendered a climate which fostered nihilistic and destructive forces. A strong, right-wing, individual-responsibility approach ultimately brought evil-doers to taste their just desserts. Those who disagreed with this summing up of the human condition, despite their numbers, had little or no voice as far as the press and the media were concerned, and therefore could not be heard. And those who cannot be heard, do not exist – at best. At worst they do not deserve to exist. After all, what matters is not what your case is, but how it is presented; and most of all, who by. If it is taken up by the best money can buy, then who can fight against it? If not, that's life. The verdict of the people has to be accepted, even if the people have nothing to do with it.

35

Peter had been ill and off school for a week. Natalia was on leave to sit two of her examinations. They came at a bad time for Peter, and she felt unhappy and guilty about it, but nothing could be done. Eleanor was even more busy than usual and had little time to spend with him, even though she wished she had. Philip managed to look in more often than he was used to, but he was used to so little that a little more than that was not much in effect. Paul was spending most of his time looking after Jonah now that Magda was dead. Peter felt betrayed, even though he knew it was wrong. He longed to escape from the house, run barefoot along the beach, chase crabs, explore the caves, be adopted by wolves, go see the grey man . . . Escape, however, was more difficult now than ever before. Eleanor had arranged for two sets of baby-sitters who took turns and stayed with him in his room all day and all night.

Although Eleanor had given up direct attempts to persuade him to 'tell the truth' about 'that man', subtle and not so subtle pressure was kept on him to do so. (The lives of so many little children could be ruined forever, even brutally cut short, because of his misguided loyalty . . .) Some very kind members of the police force kept dropping in on him to enquire about him and to have a friendly chat about the weather, the school, his friends, the grey man . . .

One rather hot and humid afternoon he fell asleep while reading a book about the meaning of dreams which Paul had bought for him, along with a number of other books he'd asked for the Christmas before last – he hadn't been around for the last one. The book was a curious mixture of voodoo fact and scientific fiction, with quotations and misquotations from someone called Carlotta, Queen of the Occult, to Sigmund Freud. He dreamed a pleasurable and frightening dream in which he was sexually assaulted by Paul; this was followed by a cross-questioning session in which his mother, a number of different doctors, policemen and policewomen, and Paul himself took turns in forcing him to reveal the truth of what had actually transpired. Eventually, after being kept interminably sleepless and on a diet of raw meat and mashed potatoes, he blurted out the name of the grey man as being the culprit, simply to save Paul, whom he loved and with whom he had enjoyed the sexual act.

He woke up drenched in sweat, his heart hammering away in his chest and a sharp stabbing pain in the back of his neck. His pupils felt as if they were being pitilessly squeezed from within. He could hardly open his eyes, and when he did he could not focus clearly. His lips were cold and withered, his throat parched and dry, the roof of his mouth scratched by a fork with ice picks for prongs, his forehead hot, his feet cold.

With full awakening came greater horror. He remembered actually telling one of the policemen something about the naked grey man. He could not recall exactly what he had said, but he could remember with vivid clarity the satisfied look in the officer's eyes, the flicker of a smile on his lips, and the nod he gave his fellow officer as they both hurriedly left the room, turning off the little tape recorder which they always had with them.

Was it all in the dream? Even if it was, the dream was reality. Of this there was no doubt in his mind.

He got out of the cane chair in which he had been propped up, and walked across the length of the room to the bathroom, followed by the watchful gaze and the murmured concerns of the woman sitting with him that day. Once inside the bathroom he took the key out of the door, then slammed the lavatory seat hard, having placed a towel over the bowl to make the bang sound like the thud of a falling body, and emitted choking rattling noises from his throat. The woman came rushing to the door of the bathroom, called his name, then pushed her way in. Peter waited till she was well in, then ran out and locked the door from the outside. He was well down the corridor before the woman even realised that he had given her the slip with one of the oldest tricks in the book.

He ran round the balcony, down the spiral staircase and was out through the hole in the garden wall without being seen.

The grey man was in great danger. He had to be warned.

36

There was an extra strong police presence in the shanty town that day. Pairs of constables on foot paraded the streets, patrol cars started and stopped at every turn, groups of men and women of the force gathered by the foot of the mountain, near the caves; the largest group huddled close to the cave of bones.

Word was about that they were out to get Diamond Eyes. Someone had squealed lies. All the children knew who that someone was. Littloo had made sure of that.

They were all gathered behind a large tree, hidden from the path that cut its way through the base of the mountain and led out to the blue caves. Some were smoking cigarettes, some talking, some chewing, one was repeatedly spitting into space, when they saw the slight figure of Peter, more pale today than golden, come stumbling through the grass, which in sections was taller than he.

'Look who's here!' exclaimed Littloo with a mixture of genuine surprise and angry disdain, 'Little Judas himself!'

Electric excitement pulsed through the previously lethargic group like a rattlesnake's tail.

Saul, the biggest in the group, nearly six feet at thirteen, broad as a block of flats and with a thick sturdy neck, jumped off a rock and shouted, 'Where? Where?' His shock of blond hair leapt with a life of its own.

'There. Right in front of your eyes, you big clod,' said Bod, the oldest at fifteen. Sara and Jony, the only two girls, sniggered, and Toby, the youngest of the lot, giggled.

Peter, who had started off running but by now was having trouble keeping his steps in line and in balance, hardly saw the gang through blurred eyes as they approached him, the leaders swaggering and blocking his path. He walked straight into the big boy who had deliberately placed himself directly in Peter's way.

'Look who we have here! Little Judas himself!' said Littloo again. His reading of the Bible had been thorough and regular when his mother was with them. Even now, reading the scriptures was the only way he kept the memory of his mother alive.

'Yes, Judas!' screamed Toby at the top of his high-pitched voice, even though he wasn't quite sure who Judas was. Perhaps he was the city boy whose family had been planning to move next door before the rains – hadn't seen or heard from them since. Maybe they were here now, with their son Judas. Actually, Toby was quite pleased to see someone smaller even than he, but he had to act nasty to keep up with the others.

'Judas. Judas. Judas. Judas. Judas . . .'

Anger and envy for the rich little spoilt bastard, mixed with anger and disgust at the idea of betrayal, compounded by proxy worries of parents who were without jobs or homes – all ground themselves into their chants.

Peter found himself in the centre of a contracting circle of very angry, very eager, very righteous young bodies.

37

By this time Eleanor had been informed at her emergency number that Peter had managed to escape, almost certainly to see the grey man because he had been mumbling his name in his sleep only a short while before. Police had been alerted and officers on duty in the shanty town had been instructed to take immediate but cautious steps to take the man into custody.

The information which had started as 'the boy might have gone to him' turned to 'the boy has gone to him' to 'the boy is with him' to 'the boy has been taken by him'. The instructions to take 'immediate but cautious steps' gradually became an 'urgent need to act with required and necessary force'.

Within minutes the known exits from the bone cave were ringed by a circle of very angry, very eager, very righteous police officers.

38

Eleanor began arranging for a helicopter to take her to the shanty town. She wanted to personally supervise the hunt for the . . . the *man*. She couldn't, wouldn't call him Diamond Eyes, nor the grey man. But she resisted the urge to say pervert or beast or sex-fiend or pederast. She was so angry at him that for a moment she forgot that Peter was missing.

39

There are conflicting accounts as to the manner of the grey man's death. Even the early police statements gave two different explanations. One: the man was shot dead while attempting to 'charge his way through' the police cordon in a bid to escape: two: the man fell over a ledge and broke his neck while attempting to escape through one of the tortuous routes in and out of the cave. Later, only the second of the two was officially and formally circulated as being the 'correct' one.

What is known is that when Inspector Sylvio's men later went to recover the body it had disappeared from inside the cave, and no amount of extensive searching gave any clues as to what could have happened to it.

Neither were the police and the host of local and national volunteers able to find Peter, or discover any clues as to what could have happened to him. Even Littloo and Saul could not tell what had happened to him, even though they were the ones who had made it happen to him. When, a few hours after their encounter with him, they scuttled back through the black body of the night to where they had left his golden body, it had disappeared too. The tree stood forlorn and naked, despite the arrival of spring.

The government decided to 'temporarily shelve' the implementation of the Delta Valley Development. The extreme events surrounding the death and disappearance of Diamond Eyes and the disappearance of Peter, not to mention the fate of Magda and her sons and that of Jonah's children, had brought so much publicity to the area that it was considered best left alone for some time. Trusting in the fickleness of public memory, the ministers and the civil servants concerned were hoping to return to it later. In the circumstances it would have only given added impetus to the Don't Vote Crusade of Jonah and co.

Most of the storm damage to the houses and to the lives of the people of Gulroza was repaired, and life began gradually to return to 'normal'. But it was never the same again. The fact that a man and a child were often seen to walk upon the river, or to stand upon the highest point on the mountain, or to call on the houses of local people and ask wordlessly for some food sent through the place the cold air of a haunting fear as well as establishing the warm aura of a sacred and profound mystery.

I kept making my regular trips to Calvary and back, for all the good they did.

The election took place according to schedule, and the government were returned to power with a greatly reduced share of votes and a greatly increased majority.

Eleanor and Philip retained their seats, but their marriage could not stand the strain of Peter's disappearance and the accusations and counter-accusations it engendered. They split up shortly afterwards, though no divorce proceedings were initiated by either party.

Jonah recovered fully, married Tamar, and with the help of her university friends and his own followers and friends, re-started the Don't Vote Crusade with renewed vigour and prophetic fervour. Paul joined him openly and aggressively, moving permanently out of his sister's house and choosing to stay on in the camper parked next to Magda's house. The campaign for consensus politics was on its way again.

Littloo started getting violent fits of aggression followed by long periods of depression, and spent most of his time in and out of various institutions. Saul was beaten up once too often by his father, and he hit back, nearly killing the man. He ran away after this unpleasant but eagerly-talked-about 'family fight', and was never seen or heard of again. The spate of child sexual molestations stopped after that, for some time. The police closed their files and their minds, and attributed this respite from the incidents to the death of the grey man. It was described as a further vindication of their action in 'dealing with him with the necessary force demanded by the circumstances'.

40

The early rays of the late December sun cutting their way through the artificially-frosted window titillated Paul's naked body with hot, pointy fingers, rousing him from a fitfully disturbed sleep.

Contrary to his usual habit he took a long time to fully shake off the night and take in his surroundings. During his life as a traveller and a wanderer he had woken up at the strangest of places and with the oddest of bed-fellows, but usually within seconds of opening his eyes he was ready for the day, whether it involved a hasty exit or a lingering stretch inside the covers or a bout of early morning oat-sowing.

It was different that day. The cool comfort of clean cotton sheets was not his last memory of last night. In fact, last night was not his memory of last night. It was only when he saw the ribbons and bunting and snow-clad fairies surrounding the window frames and a big grinning cardboard cut-out of

Santa Claus floating above his head, hanging from the ceiling at the end of a long white rope – Eleanor's annual joke – that he realised it must be the morning of Christmas Eve.

With that realisation, another memory flashed through his overloaded and out-of-sync mind. Was it the memory of an unfulfilled desire, or of a *fait accompli*? Or simply that of a promise? He shook his brain inside his skull, re-tuned his optic nerves and adjusted the time-clock that beat its seconds in time with his heart-beat.

He had promised to take Natalia out to the meadows, to paint her in naked splendour. He knew a quiet area by the river where nobody much came at any time of the year, so early on the morning of Christmas Eve they were bound to have it to themselves. He had been looking forward to the day for some time. Why was he not excited about it now? Was he after all starting to grow really old? Or was it merely the soporific effect of the droning air-conditioner?

He raised himself out of the bed, struggled into a pair of tatty old jeans, and went to the window and threw it open to breathe some fresh air into his lungs, to get some of the old life back into his body. He choked upon a scream.

There, in front of his eyes, hanging by the neck from a high branch of the tall acacia tree, at the end of a long white rope, swayed the frail, naked figure of Peter, JUDAS written in letters of blood across his bony little chest. His body was lacerated and bruised, his face and head battered and kicked in. Even as Paul stared at it in paralysed disbelief, it vanished before his very eyes.

He ran down to Peter's room and nearly kicked the door open. There, before his very eyes, in a room full of all kinds and varieties and colours and shapes of Christmas decorations, slept peacefully in his bed the frail little body of Peter. He went close enough to make sure, then feeling very foolish started to leave the room. It was only when he cast a last backward glance towards the bed that he saw a red inflamed rope mark going round Peter's neck. He ran to the bed and shook the boy, who woke up, looked uncomprehendingly at Paul and said, 'They have killed the grey man, Paul.' He looked and sounded tired, almost like an old man, a grey old man. '*I* have killed the grey man, Paul,' he added, barely audible.

Paul did not know what to say to that. He just managed, 'Eh!' But he was relieved to see that there were no rope marks round Peter's neck. It was just thin and chicken-like, as usual. Of course it had to be. How foolish and *morbid* of him to . . . He didn't even want to think about thinking it, imagining it, imagining what he saw from his . . . What party did he go to last night, and what did he drink or inhale or smoke?

In a corner, under Peter's very own Christmas tree, Trix whimpered and wagged her tail but did not get up. Now what was so unusual about that? Why was the sight like grit in the eye? Of course, Peter was not supposed to have her in his room at night, but so what? Perhaps he had got a special Christmas dispensation from Eleanor.

'What are you talking about? What grey man?' Even as he asked, a certain doubt began to invade his certainty of ignorance. Perhaps he knew, knew that there was something to know. But he couldn't be sure.

Peter raised his hands to his throat and massaged his neck, 'My throat hurts,' he said, having difficulty swallowing. 'I feel I am going to die.'

Paul was not too upset at these words. He knew Peter went through phases of being obsessed with death. Considering the time he had spent in hospitals, perhaps it wasn't so strange. But it was a bit odd, especially his choice of books. He had had to look round half of Bremmin to get the ones he had asked for this Christmas. Such weird titles. Sometimes he really worried for the boy.

'You are *not* going to die, PT. You will be fine, take my word for it. Here, drink some water, that should make you feel all right. You have just got a parched throat.'

Paul picked up the glass of water which Peter always kept by his bedside, lifted Peter up by the shoulders, and put the glass to his lips. As Peter drank, Paul wound his arms round him, pressed his bones firmly against his body and said with the utmost love in his voice, 'A little bit of water, and you'll be fine. Take my word for it.'

After Peter had taken a few sips of the water, he began to look much better. 'He said he'd come back. Do you think he will?'

Paul felt himself becoming confused again. *Ought* he to know the answer to that? He thought it safer to change the subject. Perhaps the mention of the books would further cheer him up. 'Oh, and guess what, PT. I got all the books you wanted. All but one. I had to practically travel round the world to find them. Where do you get those titles from?'

Paul had hoped Peter would jump up enthusiastically and demand to see them then and there, as he always did when he got him some books. It seemed to have the opposite effect. He lost the slight colour he had gained, taking Paul's evasion to be a negative reply to his question. He smiled a tired smile and said, 'Thank you, Paul.'

Paul decided it would be best to let him sleep on for a while.

As he was on his way out he turned round and made another attempt to clarify what was bothering him, 'Who is this grey man? *Grey* man . . .' But Peter had gone back to sleep.

He met Natalia in the corridor. 'I am ready when you are,' she said.

'Oh God!' Paul remembered. 'Damn. I promised Jonah to arrange bail or whatever to get Ishmael out for Christmas.' No wonder his mind was so mixed up that morning. Conflicting promises, conflicting loyalties, conflicting temptations. Conflicting times.

'It's Christmas Eve. You'll hardly find anyone venturing forth to be helpful today.'

'I know somebody who knows somebody . . .' began Paul.

'One day more –' she was beginning to get angry and nearly said 'won't kill him', but restrained herself. 'One day more won't make much difference. He's probably lined up a jolly party with his cell-mates.'

'That's part of the trouble. He is not in a cell with anyone, just all by himself in police custody. No charges have been brought yet. Been there for three days now.'

'Well then, I'll change back,' said Natalia, unable to keep the hurt out of her voice and pointing to her jeans and trainers. Eleanor's rule was that Natalia should always be 'properly' dressed in the house.

'No, wait.' said Paul.

They stood facing one another down the length of the corridor. I went over to her and held her hand as I went over to him and held his hand. Neither rejected my hand.

'Christmas Day would be just as quiet by the river. Quieter.' I entreated, I tempted.

I think they heard me. He certainly looked at me. At least he looked at the past, that could be the future; and at the future, that could be the past.

'Are we going then, or aren't we?' said Natalia.

41

The man lay curled up on the beach like a grotesque grey ball with its air booted out.

He was naked, except for a black hood over his head and face. His penis had been crudely carved out, so had his tongue. The wounds had healed. His buttocks were fire-branded, his nipples razor-slashed. The burns and cuts were healed.

The quivering shoreline skirted uncertainly round him: back and forth, back and forth, back and forth . . .

Spewed out by the ocean? About to be swallowed up by the waves? Fallen from grace? All set for ascension? Violated by humankind in a most vile manner? Out to subvert the world with self inflicted hell?

Adam Zameenzad
The Thirteenth House

For Zahid, life is a constant struggle against chaos. His wife confuses him; his sick, silent son terrifies him; his poverty threatens to overwhelm him. In the background, the political and religious turmoil of native Pakistan seems merely to mock his troubled state of mind in cruel mimicry.

But when Zahid finds a new house to live in, he allows himself a flutter of optimism. True, there are rumours about the house, silly rumours . . . but he feels it is a turning point. Soon after moving in, he meets the Sha Baba, a potent and splendid guru who offers him a vision of happiness.

But happiness is not what fate has in store for Zahid, and the comic progress of his life carries him stumbling towards tragedy.

'Fine, narrative wryness of the R. K. Narayan sort. The wryness, though, never once stifles the power' *Observer*

'If ever comedy was black, this is' *Guardian*

'Ghost story, nightmare, vision . . . It transposes the reader from a world where even the traumas of political upheaval and police brutality – however appalling – are at least solidly real, to an insubstantial, shimmering world where nothing is what it seems and where the significance of people, events and things trembles tantalizingly just out of focus . . . A forceful, moving and confident debut' *Times Literary Supplement*

Flamingo

Adam Zameenzad

My Friend Matt and Hena the Whore

A continent of permanent revolution, of marauding rebels and despotic governments, yet one of love and laughter, compassion and humanity: this is the Africa of today.

Nine-year-old Kimo, wide-eyed witness to its brutality, is starved out of his home village by drought. Desperate for help, he sets out for the big city of Bader in the company of his resourceful friends, the visionary Matt, pragmatic Hena and dreaming Golam. Their journey takes them through a country paralysed by the horrors of civil war, horrors which soon tighten their grip around the frail hopes of the starving foursome . . .

Buoyed up by laughter, weighed down by tragedy and violence, *My Friend Matt and Hena the Whore* is an impossibly touching, quite extraordinary accomplishment from an outstanding new writer.

'Truly astonishing' *i.D.*

'Outstanding . . . into this odyssey of nightmares and magic the author manages to weave a thread of humour which is the most remarkable achievement of his horrifying book' *Sunday Times*

'Beautifully written, imbued with enormous integrity and insight, his book is a plea for us to exercise humanity towards our fellow humans; it is in the characters' expressions of love and care that we are offered a glimmer of hope, both for the present and the future' *Time Out*

'It would be hard to overpraise the achievement . . . a truly remarkable novel' Adam Lively, *Punch*

Flamingo

Sharman Macdonald

Night Night

Frances, tired of winter and dark days, dreams about the tattooed man who won't make her plead for love. Her husband, Joey, a gaunt and haggard boy of forty, chops down the Tree of Heaven she has lovingly planted, and dreams of a fat wife in an apron cooking bacon, eggs and fried bread for his breakfast. Aaron, their son, dreams of the Libyan bombings, of planes and explosives. Fat Mia, the baby, is sublimely indifferent. Only Nat-Nat, womanly and wise beyond her years, doesn't dream.

When Joey gives up his struggle to be a painter for the more financially rewarding work of a commerical artist, his world seems secure. Yet superficial prosperity doesn't hide a lurking malaise that climaxes with a random bomb threat to their home. As the neighbourhood empties to the village hall, and a panoply of superbly imagined, heartbreakingly real characters unfolds, Joey stands to guard his house and meet his fate.

Night Night is an exhilarating fantasy that interweaves domestic shambles with a menacing parable for the bewildered eighties . . . a funny suburban nightmare about loss of faith and direction.

'A surreal purity of vision which is often disturbingly amusing' – *Time Out*

Flamingo

PENELOPE FITZGERALD

Offshore

Winner of the Booker Prize

'This is an astonishing book. Hardly more than 50,000 words, it is written with a manic economy that makes it seem even shorter, and with a tamped-down force that continually explodes in a series of exactly controlled detonations. It is funny, its humour far more robust than it at first appears, but it has in addition a sense of battles lost, of happiness at any rate brushed by the fingers as it passes by, of understanding gained at the last second. *Offshore* is a marvellous achievement: strong, supple, humane, ripe, generous and graceful.'   Bernard Levin *Sunday Times*

Human Voices

'One of the pleasures of reading Penelope Fitzgerald is the unpredictability of her intelligence, which never loses its quality, but springs constant surprises, and if you make the mistake of reading her fast because she is so readable, you will miss some of the best jokes. I wish it were longer . . . for it is certainly a very funny novel about the BBC, and that in itself is an occasion for joy.'   Michael Ratcliffe *The Times*

Flamingo

GARY ZUKAV

The Dancing Wu Li Masters

Gary Zukav's guide to the mind-stretching mysteries of the new physics points out striking parallels with modern psychology and eastern mysticism.

'It is hard to imagine a layman who would not find this book enjoyable and informative.'

MARTIN GARDNER, author of *The Ambidextrous Universe*

'It is to be recommended highly, both for those who want to understand the essential significance of modern physics and for those who are concerned with its implications for the possible transformation of the human consciousness'   *TLS*

'For those who know little or no physics this book is an excellent guide into the magic of modern physics . . . I recommend it thoroughly. I recommend it to physicists too'

Quarto

Flamingo

Feeding the Rat

Profile of a Climber

Al Alvarez

'The rat is you, really. It's the other you, and it's being fed by the you that you think you are.'

Pushing yourself to the absolute limits of physical and mental endurance, taking risks where what you might lose seems out of all proportion to what you gain, sating that ineluctable hunger for danger, but, above all, getting a kick out of life: this is the very essence of what climber Mo Anthoine calls *Feeding the Rat*.

An adventurer who courts danger with a vengeance, anarchic iconoclast, determined to distil the very best from a life rich with possibilities: whether climbing the massive overhanging prow of Roraima surrounded by rabid vampire bats or stranded overnight in sub-zero temperatures on an eighteen-inch ledge, Anthoine remains a gambler for the highest stakes.

With warmth and humour, vivacity and penetrating insight, co-adventurer Al Alvarez scales the heights of Anthoine's epic climbing career, laying bare the wit and resourcefulness of a true individualist.

'Every year, Mo Anthoine needs to flush out his system. He calls it feeding the rat. The way he describes it, it sounds almost like making love' *Observer*

'The wild side of mountaineering . . . Mo Anthoine comes to vivid, rude life as a radical inhabitant of Alvarezland, where the individual is forever pitted against the shallow judgments of the system and wins through only by robust refusal to be other than he is . . . This is writing of power and originality' *Guardian*

FLAMINGO

Flamingo

Flamingo is a quality imprint publishing both fiction and non-fiction. Below are some recent titles.

Fiction

- ☐ Home Thoughts *Tim Parks* £3.95
- ☐ Human Voices *Penelope Fitzgerald* £3.95
- ☐ Offshore *Penelope Fitzgerald* £3.95
- ☐ Nelly's Version *Eva Figes* £3.95
- ☐ The Joys of Motherhood *Buchi Emecheta* £3.95
- ☐ The Thirteenth House *Adam Zameenzad* £3.95
- ☐ My Friend Matt and Hena the Whore *Adam Zameenzad* £3.95
- ☐ Night Night *Sharman Macdonald* £3.95

Non-fiction

- ☐ The Dancing Wu Li Masters *Gary Zukav* £4.95
- ☐ The Book of Five Rings *Miyamoto Musashi* £3.95
- ☐ Home Life *Alice Thomas Ellis* £3.95
- ☐ More Home Life *Alice Thomas Ellis* £3.95
- ☐ In the Ditch *Buchi Emecheta* £3.95
- ☐ Uncommon Wisdom *Fritjof Capra* £4.95
- ☐ The Turning Point *Fritjof Capra* £3.50
- ☐ The Tao of Physics *Fritjof Capra* £3.50
- ☐ Feeding the Rat *Al Alvarez* £3.95

You can buy Flamingo paperbacks at your local bookshop or newsagent. Or you can order them from Fontana Paperbacks, Cash Sales Department, Box 29, Douglas, Isle of Man. Please send a cheque, postal or money order (not currency) worth the purchase price plus 22p per book (or plus 22p per book if outside the UK).

NAME (Block letters) _____

ADDRESS_____

_____

_____